ELEVENTH HOUR

A Kit Marlowe Mystery

M. J. Trow

CRÈME de la CRIME

This first world edition published 2017
in Great Britain and the USA by
Crème de la Crime, an imprint of
SEVERN HOUSE PUBLISHERS LTD of
19 Cedar Road, Sutton, Surrey, England, SM2 5DA

Trade paperback edition first published 2018
In Great Britain and the USA by
SEVERN HOUSE PUBLISHERS LTD
Eardley House, 4 Uxbridge Street, London W8 7SY

British Library Cataloguing in Publication Data
A CIP catalogue record for this title is available from the British Library.

ISBN-13: 978-1-78029-093-5 (cased)
ISBN-13: 978-1-78029-579-4 (trade paper)
ISBN-13: 978-1-78010-877-3 (e-book)

ONE

The linen stretched over the tenter-grounds like winding sheets, ghostly pale under the Norton Folgate moon. Kit Marlowe, quill in hand, watched them from the window. He heard the watchmen call the hour, echoing from street to street and across the fields to where the windmills turned and groaned in the half-darkness.

He spun sharply, dipping the quill quickly into the ink and scrawled, still standing, along the parchment—

'Albeit the world think Machiavel is dead,

Yet his soul but flown beyond the Alps . . .'

The Alps. Nicholas Faunt had crossed them. So had Thomas Phelippes; all the old man's golden lads. Would Marlowe follow them? That all depended on the Queen's Moor, the Spymaster and whatever game he was playing tonight.

Francis Walsingham lay propped on his down pillows, listening to the rasping of his own chest. His lips hung slack, as they had for six days now since he had first fallen into an apoplexy, or so they called it. His mind was sharp but his body did what it would. He tried to chuckle as the thought came to him that this was childhood, come again, but the sound came out in a series of grunts. His chin glistened with the saliva he could no longer control; gentle hands dried his face for him but it was stemming a tide only death could force to ebb. For this childhood would not be followed by growing, but only by diminishing. And yet, he couldn't let go. Not yet, not with the Irish business unfinished. It had been there when he first entered the Queen's service; it was there still. Thomas Wyndebank had been to see Her Majesty, to tell her that Walsingham, who had watched her back for all those years, was facing the end. She had looked at him, cold, unfeeling, with her painted hair and painted face, white with lead. There was no one else; the Irish business must be dispatched, and quickly. She had paused for long enough to let Wyndebank hope and then had dashed it. And it must be dispatched by Walsingham.

Her letter lay beside him on the table, glowing in the candle-light. Cattle. And corn. And secret Papists hiding behind every one. The wind along Seething Lane rattled the window frames. And Walsingham shivered with them.

'To some, perhaps, my name is odious,' Marlowe's pen left its black train for all time, 'But such as love me, guard me from their tongues, And let them know that I am Machiavel, And weigh not men, and therefore not men's words . . .'

'Sir Francis.' He heard the words but couldn't, at first, place the voice.

'Who's there?' the Queen's counsellor asked, half afraid of the answer.

'It's me, sir. Mylles.'

'Mylles.' Walsingham breathed easier. His chest was tight and there was a flight of stairs stretching ahead of him in his fevered mind. He frowned for a moment, focusing. 'I thought you'd look . . . different.'

'Shall I call Lady Walsingham, sir?' the secretary asked. He had seen men die before. But this wasn't a man. It was Mr Secretary Walsingham, the living sword of the Jezebel of England. If the country stood safe tonight, uninvaded, deaf to the Gregorian chant and unaware of the sweet taint of incense, that was because of Francis Walsingham.

'No, no,' the Spymaster's hands fluttered under his covers. Mylles noted the greyish-yellow of the man's skin and the sunken hollows of his cheeks. He had aged twenty years in the last six days. 'Let Ursula sleep.' A sudden thought occurred to Walsingham and he peered into the growing dark, peered up into his servant's face. 'Everything is all right, Mylles, isn't it? All's in place?'

'It is, sire.' The man placed a gentle hand on his master's shoulder and smiled down at him, his voice soft and soothing. 'Listen.'

Walsingham did. In the passageways of his mind, as along

Seething Lane below his window, the watchmen told the hour. All was well.

'You see,' Mylles summoned a laugh from somewhere, pleased with the watchman's timing. 'We can't *all* be wrong.'

'Let Ursula sleep,' Walsingham said again. 'I'll see her at breakfast.'

'Admired I am, of those that hate me most . . .' Marlowe wrote furiously, dropping ink along the rough edges of the parchment. He could hear Tom Watson snoring in the next room – or was it the girl he had with him tonight? Either way, it made no difference. The Muse was with Marlowe tonight, leaning over his shoulder, breathing air and fire into his pen. She would not leave him now . . . 'Though some speak openly against my books, Yet they will read me, and thereby attain To Peter's Chair . . .'

Peter's Chair. All his life, Christopher Marlowe had been afraid of that chair. It housed the anti-Christ, the Devil's vicar-on-earth, who had sent scattered killers against the Queen and an entire Armada to bring England to heel. But Machiavel could face that chair and the great beast who sat on it.

'And when they cast me off,' Marlowe scratched on, ink flying, 'Are poisoned by my climbing followers . . .'

Walsingham's breathing was the only sound in the chamber now. The watchmen had gone and the first sparrow had not roused itself from the huddled roofs. London slept. Seething Lane slept. Francis Walsingham did not.

'I count religion but a childish toy,' Marlowe wrote, 'And hold there is no sin but ignorance. Birds of the air will tell of murders past, I am ashamed to hear such fooleries!'

He shuddered suddenly, as though something nameless had crept over his grave and touched his soul. He looked up at his own reflection in the leaded panes, the dark curls, the smouldering eyes. For the briefest of seconds, he thought someone stood at his elbow, like the scythes-man that comes to us all. He half expected to see Tom Watson, yawning, scratching himself, the pre-dawn poet in search of a rhyme. But his steady snores through the wall told him it wasn't so – and when he looked again, there was nothing. Nothing.

'Mylles.' Walsingham had difficulty framing the name.
'I'm here, Sir Francis,' the man assured him through his tears.
'I'm sorry,' the Spymaster said.
'Sorry, sir?' Mylles frowned. 'Whatever for?'
'In all the years you served me, faithfully and well, I never called you by your given name. Never called you Francis.'
Mylles tried to laugh. 'It would have been too confusing, sir,' he said. 'Too . . .' But the Queen's Spymaster wasn't listening. Not any more.

There was a crash as something hit the window just by Marlowe's head. The pen leapt from his hand and rolled across the page, leaving a stuttering, limping snail trail of ink as it went. The poet looked up, eyes wide, and saw, printed in the grease of its feathers, ethereal in the candle's gleam, the image of an owl, wings outspread, beak agape, as it had struck the window, misjudging the distance to its imagined prey, the tiny gleam in Marlowe's eye as he flew with Machiavel over the peaks. The bird itself had gone, flown back to its frowsty, bone and fur-filled nest in the tower of the old Crutched Friars, to nurse its aching head until hunger drove it out once more. But Marlowe couldn't shake the foreboding which had been standing at his side since darkness had fallen. He wiped his pen, stretched, yawned and rolled into his bed. He would lie sleepless still, but a man's body must rest, even when his mind cannot. The foreboding stood behind the hangings, breathing softly, waiting for dawn. Outside and far away, a clock struck the quarter hour; eleven o'clock and black as pitch, with a late frost pricking the night with cold stars.

The door clicked open and a roisterer crept in, his plumed cap in his hand, his Colleyweston cloak glittering with gold embroidery in the candle's flame.
'Master Faunt.' Mylles turned in surprise in that most precious and personal moment, never to be given to anyone twice. He stood upright and fought to take a grip, sighing heavily. 'You're too late, I fear.'

Nicholas Faunt crossed the room in two strides and looked down at the husk of Sir Francis Walsingham. The man who had held England, not to mention Nicholas Faunt, in the palm of his hand looked, suddenly, surprisingly, so small.

'Fetch Lady Walsingham,' Faunt ordered. For a moment, Mylles dithered. Then he nodded, clicked his heels and made for the door. Instinctively, Faunt, the projectioner, took up the goblet on the bedside table and sniffed its contents. He frowned.

'Is there nothing you can do for him, Master Faunt?' Mylles hesitated at the door. He knew the sound of a man's last breath when he heard it, but nothing was cut and dried in this house of secrets and lies.

'Yes,' Faunt said, tucking the empty goblet into his purse and doffing his hat, finally, to the man for whom he had worked for so long. 'Yes, there is.' He looked up at the secretary, his face a grim mask of determination. 'I can send for Kit Marlowe.'

TWO

Francis Walsingham had haunted the corridors and secret corners of his home for so long, slipping on silent foot from room to room, materializing at the elbow of the gossip and spy so often that it was hard to dismiss his shade. His family were sitting, eyes wide with grief and shock, trying to warm themselves at the thin flames in the enormous grate. His widow, Ursula, was all in black, his daughter too. The clothes had come out of the press so pat, so ready for this day, it was as if they had been expecting it and, in some ways, so they had. But not like this. Not so sudden, so soon. A knife in the ribs from one of his projectioners, turned by an enemy; or a rope around the neck, pulling him down to the earth in his beloved garden, where he walked alone at dusk. But this end, this choking death in his bed, this was not what they had seen for him. Each of them, in the quiet of this house, in the quiet of their hearts, had been mourning him for years, against this day. It seemed as though the whole house wept.

It wasn't like Christopher Marlowe to sleep in late. He left that to Tom Watson, who caroused almost for a living and had hardly seen a morning hour since he entered man's estate. For Marlowe, sleep was an optional extra in his life, something to do when nothing else presented itself and yet this morning, he was dead to the world. He didn't hear the hammering on the door, only stopped when Agnes flung it open, dragged from her early kitchen tasks. He didn't hear the booted feet on the stairs, the crash as his bedroom door was flung wide. The first thing he knew was being hauled upright in his bed, the grey dawn light outlining a silhouette he knew.

He shook himself free and tweaked his shirt back into place, pushing himself upright against the head of the tester. 'Nicholas,' he said, trying to shake the sleep from his eyes. 'To what do I owe the pleasure?'

'Walsingham is dead.' The words fell like lead in the cold room.

'What?' Marlowe had heard full well what Faunt had said and yet somehow it didn't really make any sense. Three simple words, but for some reason they sounded much like gibberish to him.

Faunt shook him impatiently. 'Shake off your sleep, Kit,' he said. 'Sir Francis is dead. This six hours, dead.'

'I knew he was unwell, but . . . dead?' A thought suddenly struck the poet. 'Murdered?'

Faunt stepped back, into the faint light from the window. 'It would depend on who you ask.'

'I'm asking you.'

'Then . . . yes. Murdered.'

'And if I ask someone else?' Marlowe needed to have all the information at his disposal, even though he had not often found Faunt to be wrong.

Faunt crossed to the window, where the first light of a new day was creeping over the steeples and the gables. 'The Papists will tell you it was God – their God, of course – exacting His justice at last. They'll have the old man uttering curses with his dying breath before Satan's emissaries dragged him off to Hell.'

Marlowe looked at Walsingham's right-hand man and raised an eyebrow. 'It wasn't like that?' he asked.

Faunt turned to him, a grim scowl on the tired face. 'Of course it wasn't like that,' he said. 'Mylles was with him, at the end.'

'A good man, I believe,' Marlowe remembered.

'One of the best.'

'And the family?' Marlowe asked. 'How are they taking it?'

'Ursula's a stoic. She'll do her crying in private but never in front of me. Frances has lost her father as she lost her husband . . .'

'Some have sorrow thrust upon them,' Marlowe murmured.

'And some have problems thrust upon them,' Faunt echoed. 'And that would be us.'

Marlowe lifted his head and squared his shoulders. 'Us?' he said. Faunt looked at him levelly. It had always been an uncertain world. With Walsingham gone, it was like staring into an abyss.

'I always assumed you were us, Kit,' he said softly. 'In the breach, within the meaning of the Act, whatever phrase you damned playwrights want to play with.'

'And the problem of Walsingham's death?'

Faunt turned back to the window, watching the first draymen of the morning, scratching and coughing their way along the winding lane below. 'If you're thinking of the succession to Spymaster, as it were, your guess is as good as mine. The Giffords must be considered, I suppose, that bugger Anthony Bacon. I'm sure Burghley will decide eventually. In the meantime, Marlowe, it's me. You'll have to live with that.'

'Let me put it another way,' Marlowe smiled. 'The problem of Walsingham's *murder*.'

'Ah.' Faunt hauled up the goblet from his doublet. Its silver inlay gleamed in the light from Marlowe's candle and flashed as Faunt threw it on to the bed. 'This is your Holy Grail,' he said. 'If I'm right, it's a poisoned chalice. Will you take it up?'

Marlowe hesitated. He had been given impossible tasks by Walsingham before, often via Faunt. But this one made the hairs on the back of his neck prickle. He reached forward, lifted the cup and sniffed it. Fortified wine, certainly. Herbs of some kind. But something else; something an old man, ill and careless, might have missed. Walsingham, who had been so careful all his life, may have blinked at last. The cold, grey eyes that missed nothing for so long, just *might* have missed this; the dark phial in the liquid, the bringer of sleep.

'Why have you brought this to me?' he asked.

Faunt looked at him. 'You have a knack for these things,' he said. 'A nose for treachery – and I mean that in the nicest possible way. I want to know what was in that cup and who put it there. But you'll have to tread softly. There are a few thousand Papists in this great country of ours, not to mention those over the seas, who wanted Walsingham dead. I can hear the bells of joy ringing now, can't you? In Madrid and Rome and Rheims. The ways of the Lord are strange, Marlowe; we both know that.'

Marlowe chuckled, in spite of the solemnity of the hour. 'And we both know that the Lord put nothing in the cup, Nicholas. A man did. You want me to tell you who.'

Faunt nodded. 'And then, I want you to bring him before Her Majesty's Justices,' he said, 'Master Topcliffe will do the rest. It's astonishing what truths a man will divulge when he's about to have his fingernails ripped out.'

'And what lies,' Marlowe reminded the man.

Faunt ignored him. 'I must be at Placentia,' he said, tugging his doublet straight. 'If Her Majesty finds out about Walsingham's death before I get there, there'll be Hell to pay.'

'Hell, Nicholas?' Marlowe turned the chased cup in his hand. 'Do you know, in all the time we've known each other, I didn't have you down for a superstitious man.'

Faunt tapped the side of his nose. 'For all his cynicism,' he said, 'Francis Walsingham was a godly man. A Puritan through and through. I'm going to miss him.'

'So am I,' Marlowe suddenly realized. He caught the look on Faunt's face. 'But don't worry, I'm not going to miss his murderer.'

'You can resolve that?' Faunt asked. 'The poison, I mean?'

'No.' Marlowe shook this head. 'But I know a man who can.'

Thomas Sledd was yelling at someone slung by ropes high in the ceiling of the Rose. Thomas Sledd was always yelling these days, or so it sometimes seemed. Only when he was at home with Meg and the new baby could he drop his voice and coo like any suckling dove. But cooing here wouldn't get a show put on and, as Philip Henslowe told him every day, often several times and with additional jabs to the chest: the show must go on.

'How many times do I have to remind you, you jobless idiot?' Sledd asked rhetorically. 'You don't work up there without tying your tools to your belt.' This time it had only been a leather mallet that had dropped unexpectedly at his feet, but even that would have fetched him a nasty one had it collided with the top of his head.

A formless grumble came from above his head.

'Oh, sorry, my apologies,' Sledd said, sarcasm dripping from his lips. 'But when I called you a jobless idiot, I was indeed telling the truth. Get down the ladder now and hand in your paintbrush. Your set-painting days are over, Peake. Painter of the Revels, my arse!'

Again, the grumble.

'I don't believe you can actually do that,' Sledd observed, but stepped back a couple of long strides nonetheless. He cannoned into someone standing in the wings and turned sharply, another reprimand ready.

'My apologies, Tom.' Marlowe smiled as his friend swallowed his annoyance. 'I was in your way. Is everything going well?'

'I am surrounded by idiots,' Sledd told him. 'Incompetents and fools.'

'So, nothing too different, then,' Marlowe said, putting an arm across the stage manager's shoulders. 'You know if nothing went wrong you would never rest, waiting for the other boot to fall. What this time?' He cast his eyes up to the roof, where the grumbling was continuing unabated.

'Some idiot of a scene painter dropped his resting stick thingie. Nearly hit me on the head.'

'But it missed you, Tom,' Marlowe said, grinning. 'Look at that as the good news, not the bad. And Peake is a good scene painter. That portrait he did for the parlour scene in *Linkum-Stinkum* had a damned sight more life in it than any of the actors, that's certain. Give him another chance.'

Sledd looked mulish.

'Go on, Tom. You know you want to. Tell him he can stay if he makes a portrait of Meg and the baby. Think how fine it would look above your fireplace.' He sketched the scene in the air in front of them with the wave of his arm. 'An heirloom in the making, if I am any judge.'

'But he dropped . . .'

'Not on purpose, Tom.' The playwright gave the stage manager a little push. 'Go on. I'll wait for you here. I need a word.'

Sledd's eyes brightened. 'Have you got those new pages for me?' he said, turning as he hurried off to catch the artist, who had reached the bottom of the rickety ladder.

'Hmm. That is rather what I needed a word about . . .' Marlowe made a rueful face and waited as Sledd berated Peake some more, just for the look of the thing.

'Well, that's him told.' The artist was making his way back up into the flies. A Painter of the Revels couldn't afford to cross theatre managers, or the men who ran their stages. 'Are you telling me that you haven't got the pages? We need to get the rehearsal started today. It's bad enough getting Alleyn and Burbage together in one room as it is. If one is ready, the other isn't. Shaxsper isn't worth the space he takes up, always wandering around with inky fingers and his head in the clouds. Henslowe has already cut my budget by almost half and this latest thing needs walk-on parts I just can't afford . . . Kit, why do you always write for a cast of thousands when the stage isn't more than ten paces across and my stipend won't stretch beyond three lads and a dog?'

'Tom, Tom, calm yourself. Worse things happen at sea.'

'Yes, and that brings me to that wreck scene you wrote. How can I have a ship sink on stage night after night? The carpentry fees alone . . .'

'I'll look at that for you,' Marlowe soothed. 'But, Tom, I have serious news. Sir Francis Walsingham is dead.'

Tom Sledd stopped and goggled at his friend. 'Sir Francis *Walsingham*? Sir *Francis* Walsingham?'

'The same. As far as I know, the one and only.'

'But . . . what happened?'

'The story goes that he died of apoplexy. A stroke, or so they say,' Marlowe told him. 'And why not? He's had them before. He hasn't been well for a long while.'

Sledd waited. He could hear a 'but'.

'But . . . Nicholas Faunt thinks . . .'

'Ah. Master Faunt. I did wonder whether he might come into this story.'

'Faunt thinks there may have been some dirty dealing. When the Queen's Spymaster dies, it can't be simply death, can it?'

'Sometimes it can.' Tom Sledd had seen a lot of death in his short life and, though it was sometimes untimely, it was more often than not simple.

'My mind is open, Tom,' Marlowe said. 'Part of me is tired of the spying, the dodging, the ducking, the suspicion. I feel it's time I lived a simple life. Writing; perhaps even a little acting, now and again.'

Sledd's smile became a little fixed. Marlowe wrote like a dark angel, looked like one too, come to think of it, with his flashing eyes and his curls. His voice could charm the birds from the trees, but he acted like the bough they perched upon, whenever he stood on the wooden O. There was something about the leg and the set of his shoulders that made him look as if he had a broom up his backside. But he loved Kit Marlowe like a brother, so he said, 'That would be wonderful, Kit. Let me know whenever you want to strut your stuff.'

But Marlowe was in full flight. 'But another part of me, the stronger part, knows that Faunt is right. Sir Francis was old and ill, it's true, but this death seems wrong, somehow. I won't rest until I have at least tried to solve the puzzle, if puzzle there proves to be.'

There was a silence. The two were walking through the groundlings' pit towards the door, Sledd noting automatically the mess the cleaners had missed and making a mental note to bawl someone out, on principle. Then, he couldn't keep quiet any longer. 'So . . . my pages?'

'Yes.'

Sledd waited again. Whenever Marlowe used one word where a couple of dozen would do better, good news rarely followed.

'I think I meant to ask . . . do you have my pages with you?' He poked the front of Marlowe's doublet, hoping for the crackle of parchment beneath, but all he got was the whisper of velvet and brocade.

'Not *with* me, no.' Marlowe could have been more evasive, but this was Tom Sledd and, as he knew all his tricks, the effort would be wasted.

'So . . . they're at home, then. Shall I send someone to get them, perhaps?' Hope was dying in Tom Sledd's breast.

'They are not at home, not precisely.' Marlowe smiled, bleakly.

'You haven't written my pages, have you, Kit?' Tom Sledd had had many disappointments in his life; one more wouldn't hurt.

'No. That is to say, I have jotted down a few ideas. But last night . . .' How could he explain last night, even to Thomas Sledd, his companion of many a bumpy mile? He couldn't even begin. 'I left them with Tom Watson.'

'Tom *Watson*?'

'Why ever not?' Marlowe was rarely polite either to or about Watson, but it wasn't for others to point the finger at his house companion. 'Wykehamist, Oxford scholar, man about several towns. His poetry can make angels weep, when he is on song.'

Sledd stopped in his tracks, unaware of the rotting apple slowly disintegrating under his heel. 'Indeed, my point exactly. When he is on song. Rather than on some wench he has found in some alehouse. And how often does that happen?'

'He slept alone last night, I know this to be true.' Marlowe could spin a lie and leave no trace, but even as he spoke he knew this one would never pass muster.

'Tom Watson hasn't slept alone since he was fourteen – at least by his own boasting – and I see no reason to disbelieve him,' Sledd said. 'And I doubt last night was any different. And anyway, I heard he's . . . what do the authorities call them? "One of the strangers that go not to church"?' He sighed and clapped the playwright on the back. 'But I know you must do what you must, Kit. Sir Francis deserves your attention more than we poor mummers.' He looked up at Marlowe under his lashes, to see if there was even a slight slick of remorse on the man's face, but there was none. 'Does Master Watson even know that he has the lines to attend to?'

Marlowe smiled a rueful smile. He knew his Toms, both Sledd and Watson, and knew therefore that something would work itself out, somehow. 'I left my notes on the kitchen table. Agnes will give them to Tom, when he wakes.'

Tom Sledd barked a laugh that had no humour in it. 'Does he know Will Shaxsper will write them if he doesn't?' he asked.

Marlowe stepped back in admiration but, unlike the stage manager, did not end up with a boot smeared with discarded fruit. 'Thomas Sledd,' he said, laughing. 'We will make a Machiavel of you yet! Send to Norton Folgate with that news and I can guarantee you will have your pages before nightfall. Now, I really must be away. For one thing, that urchin you employ will have sold my horse if I don't get back to him soon. And for another, I need to get to Dr Dee in Winchester and it is a good ride away yet.'

Tom Sledd dearly loved magic. He tried sleight of hand for himself whenever he got a moment alone, but the flights of butterflies and birds of which he dreamed always turned into damp paper in his hands. 'Dr Dee? Why there?'

'If there is a puzzle to be solved, there is no better place to begin, surely? And there is a puzzle, Tom. A puzzle I owe it to Sir Francis to solve. So,' he clapped the man on the back, 'I'm off. Send your message to Tom Watson and I'll be back before first night.' He rummaged in his purse and came out with a guinea between his finger and thumb. 'Don't tell Henslowe, but take this. Buy yourself a couple of walking gentlemen; people my stage a little.'

Sledd gaped but didn't say no.

As Marlowe slid through the wicket in the great door of the Rose, he heard the theatre owner's Stepney vowels from above.

'Don't tell Henslowe what? Tom? Tom! Don't tell Henslowe what?'

Marlowe smiled and pulled the door gently closed. It was good to think that, whatever else was ill with the world, there would always be Sledd and Henslowe.

THREE

I f the nights were still cold in this late-coming spring, the days were warm and the sun shone on Marlowe's back as he set off for the west. Winchester beckoned with its pile of grey masonry. The choirboy in Marlowe was never far from the surface, though he would die rather than admit it and he hummed under his breath the soaring Tallis of his youth. Half his life had gone by since his voice had broken but, in his head, he could still soar to C above middle C without having to draw a breath. The miles were eaten up under his horse's hoofs on the Portsmouth road and, before the sun began to sink low enough to shine into his westering eyes, Winchester's water meadows were alongside his path and the ancient almshouses of St John's Cross were before him, early lamps shining in their windows.

Marlowe had found out easily enough that Dee and his little family had holed up in Hampshire after his return from exile in Germany and, with a little more digging, that he was in Winchester. The rumour flew that the Queen's magus sought retirement from the world, to become the Master of St John's and watch the Heavens for signs of God. But precisely which house currently housed the Dees was a question too far even for him. But there were only twelve almshouses, to be sure, so it would be, at the worst, a process of elimination. He knocked on the first door, the one at the right-hand end of the row. After a long pause, it creaked open but, to Marlowe's discomfiture, there was no one there; perhaps, he reminded himself, he shouldn't be surprised at that; he may have happened upon Dee's house at first try.

'Doctor?' he said. 'Dr Dee?'

'There be no doctor here,' a crabby voice said, from around the level of his waist. He looked down, into the malevolent eye of a very, very old man, dressed in grey fustian with a Piccadill set rakishly on his matted hair.

Marlowe looked down and spoke more clearly. 'I am looking for Dr John Dee,' he said. 'The Queen's magus. I believe—'

'No business of mine what you believe, sonny,' the man said and spat with terrifying accuracy on the flagstone just by the playwright's right foot. 'But I tell ye, there be no doctor here.' He made to close the door, but Marlowe leaned on it and prevented him as easily as he would a child.

'I see that he doesn't live here,' he said. As soon as he had seen the simple room beyond the door, the fireplace with one stool beside it and a truckle bed, its doors open ready for the impending night, he had known that. 'But I wondered if you could tell me where he *does* live.'

'I tell ye . . .'

A coin was suddenly in Marlowe's fingers, catching the last rays of the dying sun.

'. . . that the doctor, he do live up that way.' A gnarled finger came around the door and pointed along the row. 'You do go along here, then follow the wall until you come to the tumble-down bit.' The old man stopped to clear his throat, limbering up for another spectacular expectoration, but Marlowe was ready for him this time and stepped smartly to the left. 'You go along through the breach and he do live in the house there, under the trees.'

'Thank you,' Marlowe said and allowed the old creature to snatch the coin. 'I'm very grateful.'

'We been expecting you, or your like, at any road,' the pensioner said, closing the door.

Again, Marlowe was too quick for him. 'Expecting me? How so?'

The door relented by just a crack and the eye measured him from crown to toes. 'Well, some fellow me lad, no better nor he should be. 'Tis only common sense the doctor he can't be the feyther.'

'Feather?' Even as he spoke, Marlowe knew this conversation could only get more complicated than he had time for.

The old man straightened his cap and looked up at Marlowe. Speaking slowly, as though to an imbecile, he said, 'Fey-ther. Of the babby. 'Tis certain sure the doctor be too old for that. Some young blood from up Lunnon, that's what we reckon, did do the business with Mistress Jane.' A horrible noise rose from the ancient throat and Marlowe realized the man was laughing. 'And I reckon, 'tis you. Got the itch agen, have ye? Well, she been brought be bed these six weeks 'n more, so perhaps she be itchin' too. I should run along, sonny, 'twere I you, see your babby and give her a good . . .' This time, a cough seized him and seemed reluctant to let go. Marlowe took advantage of the break in the narrative to make his escape. He couldn't help a chuckle as he walked his horse along the wall and through the breach. Unlike the pensioner, he didn't doubt that Dee could well be the father of the child. He had means for all kinds of miracles and he wouldn't even have had to break a sweat. He walked towards the lights of the house under the trees, congratulations already on his lips.

He rapped on the door and listened intently for signs of life from within, but there was nothing. He counted to twenty and rapped again and this time was rewarded by hurrying footsteps. The door was wrenched open and a red-faced woman appeared silhouetted against the light, a frantic finger to her lip.

'For the Lord's sake,' she hissed, 'stop that racket. We have only just this minute got the baby off to sleep. That one, she has the devil in her if I'm a judge; she does nothing but scream from morning to night. So hush, master, hush.'

Marlowe bit his lip to show his remorse and that he intended to be as quiet as a mouse. He leaned in and whispered to the maidservant. 'I'm here to see the doctor.'

The maid looked up appreciatively at the curve of his cheek and lip, the bright sparkle of his dark eye, the curl of his hair. She breathed in the clean smell of leather and horse, of wind and weather; it made a change from baby posset and damp napkin. He didn't look ailing, but the doctor had made it plain – if anyone comes asking to see him, she must be sure to let them know that he wasn't *that* kind of doctor. She was to say what she said now to Marlowe. 'The master is not a doctor of physick, sir.'

'I don't need *a* doctor,' Marlowe said with a smile. 'I need *the* doctor, Dr Dee.'

A door squealed open down the hall and a head peered out. With it came the sound of a screaming infant. Above the squalling, a voice Marlowe knew asked, 'Who is that, Anne?'

The girl turned with a bob. 'It's a gentleman asking after a doctor, sir,' she said, in a voice made husky by long whispering.

Dee flapped with his hand. 'Have you told him . . .?'

'Yes, master,' she said. 'He says he doesn't want a doctor, he wants the doctor.'

Dee was silent for a moment and then said with a chuckle, 'Ask him, Anne, if he is Machiavel.'

'Master?'

Dee flapped again. 'Go on, ask him.'

From the room behind him, a female voice raised in protest could be heard above the child's wailing.

She turned to Marlowe and began. 'Sir, are you Mac . . . Mac . . .' She was puzzled. He didn't look ill, but neither did he look at all Scottish.

'Yes, Doctor,' Marlowe said, in the same stage whisper as the others employed, 'Yes, I am Machiavel.'

Suddenly, the hall was full of swirling robes, snow-white beard and cries of delight. 'Kit! Kit! Come in and meet my new darlings! I have missed you! Where have you been?' Dee thrust the maid aside. 'Anne! Fetch us wine. Fetch us food. Warm the second-best bed.' He turned to Marlowe. 'You'll stay with us, I know.' He glared at the maid, who spun round on the spot in confusion. 'Go on, go on, stupid girl. Drink. Food. What are you waiting for?'

Released from the madness, the girl ran for the kitchen door and sanity. Dee threw his arms around Marlowe and pulled him excitedly down the hall to the door which still stood wide.

Marlowe was manhandled in and the door was pulled to behind him. He had heard that Dee had remarried, having lost his beloved Helene but he was not really ready for how different a path he had taken. Where Helene was fair as the sun through mist and as gentle as a milk-white doe, the woman who sat in the glow of the fire was all dark and spark. She had a baby over her shoulder and bounced it hard, patting its back with blows calculated to stun a less hardened child. She was ruddy of cheek and sharp of feature, but the look she bestowed on her husband could not have been more loving. She probably was a few years Marlowe's junior, but was old in judgement;

she had his measure in the time he took to walk across the room and bow deeply, reaching for her free hand to kiss it.

'Master Marlowe,' she said, with no introduction necessary. 'I have heard so much about you I feel I know you already.'

'Then you know more than I,' Marlowe said, 'for I often think I scarcely know myself.'

'Jane,' Dee said, flustering himself into the opposite chair from his wife and reaching out, 'give Madimi to me and let me soothe her if I can.'

She gave him a look with a cocked eyebrow. 'Are you sure, John?' she said. 'I know she interferes with your train of thought.'

If there was sarcasm there, Marlowe could not hear it. Although Jane and Helene could not have been more different, Dee had found another woman to love him without question. It was a skill no one would have given him credit for, but here was living proof. He stepped forward, his arms out.

'May I hold her, madam?' he said. 'We poor bachelors have all too little to do with babies.'

With a chuckle, Jane Dee handed over her damp and furious daughter, whose screams redoubled. 'I will leave you, gentlemen,' she said. 'I will take this opportunity, John, to take a nap, if I may? Last night was a little trying, to say the least.' She turned a dazzling smile on Marlowe and he could see why Dee had fallen in love with her. It was as if a thousand candles had burst into light in that little room.

As she swept out, Marlowe juggled the child into a more comfortable position for them both and sat down.

Dee raised a quizzical eyebrow. 'We poor bachelors, Christopher?' he enquired. 'I never had you as someone who bemoaned his single state.'

The playwright smiled and shook his head. 'You never know, Doctor,' he said. 'Perhaps I am at that peculiar age, when all men look to their futures and want to leave something of themselves behind. For every year they swell and yet they live. Now all are dead; not one remains alive.'

'Not you, Kit,' Dee said, leaning over to pat the younger man's knee. 'You will never die.'

'A sobering thought,' Marlowe said, bouncing the child absentmindedly in time to the doxology he sang in his head.

'To live on when everyone you love is dead. Who would want that? Another quote, probably.'

Dee bent his head. 'Who indeed,' he muttered, as if to himself. Then, he brightened. 'You have a knack, Kit. Listen to Madimi. She is almost quiet.'

And sure enough, the child had subsided into hiccups and was mumbling on her fist over Marlowe's shoulder.

'I do seem to have quietened her,' the poet agreed. 'Accidental, I assure you.' He carried on bouncing gently and soon even the hiccups had passed and he gave the child into the eager arms of her father, whose face brightened as he looked down at his dear, his darling. 'Madimi. It's not a name I've met before.'

'Nor will you again. A child spirit. The great magus Agrippa was visited by her.'

'And now she has visited you,' Marlowe smiled.

After a while, the doctor spoke. 'You didn't just come to see my new family though, did you, Kit?' He had returned to the half-whisper which this child had imposed on the household.

'No.' It was no good trying to dissemble. 'Sir Francis Walsingham is dead.' There was no point in trying to break it any other way than directly.

Dee had to swallow his cry of surprise. 'What?' he mouthed. 'When? How?'

Marlowe shrugged. 'When? Two days ago at the eleventh hour. As to how, it depends on whom you ask,' he said. 'Without bothering you with all the alternatives, which couldn't matter less, the important one is the one which Nicholas Faunt and I believe in.'

Dee knew the answer to the question before he asked it, but asked it nonetheless. 'Which is?'

'Murder.'

Dee looked down at the sleeping face of his daughter, still red from crying, tears dried on her velvet cheeks. Her lashes, the improbably long fringes of childhood, lay finally at rest and her mouth was a rosebud that surely could never open in an infuriated roar. Not for the first time, Dee wondered how a single world could hold something as beautiful as his daughter and as black and ugly as death and murder. 'Apart from the fact that Faunt sees murder and mayhem behind every tree in a wood, every arras in a room, what reasons have you?' he murmured.

Marlowe reached beneath his chair for his travelling bag and pulled out the cup from which Francis Walsingham had taken his final drink. It was still wrapped in the cloth Faunt had snatched up in the death chamber. 'We have this,' he said, revealing it.

Dee leaned forward. He was puzzled. It was a substantial cup, right enough, but scarcely heavy enough to kill even a sick man with, surely. Marlowe guessed his thoughts.

'We suspect poison,' he said and Dee leaned back again, nodding. 'There are the lees of wine in here, dried on the side and in the bottom. I thought . . . *we* thought . . . that perhaps you could find out what it is.'

Dee smiled. Of course he could find out what it was. There wasn't a poison on earth he didn't have in a bottle on his shelves. His study wasn't a patch on the one he had had at Mortlake and his library – his dear, lost books – would never exist again, except in his memory and in his dreams, but still . . . knowledge is knowledge and that could never be smashed and burned. And he had such plans for St John's Cross, a new study, a . . . but now was not the time. He held out his hand for the cup, but snatched it back. 'Not with Madimi here,' he said. It was not possible to be too careful. Although he was surrounded now with a loving family, Helene's dear, dead face came to him every night in his dreams, her smile sad, bringing with her loss and longing. 'Take it through to my workroom; it's that door, there. A small thing, you will think it, but when I am Master of St Cross, oh,' his eyes lit up, 'oh the laboratory I will have!' There, he'd said it anyway.

Marlowe got up quietly; the sleeping Madimi had cast her spell over him too. He pushed open the door in the corner of the room and stepped into the dark. Without lighting a candle, he used the borrowed light from behind him to find the corner of the table and put the goblet down carefully. Dee was right; it was a small thing. Just a table and a few rough shelves on the wall, but it did seem to hold the spirit of the old Dee magic, despite being a shadow of its former self. Trying to suppress his feeling of disappointment, he softly closed the door and resumed his seat by the fire.

In the dark workroom, up in the rafters, the stuffed cockatrice turned its head to stare through the gloom at the jewelled cup, waiting patiently on the table to divulge its secrets.

Was there really a man there? It seemed so, but his face changed, now smiling, now scowling. He looked at Thomas Hariot first with his right eye, then with his left. Hariot crouched before his perspective trunk and touched the wheel, feeling the brass slide under his fingers. He straightened, away from the powerful lens and looked up at the night sky. There were the stars, as familiar to the mathematician as the beads on his abacus. The lights from God's heaven? Perhaps, but it was not as simple as that and the little voice inside Hariot's head whispered to him again, 'Find out more. Find out more.'

He crossed the room to where the trunk stood, angled to the stars, pointing at the moon. The latest letter from Tycho Brahe at Hven intrigued him, but it gave no answers. The Dane was as in the dark as he was and just as careful. Knowledge is power; they all knew that. But *this* knowledge, the secrets of the night, was far more than that. *This* knowledge could get a man killed.

There was a knock at the door. Three, in fact, followed by a pause, then a fourth. That was the knock of the magus, of the doctor, but Thomas Hariot was a careful man. It was late. Would the doctor have ridden this far to see him, at this hour? He snapped shut the trunk's lens cover and hauled the heavy brocade over it, just in case.

'*Quis?*' Hariot's Latin was as simple to him as his English. He could have used Algonquin, but that would have been pretentious.

'*Ego,*' came the muffled answer.

The mathematician unlocked the door and a messenger stood there, cloaked against the night, a letter in his hand.

'Carter,' he nodded, taking it.

'Master Hariot.' The man half bowed.

'Where, exactly?' Hariot asked.

'Durham House, sir.'

Hariot looked down at the doctor's seal. 'I'll be there,' he said.

*   *   *

The April sun was already high by the time the party reached the high ground. Ralegh, as always, was first to the hilltop – if only because Ralegh was who he was and he was always first everywhere. He reined in the bay gelding with its straw-velvet livery and patted the animal's neck. Through the boughs of the elms, quickening now with the season, he saw London lying below him, straddling the river, a silver slash across the land. Paul's looked grey and solid, its spire lopped by the lightning. Ships without number cluttered the Queen's Wharves, their spars like hedgehogs bristling against the pearl of the morning. Every time he saw a race-built galleon, Walter Ralegh's heart leaped. He saw leafy Roanoke again and the copper-coloured heathens whose home it once was. He saw the stockade of raw-cut timbers, smelt the fragrance of the pine. All the magic, all the wonder of the New World that he had helped carve from the Old.

The hawk on his wrist twisted its jessed head, looking at him with blind eyes. Its claws, like black steel against the leather of his gauntlet, tightened and flexed as its wings fluttered. The bird smelled blood. It heard, as Ralegh could not, the beat of wings in the air, the rustle of feathers in the high wood. One movement from Ralegh, with the hood gone and the arm flung free and it would be away, soaring through the air like a musket ball, faster than the eye could follow, to crash and thud into the quarry, the hapless turtle-dove flying homeward to its nest. The dogs smelled it too – the scent of death in the morning. They yapped and snarled around the horses' hoofs as Ralegh's party joined him, panting with exertion after the long chase up Shooter's Hill. The hounds' patient eyes belied their tongues, lolling on the ground as they sniffed and snorted. Their heads came up and they watched the sky, waiting for the command from their lord.

But the command never came. A horseman was galloping up from the heather, sending clouds of dust as he rode. The black speck billowed and sharpened into a messenger, his cloak flying, the haunches of his horse flecked with foam.

'Steady,' Ralegh spoke softly to his hawk and his horse, both animals reacting instantly to the thud that beat a tattoo on the ground.

'My lord!' The messenger doffed his hat as he reined in, as blown as his horse. He handed Ralegh a letter, with a seal the huntsman knew well.

'How touching,' Ralegh smiled, steadying the hawk that flapped and squawked at this unwarranted intrusion. 'Thank you, Carter. A letter from the doctor. And here's me, feeling as fit as a flea.'

He was sure his heart would break. But then it had broken before. Never before like this, however. His Lucilla had filled his thoughts now for so long, he had forgotten everything else. He heard her laughter in his bridle bells, saw her smile in the rays of the sun, heard, even here in his library, the swish of her satin gown. But now she was gone. A letter had come, in her elegant hand. She loved him, she said, as a brother, as a friend. It was all her father's fault. Her father had chosen a husband for her long ago, when she was still in her hanging sleeves. She had no choice in this. It was the way of the world, at least for people of their class. 'Dearest, dearest Henry,' she had written. 'It is for the best.'

For the best! Henry forced himself upright, off the ottoman that lay in the corner and crossed to his books. Hariot probably had some arcane method of counting them by eye. There were nearly two thousand of them here at Petworth, but there was only one he wanted tonight: a book of Ovid's poetry, translated by one Christopher Marlowe. Owning two thousand books was one thing; finding any one of them was something entirely different. Please God, let the new librarian make sense of these shelves soon. He slid the steps nearer and climbed. There it was, the slim volume on the . . . Damn! His fingers hooked on the wrong spine and a heavier tome altogether crashed to the floor. It thudded on to the priceless Persian, the corner digging a gouge into the deep, silk pile and it lay there open, tantalizing.

A more ordinary man would have picked it up, straightened the pages, put the book back. But he was no ordinary man. He was Henry Percy, the ninth Earl of Northumberland, for God's sake. Men called him the wizard earl and there was a reason for that. He opened the page, deliberately not looking at the book's title. The colours of the rainbow lay there on the vellum, the myriad light of reds and blues, oranges and greens and the cause of the curve against the darkness of clouds.

Henry Percy smiled, but it was not an easy smile. Nothing happened for nothing. He had been looking for Ovid, via Marlowe and he had found Alhazen, the old Arab, a book he had forgotten he owned. He felt a shiver, as though the rain of that magic bow was falling on his shoulders, chilling him to the marrow.

'My lord?'

Percy dropped the book again and noted that this time it landed closed on the carpet. 'Who are you?' He controlled his stammer, if only because he had not had time to worry about framing his words.

'Carter, my lord. From the doctor.'

'The doctor?' Percy took the outstretched letter and nodded. He felt the skin of his head crawl. So that was it. The book. The page. The rainbow. Nothing was for nothing. There was a purpose to it all.

'Thank you, Carter,' the earl said. 'See my man for your trouble. Some coin. Food at least. And rest.'

Carter was affronted. 'Thank you, sir, I have no need of that. I have others to see.'

'Others?' Percy blinked, already opening the letter. 'Oh, yes. Yes, of course.'

The world looked strange through the eye-slits of a visor. The lists twisted and arced between the blackness and tents reeled, their colours blurring now red, now white. He wasn't watching any of this. He was focused on that shield, his target at the far end. His opponent was a bigger man, heavier and taller and better horsed. But what did they say? The bigger they are, the harder they fall? He hoped so.

The helmet was still a problem. He'd had the straps adjusted, but the beavor rode up, pushing his chin too high and restricting his vision. The pauldron re-panelling had worked well, though, freeing his arm, and he brought down the oak lance as his horse kicked off with its hind hoofs. He felt it snick into place on the iron rest and braced his back. Instinctively, he straightened his legs ready for the impact. He had won before; he had lost before. Once he had been unconscious for two days and that silly old priest had been fussing around him, with bell, book and candle – a little *too* anxious, it seemed to him, to issue the last rites.

He knew the horror stories; how Henri of France had gone down on what was supposed to be a sporting occasion, a holiday. How the lance had smashed through the eye-slits of the visor, into his eye, into his brain. And not only had Henri bled to death that day, but his country had been drained of blood for thirty years because of it. His opponent had been aiming for the shield, as all jousters did. But the lie of the ground, the mole-hill, the jitteriness of an inexperienced horse; any and all of that could mean that the lance tip could go anywhere. Into a man's brain. Into a man's soul.

The noise was deafening now inside the steel, the rising thud of the horses' hoofs as they reached the gallop. He saw his lance tip come into line with the shield – Edward Dymoke's shield, the champion of all England, its lions snarling in the sun. Only a practice bout, he kept telling himself as the moment came. Nothing to die for here. He felt the thud hit his left shoulder, saw his lance tip bounce uselessly off Dymoke's shield. His horse jerked to the right, carrying him away from the barrier, wheeling as he gripped the reins for dear life. His lance had gone from his grasp and for one long, horrifying moment, he couldn't breathe, the air punched from his lungs. His left arm was still hooked under the shield but the sloping wood had all but shattered and a splinter had embedded itself into his thigh, just beyond the rim of the cuisse. It wasn't bleeding yet, but it would when he wrenched the wood out.

He saw Dymoke reining in at the far end of the field, wheeling his horse to face him again. But he saw a second horseman, unarmoured, alone, cantering across the tilt field into his view. He threw up his visor and breathed again, letting the precious air fill his lungs.

'My lord,' he heard as his ears stopped pounding with his blood. 'My lord, are you all right?'

'Carter?' he squinted at the man. 'Is that you?'

'It is, my lord. Are you hurt?'

'No, no,' he said. 'It's nothing.'

There was another horseman at his elbow now. 'Ferdinando?' He leaned over, steadying the man in the saddle. 'Anything untoward?'

'No, Dymoke, no,' he said. 'Another day, though, eh? Got to get my breath back.'

'Absolutely,' the Queen's champion said, unhinging his helmet. 'Never let it be said I didn't give Lord Strange every opportunity. Better luck next time, eh?'

Strange tried to straighten himself and recapture what dignity he could. 'I haven't been well,' he said. 'Next time, indeed,' and he watched the champion salute and ride away.

'The doctor, I assume?' Strange said to Carter.

'Could there be another, my lord?' the messenger asked.

He had drawn the circle on the cold stone of the floor and the pentagram inside it, to keep him safe. He sat at its centre, the book open on his lap, watching the flames dance in the grate. The coal had cost him dear, brought all the way from the Tyne, but he'd had no choice; mere timber would not suffice and with Irish peat there was no flame at all. The reflection on the mercury sent myriad lights darting and sparkling on the ribbed vault of the ceiling.

He took the knife carefully in both hands, kissing the silver of its hilt. Then he thrust out his left hand, pulling back the velvet sleeve so that his vein was exposed. He sliced the skin and watched the blood ooze, beading the cut, then spurt, spattering the robe, the blade, the book. He noted carefully where the first drop fell. Asmodeus. So it must be. Asmodeus.

'Lord,' he intoned, his voice the only sound in the room now that the coals had settled. 'Demon of the Shedin, Master of the Gaming House of Hell, show me your face.'

He held out both hands as the blood still trickled, intoning the ancient Hebrew over and over. 'Show me the ram and the bull. Let me feel your fiery breath.'

There was a thud at the door and he visibly jumped, his pulse racing.

'Who's that?' He was almost afraid to hear the answer.

'Carter,' the muffled voice came back through the oak. 'Dr Dee's man. I have a letter for you, Dr Salazar, from the magus.'

'Slip it under the door,' Salazar commanded. 'Now is not a good time. I am expecting guests.'

FOUR

Tom Sledd always assured everyone he was not an impatient man. He thought that perhaps, if he said it often enough, it might even turn out to be true. Little did he know that in fact he did have wells of patience which few ordinary mortals could plumb; after all, he had lived almost his whole life with theatrical folk, from mummers on street corners, begging for food, up through the travelling players on the road, or higher still to the exalted ranks – as they saw themselves – of the company of the Rose. As he often remarked to Master Sackerson, the moth-eaten bear still kept by Philip Henslowe outside the theatre to amuse the crowds, they were nothing special, God above knew, but they were all he had. Once he left the warm nest of his home along Bankside, he needed the smell of glue, sawdust and ego as a fish needed water. But today his patience, far from filling a well, would have been hard pressed to wet a spoon.

'Has anyone . . .' He realized that his voice was high and tight, so he consciously relaxed his throat and unclenched his teeth. He had played heroines before his voice broke and he didn't want to be reminded of that. Several octaves lower, he began again. 'Has anyone seen Tom Watson this morning?'

In a storm of weeping, one of the dressers put her apron to her eyes and rushed from the room; a girl who, Sledd suddenly realized, had been putting on a lot of pounds lately.

Sledd sighed. 'Apart from Emily, I mean.'

Heads shook and shoulders rose, but otherwise, no one really cared.

'He was meant to be delivering some pages to me by yesterday at the latest.' He looked around, hoping that someone would suddenly brandish a sheaf of paper in the air and all his troubles would be over. 'No?' Sledd slumped and turned towards the stairs. He would have to share this with Henslowe, always a court of last resort. Where Tom Sledd kept everything inside, Henslowe let it all hang out, inkwells, goblets, plates and, in one never to be forgotten example, the theatre cat had all flown across the room at one time or another. But instead of a clear path to the staircase, he found his way blocked.

'Tom.'

'Will.' Damn. He had hoped to keep Shaxsper out of this. He might come up with the odd useful line from time to time, but really he should stick to being a second-rate actor and not try to be a fourth-rate playwright.

'Pages? You didn't ask me. I could do you some extra pages if you need them.' The Warwickshire man's smile was chilly and fixed.

'Ah. Yes. I know you are always ready to help, Will, but, ah ha!' to his horror, the stage manager heard a slightly hysterical laugh break through, 'Kit had already made arrangements, you see. I, ah, I didn't like to interfere.'

'Arrangements?' Shaxsper's voice was level but it was clear that his temper was reaching Henslowe levels.

'Tom Watson is writing some extra bits. Wykehamist. Oxford scholar. Local colour, that kind of thing. You remember, Will.' Sledd risked a friendly buffet to the man's shoulder, but it was like punching an iceberg. 'We all thought that we needed a few lines to let the idiots . . . the groundlings, I mean, bless their little purses . . . know what is going on.'

Shaxsper looked coldly at Sledd. 'Watson knows a lot about Malta, does he? A lot about Jews?'

Sledd had had enough. 'As much as you do, I expect, Will. And if he needs a little help, no doubt Master Thomas Walsingham's library will be of no little help.'

Shaxsper flounced as only a frustrated playwright could. 'There's no need for that, Tom,' he said, with just a hint of a whine in his voice. 'Patrons don't grow on trees, you know. It's not for want of trying . . .'

Sledd patted him on the arm. 'I know, Will, I know. But, when you do finally manage to find one, can you do me a small favour? I would be so grateful.'

'If I can.' Shaxsper was close to being mollified. 'What?'

'Find one who isn't called Thomas. It's getting a bit complicated around here.'

*   *   *

Kit Marlowe was tired and road-stained as he tied up his horse in the stable at the end of Hog Lane. For much of the previous night, he had sat crouched on a stool in the inner sanctum of the Queen's magus, watching fascinated as the man mixed liquids, drained phials and scribbled furiously with his quill at each bubbling, every change of colour. He had watched Dee work before and he knew the man's powers. But there was no dark mirror that night, no roar of thunder or flash of light. No spirits came to him and gripped him by the hair. And, hours later, the result came as pure anti-climax.

'I don't know, Kit,' the magus had said.

Marlowe had looked at him, the skullcap, the long white beard. Above all, he had looked into the man's eyes, those mirrors of the soul. He saw fire, he saw death, he saw magic. What he did not see was a man stumped, a scholar beaten by *Scientia*, wisdom.

'Your best guess, then,' Marlowe had challenged him.

'Guess?' Dee had snapped back. 'I am the Queen's magus. I do not guess. You'll have to wait.'

'Until?'

'Until Hell freezes over, playwright.'

There had already been a freezing. 'Kit' had become 'playwright' as the liquids of the night had mingled and changed colour. Dee had found something. Something he had no intention of sharing with a cobbler's son from Canterbury. Not yet at least.

And now, Marlowe wanted something to eat, something to drink and a nap in his own bed. Night and day had always been but one to Marlowe, but sometimes even he needed to close his eyes and indulge in some nice home comforts.

The front door was unlatched as he got to his house, but that was by no means unusual. Watson was always coming and going and Agnes needed to go marketing, so locking up was often a wasted effort. He looked around the kitchen door, but apart from the tick of the warm range and the low singing of the kettle, the room was empty and still. He hauled off his boots and left them to dry in the inglenook. A loaf of new bread was cooling on the table and Marlowe tore off the crust and slathered it thickly with butter. He leaned on the table and ate it voluptuously, letting the creamy butter coat his moustache and grease his chin. He poured some ale from the jug on the dresser and drank deeply. Even after enjoying some of the most delicious foods on offer at the boards of Walsingham and the great and good of the country, he still enjoyed the simple things the most. As he ate, he could almost hear the clamour of Corpus Christi's Buttery, the wise words of Michael Johns in one ear, the venom of Gabriel Harvey in the other. Those days seemed so long ago, but were like a winking in eternity's eye.

He shook himself. He always got a little introspective when he was tired, but he had no time for introspection just now; there was much to do. He wiped his face and hands on the apron hanging on the back of the door and started up the stairs. He let his eyes droop as he reached the landing and, by the time he was at the end of the bed, he had unlaced as much of his doublet as he intended to loosen. Sleep was in his eyes as he fell face forward across the bed.

'By all that's Holy!' Tom Watson had been otherwise engaged beneath the coverlet as Marlowe landed on him with the weight of the exhausted. Had he not been in his nightgown, it could have gone ill with Marlowe, a dagger between the ribs being the best outcome. Agnes the kitchen maid lay under him, rigid with stark terror.

Marlowe was on his feet before his eyes opened. 'Tom Watson! In my bed!' There was no point in asking what he was doing – firstly, he was Tom and secondly, it was plain for all to see.

'Kit.' Watson had his hands in front of him in supplication. 'I can explain . . .'

Marlowe shook his head. Agnes tried to slip out of the room unobserved, but Marlowe held up a finger and she froze. 'No explanations, Tom, please. It doesn't take a giant intellect to know what was going on. But I do wonder why it had to be in my bed.' He waited expectantly for an answer but none came. He turned to Agnes and raised an eyebrow. 'Anything, wench? You have surely had time to think of something.'

She dropped her head, blushing. 'Oh, Master Marlowe,' she said, quietly. 'I was making your bed, turning the pallet while you were away . . .'

'An unusual way of turning a pallet,' Marlowe said, wryly, 'though I confess I am no housekeeper.'

'I couldn't manage it, sir,' she said. 'It is too new and heavy for me. So . . .'

It all fell into place. 'So, you called Master Watson to help you.'

The girl brightened. 'That's right, sir,' she cried. 'I did. I went on to the landing and called and he . . . well . . . he came out and . . .'

'Came in,' Marlowe said, looking coldly at his lodger. 'Did you not wonder at him being in his nightshirt?'

The girl laughed. 'Master Tom is always in his nightshirt,' she said, spluttering. Then, she realized what she had said. 'I mean, Master Watson works at his writing in his nightshirt,' she corrected herself.

'That's right,' Watson chimed in. 'I was writing those pages for you, Kit.'

'Oh, yes.' Marlowe stood now with his arms folded. He felt like an angry father, come upon his child in fornication. 'The pages you were writing for me in lieu of rent. How *are* they coming along?'

Watson waved a casual hand. 'Done,' he said. 'Good as, anyway.'

'Good as?'

Watson tapped his head with a knowing forefinger. 'All in here,' he said. 'I just need to write it all down. Just about to, in fact, when Agnes here distracted me.'

The girl burst into tears. She could see her future. It involved starvation, shame, the street, tied to the cart's tail.

Marlowe made up his mind. 'This is how the rest of the day is going to work for you both. You,' he pointed to the maid, 'will get yourself straightened out. Put back on any garments you may have shed and go down and tend to the cooking.' With a grateful look, the girl fled, snatching up discarded linen as she went. 'And you,' Marlowe said, pointing this time to Watson, 'will go to your *own* room and write all those golden lines you have in your head.'

'But now you're back—' Watson began.

'I haven't finished.' Marlowe unfolded his arms and, without

Watson seeing how it happened, he had his dagger in his hand and it was pointing at his most vulnerable spot. 'When your golden lines are on paper, in your best writing, mind, you will take the pages round to Thomas Sledd at the Rose.'

Watson could hardly believe his luck. He had expected to be at least threatened with eviction, but all seemed to be well, nevertheless.

Marlowe's annoyance was abating and the humour of the situation was beginning to take precedence. He slid his dagger home into the sheath at his back and turned to the doorway, where he stopped as though poleaxed. The woman leaning on the doorjamb was not particularly beautiful, but she was stark naked and clearly as angry as they come.

'What kept you, Thomas?' she said, acidly. 'One minute you were making verses to my beautiful . . . well, never mind what . . . and the next you were giving the maid a hand.' Her dark eyes raked the room. 'Although now I wonder just what you were doing. And who,' she spat at Marlowe, 'might you be?'

Marlowe sighed. 'I sometimes wonder, madam,' he said, politely, bowing, but under his breath he muttered, 'I might be Belzebub for all you know.' He turned pointedly to his erstwhile friend. 'Thomas,' he said, 'I have another task for you, but simpler than the writing, perhaps.'

Watson tried a smile, but it didn't feel very comfortable on his frozen face. 'Name it,' he said.

'When you've written the pages and delivered them to Tom at the Rose, I want you to come back here and pack your things. I'm having a short nap and, when I wake up, I want you gone.'

'And me?' the whore in the doorway asked, in a sultry purr.

'Assuming you came in clothes, madam, please assume them and leave as well. Thomas knows the way out and I am sure he would be happy to share the knowledge with you. Now,' he ushered Watson to the door and used him to push the woman out on to the landing, 'I wish you both good day.'

Philip Henslowe was perched as always in his eyrie above the theatre, keeping more than an eagle's eye on what went on below. Everyone knew about his window, which commanded a wide view across the seats; he could estimate a house down to the last groat, as he had proved time without number to the chagrin of the occasional crooked ticket-seller. But what hardly anyone knew about were the numerous little squints he had had incorporated into the building, through which he could keep his people observed, without cramping their style by letting them know they were being watched. He chuckled now as he watched the exchange between Sledd and Shaxsper. He loved Tom Sledd like a son; Tom was as loyal as any employer could want and if he was occasionally overwhelmed by the actors, he hid it well. Henslowe treated everyone like a fairly stupid, fairly dishonest child and so far that had served him more than adequately. Sledd was beginning to understand his methods and he watched him with pride as he coped with what less discerning impresarios were wont to call 'the talent'. He was still chuckling over the inappropriateness of the term when Sledd came in, hard on his peremptory knock.

Henslowe looked up, feigning surprise. 'Tom! How can I help you?'

Sledd was suspicious. Of all the old ham actors in the building, and there were many, Henslowe was perhaps the least convincing. 'I have a bit of a problem with the next production,' he said, flinging himself down in a chair near the window and looking out, moodily.

Henslowe made encouraging noises and waited. He knew his Tom Sledd – a bit of cogitation was always the precursor to a veritable flood of information.

The stage manager chewed a thumbnail and then grimaced as he remembered he had been using glue not half an hour before – boiled hoof and horn had never been his favourite flavour. 'We need some new pages,' he said. 'Marlowe is on song, as always, of course, but he has left a little too much to the imagination in some parts and, let's face it, Master Henslowe, if there is one thing you can guarantee in any average audience, they are a bit lacking in that area.'

Henslowe looked dubious. He had heard the salacious laughter in the bawdy passages and sometimes had been of the opinion that the groundlings were pretty much filling in the blanks for themselves. For himself, he would have left no blanks to fill, but Edmund Tilney was not so much a Master of the

Revels as the Master of Let's Not Let Anyone Enjoy Themselves. Puritan bastard. Why didn't he just close the theatres down and have done?

Tom Sledd could read Henslowe like a book, so explained further. 'No, not that kind of imagination. I just mean the flying bits, the . . . poetry, I suppose I have to call it. We just need a bit of explanation.'

Henslowe waved an airy hand. 'Can't Shaxsper do it?' It amused him to tease his stage manager.

'Sshh!' Sledd put an anxious finger to his lip. 'Don't let him hear that. He'll be badgering me all the more. No, Marlowe asked Tom Watson to do it.'

'Marlowe can't do it?' Henslowe raised an eyebrow. What did he pay these people for, after all?

'He's had to go out of Town for a while,' Sledd hedged.

'Not all that spying nonsense, surely?' Henslowe said with a sigh. 'Really, Tom, I'm surprised at you. Do you really believe all that?'

Sledd blinked.

'We all know it's just Marlowe's way of getting away from time to time. Spying? Intelligencer! Tchah! He's probably got a nice warm woman tucked away somewhere in the country, some matron whose husband doesn't mind being cuckolded by the Muses' darling.' Henslowe folded his hands over his stomach and chuckled again. 'I doubt he even knows Sir Francis Walsingham.'

'He's dead,' Sledd remarked.

'Marlowe?' Sometimes, Henslowe found Sledd's conversation hard to follow.

'No! Walsingham.' But Sledd's attention was no longer in the little attic room. He had seen, far below, a gangly figure leaning over the wall of the Bear Pit, having a word with Master Sackerson. 'Watson!' he breathed and was gone.

Tom Watson rarely went into any building without first looking carefully around the door. Enemies lurked in every shadow and ranged in shape and size from the smallest serving wench to the largest outraged creditor, with all kinds of fathers, husbands and brothers in between. But the coast seemed to be clear, so he edged in carefully, his sheaf of papers held before him like a peace offering. He leapt as a voice sounded in his ear. It was the second time that morning that he had almost died of shock.

'Master Watson. My pages, I presume.' Sledd's voice sounded as though it should belong to something scaly basking on a rock.

'Ah!' Watson's nerves were on a knife-edge. He had a lot on his mind and he didn't take tension well. He had had what could only be called a tricky interview with Esmeralda, the Winchester goose who had filled his bed last night; she always claimed Egyptian blood and she certainly was showing it today. His ear still smarted where she had caught him a nasty one with the heel of her shoe. Add to that Agnes, who was feeling slighted, and Emily, for whom he was watching most carefully and it was no surprise that Tom Watson was a worried man. He supposed that he would still be welcome at Thomas Walsingham's place at Scadbury, buried deep in the Kent countryside as it was and far from London, but he had a vague feeling that he owed him a couple of poems and at least one revel.

'Well said,' Sledd said, taking the paper with a pinch of finger and thumb. 'About time. Now, bugger off.' Dressers were hard enough to come by, God knew, and letting Watson hang around was tantamount to pandering.

Watson needed no further bidding. Like a louse in the bedding, he scuttled off, hoping to find a nice warm – and more especially undemanding – home elsewhere. 'I'll be at Scadbury then,' he called, 'if anyone needs me.'

'Lovely,' said Sledd, taking the pages into the space behind the painted flats which he laughingly called his library. True, there were a few books of collected plays on the single shelf that held on to the wall more by luck than carpentry. Like many people with a skill for making things, Tom Sledd had better things to do with his time when not actually engaged in his employment than to put up shelves and other footling pursuits. In vain had his good lady been begging for the door to the press in their bedroom to be mended and it fell off and brained their little maid-of-all-work on an almost daily basis.

Tom Sledd had been brought up in the hardest of all theatrical genres, that of the travelling players. The scenery for them was whatever backdrop the town or village in question had to offer, so many a time he had played the Maid of Orleans against the wall of an inn or ramshackle fence. He had always had the dubious pleasure of playing the female parts, being small of chin, big of eye and rather fluting as to voice, back in the day. His playbooks were the old stagers, *Ralph Roister Doister* and other gems from the pen of Nicholas Udall. A couple of John Lyly's. He hadn't had to use one yet, but sometimes it had been close, very close.

He sat down now to read Watson's extra pages. They were neatly written, at least, and not at all bad. He had taken on Marlowe's style admirably, the thundering metre, the mighty line. The spelling was as accurate as you might expect for a poet who was drunk half the time and fornicating the other three quarters. Sledd nodded; yes, these extra speeches would come in very nicely indeed. He ran a few lines through his head.

> Now I remember those old woman's words,
> Who in my wealth would tell me winter's tales,
> And speak of spirits and ghosts that glide by night
> About the place where treasure hath been hid.
> And now methinks that I am one of these;
> For, whilst I die, here lives my soul's sole hope,
> And when I die, here shall my spirit walk.

Oh, yes, Sledd knew, New Alleyn would love this bit. What he'd just read in seconds, the Great Tragedian would take a full five minutes to roll out.

Shaxsper was annoyed, there was no getting away from it. He had seen that idiot Watson turn up with his grubby bits of paper; rubbish, you could tell even from a distance. He leaned on the wall over the Bear Pit and communed with its only occupant. Master Sackerson was looking a bit moth-eaten these days, even his best friends would admit, but it was spring, and in the spring, an old bear's fancy lightly turns to thoughts of moulting. To that end, the bear was standing on his hind legs and rubbing his back luxuriantly against the wall, accompanying this activity with pleased little grunts. Shaxsper watched him; how wonderful to have nothing in your mind but scratching that itch. He had an itch he couldn't scratch; jealousy of almost everyone he knew. Marlowe for being a better playwright and having more hair. Sledd for being Henslowe's favourite, having more hair and a wife who could stand him being in the house. Alleyn and Burbage for actually being able to act. It was true that the constant wigs Burbage was forced to wear for the character parts were taking their toll on his hair, but still, they got all the glory. Will Shaxsper sighed. The sap was rising, the birds were singing and here he was, leaning over a wall and talking to a bear. He allowed himself to wallow in misery; perhaps he should put the mood to work and go and carry on with the play he was mulling over. There was that Island thing that Marlowe had suggested. And surely, the Warwickshire man could make a better fist of a tight-fisted old Jew than Barabbas. Sherlock, perhaps? Yes, that was a good name. But always his thoughts ran to the historical and fluttered to rest on the soul of poor, mad old Henry VI.

He was pulled from his brown study by a polite cough behind him. He turned. Two men stood there, unalike in appearance except that they shared the same slightly weaselly expression.

The taller of the two doffed his cap. 'Master Henslowe?' he asked, deferentially.

Shaxsper was torn. It was good to be taken for a man of substance, who owned the Rose – and most of the streets around it, if even some of the gossip were true. On the other hand, Henslowe was old enough to be his father, at the very least and looked every minute of it. He decided to be moderately pleased, with a veneer of affront.

'No,' he said. 'I am William Shakespeare.' He paused. Nothing. 'Actor and playwright.'

The men stepped back in perfect unison. 'Playwright!' the shorter one said, doffing his cap also. 'I wonder, do you know Master Marlowe?'

Shaxsper sighed. 'Twas ever thus. 'We're great friends, yes,' he said, in a tone which belied the words. 'If you're looking for Kit, though, you are having bad luck today. He isn't here.'

'Oh, no, no,' the taller, rather more thickset one said quickly. 'We don't *know* Master Marlowe as such. We know *of* him.'

Shaxsper nodded. At least these two were honest. 'So,' he said, suddenly anxious to carry on his one-sided conversation with the bear, 'if you want Master Henslowe, you'll find him in the theatre. But I warn you . . . he doesn't buy anything at the door and it's no good asking for a donation of any kind; he doesn't give at the door either.'

'We're actors,' the smaller one explained. 'We saw a bill in the alehouse down there, saying the theatre is in need of extra walking gentlemen.'

Shaxsper raised a sardonic eyebrow. 'You're actors?' he asked, dubiously.

'In a small way.' The taller one blushed and looked down as he traced an aimless pattern in the dust with his toe. 'Nothing major, just a few tours in the provinces, you know.' He nudged his companion. 'What was that thing we did, Ing, that thing, you know, the one with the dog?'

His friend put a finger to his lip and looked skywards, mumming an air of deep thought with little success. 'Sorry, Nick,' he said. 'I just can't put a name to it.' He looked at Shaxsper and the eyes were no longer vague, but like daggers looking for a target. 'But we're very good.' He rammed his hat back on his head and pointed at the Rose, settling in her midday sleep before the afternoon show. 'Through there, is it?'

Shaxsper nodded. He felt a chill run down from the crown of his head to the soles of his feet.

The shorter man shook his head indulgently. 'You must excuse my friend,' he said to Shaxsper. 'He forgets his manners when he thinks there may be a role for him. The play's the thing, you know. Let me introduce ourselves. He,' and he gestured to where his companion was shouldering open the wicket, 'is Nicholas Skeres. I am Ingram Frizer. So glad to have made your acquaintance, Master Shakeshaft.' And with a purposeful stride, he set off up the slope of the lane, leaving Shaxsper alone with the bear.

FIVE

Marlowe had been to Barn Elms before, taking the darkling river where its strange eddies ran counter to the seaward flow. Neither he nor the boatman was in the mood to talk, the man cloaked and booted against the coming night. An owl hooted in the darkening woods as the boat's torch guttered in the shifting wind.

Marlowe pressed a coin into the boatman's hand and was already on the wooden planks of the jetty when he heard the man ask, 'Is it true, then? Is Sir Francis dead?'

Marlowe looked at him, for the first time *under* the hood, not at it. London boatmen, he knew, were the nosiest in the world. They kept their own counsel, but made it their business to find out everybody else's. On the other hand, it could be that the man was an intelligencer for Rome. Nobody's virtue was over-nice.

'Sir Francis who?' he asked.

The boatman scowled, muttered something under his breath and hauled up his oars, the river water flying like dark moths through the dusk, wood rattling on wood until he had vanished into the darkness.

Marlowe turned to the house. It loomed as a black bulk below the tallest elms, its windows pinpoints of candlelight. From somewhere, a dog barked and the playwright heard footsteps on the path, a pale winding way under the rising moon. His hand went to the dagger at his back; even in a house of mourning, especially *this* house of mourning, there was danger.

'Mylles.' Marlowe shook the man's hand as he became clearer with proximity.

'Welcome, Master Marlowe,' the retainer said. 'Lady Walsingham is expecting you.'

'How is she, Mylles?' Marlowe liked Ursula Walsingham. Even when her late husband was at his most devious and his temper frayed beyond repair, Ursula was always steady, reassuring. She reminded Marlowe of his own mother, radiating trust and love in a cruel world.

'She is Lady Walsingham,' Mylles said with a shrug and they both knew that said it all.

'You were with Sir Francis?' Marlowe asked as they took the path through the knot garden. 'When he died?'

'I was, sir,' Mylles said. 'And Master Faunt not long after.'

'You sent for him?'

'Not exactly, sir. He wasn't due until the next day. Came early, he said, on a whim.'

Marlowe raised an eyebrow but it was a gesture lost in the dark. 'A whim, Mylles?' Both men knew Nicholas Faunt. Whims were something he did not do.

'It's not for me to question the master's people, sir,' Mylles said. Since Marlowe was one of them, that was gratifying in a way. But in another, it wasn't. Francis Walsingham was the Queen's Spymaster, playing the most dangerous game a man could. If no one questioned his people, what, in the end, could keep him safe?

'Tell me about the last day,' Marlowe said, getting into step with the man as they reached the gravel path.

Mylles stopped. They would be at the side door in a moment and he didn't want to be talking about this when they reached it. He focused for a moment, searching Marlowe's face, reading there what he could. Marlowe could wear his heart on his sleeve or hidden up it; he let Mylles see enough to know it was safe to talk. 'He had not been well for some time, as you probably know,' he murmured, in case the fountains had ears. 'He couldn't sleep and was worried about the Irish business.'

'Irish business?'

Mylles shrugged. 'I was never quite sure what it was, sir. The Queen's business, for sure. We all did our best for him, calming him down, warming his feet. He was a troubled man towards the end.'

'How long have you been with him, Mylles?' Marlowe asked.

'These fourteen years, sir,' the man remembered. 'I was with Sir Christopher Hatton before that.'

'We'll leave that stone unturned, Mylles,' Marlowe nodded. Of all the noddies that fluttered around the court, Christopher

Hatton was the most stupid. 'Did anybody come to see Sir Francis, on the last day, I mean?'

'I wasn't there in the morning, sir,' the retainer told him. 'In the afternoon, Master Patchmore turned up.'

'Who's he?'

'Local farmer, sir. Holds property beyond Barn Elms. He's been at loggerheads with Sir Francis for years over grazing rights in the lower meadow. I saw him off.'

'So he didn't actually see Sir Francis?'

'No, sir.' Mylles scowled. 'He did not. Grasping skinflint. You'd think he'd be proud to have a man like Sir Francis as his neighbour. Master Williams came later.'

'Rowland Williams?' Marlowe checked.

'The same, sir. You must know him, I'm sure.'

Marlowe did. After Nicholas Faunt, there was no one more slippery in the Spymaster's employ and Marlowe did what he could to stay out of his way. 'What did he want?'

Mylles chuckled. The house had been a house of mourning for days, everything muffled and swathed in deepest black. Marlowe, the retainer noticed, had tied a black velvet ribbon to his right sleeve, death on his sword arm. Only certain rooms were lit now against the night; the others lay in the darkness of the coming clouds. Everyone was creeping around, afraid of their own footfalls, whispering in corners, avoiding the light. Perhaps at last Mylles could allow himself a small chuckle. 'Of all the men who wore Sir Francis's livery, Master Marlowe, I was probably the only one who *didn't* listen at the foot of a stair.'

'All right.' Marlowe folded his arms now that they had reached the side door. There were certain things that could not be discussed where walls may well have ears. 'How long did he stay?'

'Master Williams? About an hour, perhaps more.'

'Where was this, in Sir Francis's private quarters?'

'His inner sanctum, sir, yes.'

'You saw Williams leave?'

'I escorted him to his horse myself.'

'He didn't come by river, then?'

'No sir. Told me he was bound for Nonsuch.'

'And no one else came calling?'

'No one, sir. Oh, only Sir Walter Ralegh.'

'Kit. How are you?'

In her black, Ursula Walsingham looked as regal and unperturbed as ever.

'My lady.' Marlowe bowed.

'My lady!' she tutted. 'I think it's more than time you called me Ursula, don't you?'

He smiled and shook his head. 'Ursula,' he said. 'I don't have the words.'

She looked surprised. 'Yes, you do,' she scolded gently. 'You're a playwright. What do men say of you – "the Muses' darling"? "All fire and air"?'

Marlowe wanted to laugh, but in this hall of sorrow, it didn't seem quite right. 'I am paid for those words,' he said. 'The day job. They're not from the heart.'

'I know you, Kit Marlowe,' she closed to him and put a gentle hand on his sleeve. '*All* your words are from the heart. All your mighty lines.'

'But in the case of Sir Francis . . .' Marlowe began. She held a finger to his lips.

'I assume it is that very case that brings you here.'

'My lady . . . Ursula, I assure you . . .'

'Dear boy.' She took him by the arm. 'Come and warm yourself. I still have a fire in the solar for all it's April and that river freezes a man's marrow. Let me see; it will have gone something like this. Poor Francis meets his maker and Nicholas Faunt suspects murder.'

'He told you that?' Marlowe was surprised. Nicholas Faunt was a lot of things, but loose-lipped was not one of them.

'Other than his name, Nicholas Faunt has never told me anything. Anything that is true, anyway. That's why he is so good at what he does; why Francis kept him on. No, Faunt didn't have to say anything; I know how his mind works. He will have assumed poison. He will then have asked himself who, among Francis's golden lads, has the experience of things like that. The first name on his list will have been yours.'

'I'm flattered,' Marlowe said, allowing Ursula to lead him towards the marbled passageway.

'You've spoken to Mylles already?'

'I have,' Marlowe said. 'I may need to do so again.'

'Salt of the earth, Mylles,' she said. 'I couldn't have wished Francis a better manservant. Now you'll talk to me. You'll want to see the other servants. Oh, and Francis's inner sanctum, where he . . .' for the first time, her voice betrayed her, but she sniffed and swept on. 'And of course, you'll want to talk to Frances too.'

'If I may,' Marlowe said.

Ursula stopped. 'I want you to be careful with Frances, Kit,' she said. 'She adored her father and she's been through a lot lately.'

Careful, Marlowe repeated in his head. What an odd choice of word. Gentle, perhaps. Understanding. Tender, even. But . . . careful? The Muses' darling assured the widow of Barn Elms that he would.

Ursula Walsingham had been thoroughly honest; Marlowe was sure of that. But the Spymaster had been a careful man. He had warned too many of his people to be wary of what they said between the sheets; pillow talk could rack a man, drive iron into his bowels, crush his windpipe with hemp. He applied the same criteria to his own wife, not because he didn't trust her, but because the less she knew, the less she could tell. He had kept her safe always, as he had kept the Queen safe. There was a price on the head of the Jezebel of England and there was not on the head of Ursula Walsingham. Or was there? Walsingham's people were everywhere, hunting Jesuits, stamping out Popery, but there were always cracks in the pavement, holes in the wainscoting. And every man who passed in the street was a smiler with a knife.

Marlowe wandered the Spymaster's inner sanctum. He had three of these: one here at Barn Elms, another along Seething Lane where he'd died, a third at Whitehall. There were secrets in them all. Walsingham had served the Queen for nearly twenty years, since Kit Marlowe was still splashing through the puddles of cobbled Canterbury on his way to school. How many secrets

had been added over those years, chasing like ghosts in the
dark recesses of a man's mind and a man's study?

Marlowe counted four strongboxes, each one locked and
bound in brass. Ursula had no keys for these. Neither did Mylles.
Nicholas Faunt had a key, but Nicholas Faunt was not here.
Along the shelves lay books and papers, scribblings in
Walsingham's precise, neat hand. There was one book that
Marlowe recognized as code, but the fact that it was out in the
open meant that the code was obsolete and had been abandoned.
It would have been one of the many offerings of the code-
breaker, Thomas Phelippes: worth its weight in gold while
current, but burnable trash once the codes had been changed.
There were other pages of parchment too, some blank. But
Marlowe knew they were not really blank. He lit a candle in a
dark corner, away from the leaded panes of the window and
squinted to see the words that glowed there, invisibility made
visible by the candle's flame. It was a note from Thomas
Wyndebank, something to do with Ireland, cattle, estates. Ireland
was a thorn in Walsingham's flesh as it was in Elizabeth's, but
there were more pressing problems. Nothing here that could
explain a man's sudden death.

He blew out the candle, took one last look around the room
and left.

The candles blinded him at first. There were so many of them.
And this in the house of the greatest Papist hunter of them all.
He let his eyes get used to them, dancing in the little draughts
that ran through passageways and rippled through keyholes.
Beyond them he could see the half armour, blued and gilded
and chased with the arms of Sidney on the breast. Intrigued,
he drew closer. This was a shrine, that much was clear, and the
flames' reflections danced on the vambraces and pauldrons.
There was something off, though, unfinished, missing. Half
armour was commonplace, especially for portraits when a man
wanted to be seen in his finery for all time, glowing on canvas
for the ages. In this case, the cuisse-straps were still there,
buckled on to the corselet. But there were no cuisses and the
strap ends were dark-stained, the leather stiff.

'Master Marlowe.' The voice made him turn.

'Mistress Sidney.' Marlowe bowed. He had seen this girl before, when she had still been the wife of Philip Sidney. He had seen her as a widow, when Philip Sidney died. This was the first time he had seen her without her father, the man she adored. 'Please accept my deepest condolences.'

'Dead shepherd,' she nodded and crossed beyond the candles to straighten the lance-rest on the armour. 'Tell me, Master Marlowe, have you ever fought a battle?'

'The odd duel, my lady,' Marlowe said, 'but a battle, no, I have not.'

'I hope you never have to,' she said. 'It breaks hearts.'

He let the silence stand between them. She turned away sharply and looked at him. Frances Sidney, née Walsingham, was younger than Marlowe. She was beautiful, with her mother's gentle face and her father's grey, glittering eyes. Black became her and, unlike her mother, she wore it unadorned, unbroken. Ursula wore pearls and beads. Frances dressed like the night. 'You want to talk about Papa,' she said and ushered him to a chair.

'There is some doubt, my lady,' he said, once she was sitting opposite him, 'about Sir Francis's death.'

'That he is dead, or how he died?' she asked.

'Er . . . the latter,' Marlowe said. He had barely exchanged a dozen words with this woman before, but already he realized that she spoke in riddles.

'What if he were not dead?' she asked. 'What if all this,' she waved to the candles, to her widow's weeds, 'were simply a Spymaster's ploy to lure his enemies into the open?'

'Then I would catch them, my lady, as you and Her Majesty would expect.'

'Her Majesty?' Frances all but snorted. 'Look around you, Master Marlowe. Barn Elms, the house in Seething Lane, the movables thereof. Who owns them?'

'Er . . . I am not privy to Sir Francis's will, my lady,' Marlowe said, feeling increasingly uncomfortable.

'It doesn't matter what his will says,' she told him. 'Papa bankrupted himself years ago in the service of Her Majesty.' She spoke the last two words in a voice which dripped venom. 'Mama, of course, will never tell you that. She's too loyal, too

true. Me? I see things as they are . . . sometimes. None of this
belongs to the Walsinghams. We'll have to leave. Do you know
that Her Majesty has not even sent a letter of condolence?'
    Marlowe had no answer to that.
    'Why do you serve her, Master Marlowe?' Frances asked.
'The Jezebel, the prize bitch. Two years ago, she left her sailors
to rot in their hulks along the Thames and the Medway; the
sailors who had saved her realm from the Armada. No money,
no physic, nothing. Not even the thanks of a grateful Queen.
My father gave his life for that woman. I wonder – who will
be the next?'

It was dark now the April twilight had faded to night; a final
blackbird, putting the day to bed with some running trills,
stuttered to a stop as a horse clattered up the approach to the
house. The sounds of the city came faintly through the encir-
cling trees and, for all this house was on the Strand, just yards
away from the river, it might have been in the deepest countryside. The horse's rider dismounted with a flourish and beat
a complex tattoo on the door, which opened smoothly on
well-oiled hinges. The man slipped inside, cloak flying, spurs
jingling at his booted heels. The door closed again and the
blackbird finished its cadence; silence reigned in the garden
of Durham House.
    Inside the dark was even more complete. From the hallway,
with one single shielded candle by the door, it was clear even
to a newcomer which way they should go, with just one doorway
ajar, a faint light spilling like honey on the marble floor of the
hall. But no one coming to Durham House that night was a
stranger. They had all been there many, many times before,
always under cover of darkness, always protected by the shades
of night.
    The servant who guarded the door blew out the candle and
made his way with the ease of long practice across the hall
to the baize door in the corner which no one ever noticed.
Beyond it lay everything that a great house needed to run
smoothly: heat, light, bustle and people; but nothing of that
must ever show itself in the murky purlieus above. His master
loved the dramatic and paid the wages to ensure it. The maids

wore black from head to foot. The manservants were all
chosen for their pallor and solemn demeanour. When the latest
addition to the upstairs staff had turned out to have one blue
eye and one brown, he had been given an extra guinea a year,
just because. The nights when the master had visitors meant
a night off for the staff and, as soon as the last one had
arrived, Scranton the steward would shoo everyone out the
back way and they could hit the taverns in the town, all on
the master's guinea. A tight lip was a small price to pay for
such riches.

As the latest man to arrive entered the room and closed the
door, the candle in the middle of the great table guttered in
the draught but didn't quite go out. The winding sheet of wax
running down its side was pooling on the silver dish in which
it sat and made oily patterns in the lamplight. It had been
remarked upon before that using a black candle was perhaps
an affectation too far, but when black arts may need to be
called upon at any time, it paid to be careful. The five men
already round the table leaned back and their faces were in
shadow.

Ferdinando Strange, the latest addition to their number, took
his seat and looked around. He had jarred his back in the lists
and his thigh gave him gyp, so he moved carefully. Just six
of them? Why so few? Usually, some more pernickety member
would insist on a quorum, but this was far from that. Strange
amused himself for a moment with trying to identify his
companions simply from the small bit of them visible in
the faint light. Ralegh was easily identified, of course. Not
only was it his house, but the light glinting from his gold-
embroidered doublet shone on the diamonds of the rings on
the hand laid so complacently on his breast made it as clear
as if he had been wearing a label. You couldn't miss the special
man, the great Lucifer.

Strange turned his head to look more closely at the man to
Ralegh's left. No ostentation there, just a grey robe below a
white beard, fur-trimmed summer and winter and looking
a little moth-eaten these days. There was a stain on the sleeve
just where it disappeared into the gloom at the edge of the faint
light's circle. It did not take a mind of Strange's unusual genius

to know that this was John Dee; his magus's robes were unmistakable and everyone who ever went near him these days knew about the new little addition to his quiverful of children; little Madimi was well known to suffer from the colic, hence the stain. Why Dee didn't just dose the child with one of his potions and have done, Strange would never know.

Next to Dee and therefore on Strange's immediate right, was someone who was not so easy to identify. He had clearly taken steps to be anonymous, with clothes which were masterly in their nondescript styling. No diamonds here, no clues as to identity at all. Strange looked closer and smiled a little to himself. Henry Percy, as he lived and breathed. Tucked into the breast of his doublet was a letter and a scrap of red ribbon was just visible laid against one corner. Percy went nowhere without at least one love letter about his person; he had had his heart broken more times than Strange had had hot dinners; when the man finally married and made some woman permanently miserable, the sales of scented notepaper would plummet.

Turning to his left, Strange knew at once who was sitting there. That inky forefinger could only belong to one man. Strange, a man of moods and enthusiasms himself, could understand an obsession as well as the next man, unless that man was Thomas Hariot, who was never truly happy except when among his numbers and his equations. He knew the world could be reduced to columns, to arcane minutiae of facts and figures and he lived on the edge of discovery all the while. The answer to the universe and all its workings was just around the corner; it was simply a matter of putting everything in the right place, at the right time; Hariot was hardly ever really in a room. He sent his body about in the world, but his mind was always elsewhere.

Hariot's head, bent forward as always in thought, half concealed the man on his left. Only an arm was clearly visible, held stiffly on the table, the fingers flexing occasionally as if in remembered pain. Strange could hardly conceal a chuckle; it had to be Barnaby Salazar. The man was so addicted to blood rites and raising this demon and that, that there was scarce an inch of his skin unmarked by a blade and he usually was bandaged somewhere or other. But, despite his monomania, Salazar was no joke; his eyes often veiled knowledge that Strange would rather not share and he avoided close contact with the man whenever he could. There was something in his sickly pallor that reminded Strange of something that had lived too long in the dark, too long out of reach of humanity. If there was one in this company who he wished had turned down tonight's invitation, it would be Barnaby Salazar.

Strange was jolted from his reverie by the sound of Dee's voice.

'Thank you for coming here tonight at such short notice, gentlemen. As you will see, we are not quorate, but this is by no means a normal meeting. Sir Francis Walsingham died four days ago, as I am sure you know . . .'

Hariot's voice grated from the darkness. 'Don't tell me you have dragged us all here to tell us that,' he complained.

'No, not at all.' Dee was not going to lose his temper tonight. He had promised Marlowe he would find out what lay within the goblet Faunt had pocketed at the death bedside and find out he would. He had his suspicions, suspicions he was not prepared to share with the playwright, not yet. With his reduced circumstances, he had done what he could, but had got no further than discovering that there was indeed evil in the cup when Marlowe had left him. A mouse, rescued from the kitchen cat, had died instantly with just one grain introduced between its reluctant jaws; a better death than the one it had been taken from, though Dee doubted the rodent had been particularly grateful. But with so little remaining in the goblet, he was loath to use it up with little hope of success. These men, chosen with care, would be able to do more than he ever could, save by magic. And it was important that anything they found could be proved to the satisfaction of others – it would never come before a coroner, but heads must roll. Walsingham was not a man who had been universally loved, but he had not deserved to die before his time and Dee's spirits had told him that he had indeed been taken from this sphere before his span had run.

Dee took the goblet from the bag on his lap and placed it in the golden pool of light. 'This goblet held the last drink taken by Sir Francis in his last hours,' he said. 'I know it contained poison, but further than that, I have no means of telling what it might have been. Whether mineral or vegetable or something unknown to man before, who can say? You . . . gentlemen . . . with your different skills may be able to succeed where I have failed.'

Ralegh reached forward for the goblet and Dee closed his hand around the stem and held it firm.

'There are but traces left,' he said. 'If each of you can extract the smallest amount, that is all I can spare. I have promised not to let this vessel out of my possession.'

'How did you come by it?' Ferdinando, Lord Strange, needed to know with whom he was dealing. He loved all the theatricality and subterfuge of their little club – he was a patron of actors himself – but if it came to annoying anyone who could actually inflict bodily harm, well . . . he had many other outlets for his taste for the unusual without running that kind of risk. Poisoners rattled him nearly as much as witches.

'I can't say,' Dee told him. 'But suffice to say, there is no need to worry on that score. The source of this goblet means us no harm.'

Ralegh leaned forward into the light and his handsome, raffish face was lit devilishly from below. The other men around the table leaned back, shocked that one of their number should expose his identity so boldly. Knowing who everyone was was one thing; showing your face in the light was another. Ralegh laughed at their discomfiture.

'Come, now, gentlemen,' he said. 'Surely, we are all friends here. I would be delighted to try to solve your conundrum, Dr Dee. Henry; you are not the wizard earl for nothing. I assume you have nostrums which can detect even the most esoteric of poisons. Ferdinando, I confess I know little about your scientific leanings, but if pentagrams and posturing can bring results, I expect you to have the answer before dawn's light is in the sky. Thomas.' He gestured to the man on his right. 'Numbers are the key, hmm? Am I right?'

The silence round the table was palpable. Dee pulled the goblet towards him and made as though to pack it away again.

'Don't take on, John,' Ralegh said, slapping the table with an open palm and making the candle jump and flicker. 'Come with me, all of you, to my workroom and we can bottle this demon for you to all take some home. And I promise,' he leaned forward towards Strange, 'that at our next meeting, we can have frills, furbelows and as much secrecy as your theatrical heart desires. But for now, gentlemen, we have a poisoner to catch.' He pushed away from the table and took up the candlestick to lead the way. 'Shall we?'

SIX

Whitehall was crowded that day, the first of summer and the last of spring. There was a horse fair and the hoi polloi from the country rubbed shoulders with the knights of the shire, exercising their legs in their stroll from Westminster. The Watch were with them, rounding up the drunks and kicking the beggars back into the shadows. Flies bit the horses that stamped and whinnied in their enclosures. Men checked their teeth and ran experienced hands over their withers and fetlocks.

But one man had no time for the horse fair. He had a horse of his own, stabled safe in Hog Lane and this morning he had more pressing business. They watched him from the shadows of the shanty hovels that ran to the river.

'That's him, all right,' Ingram Frizer said. 'That's Kit Marlowe.'

His partner in crime was not so sure. 'I don't know, Ing.' He spat out the tobacco he'd been chewing. 'It's been a while.'

'You were as close to him as I was,' Frizer told Skeres. 'Nose to nose, we were, in the aisle of Paul's. That man got us put away. I'd know him anywhere.'

'We've got to be sure, Ing,' Skeres warned.

'Oh, we'll be that, all right. Hang on, where's he going now?'

Marlowe was striding past the horse-lines and the fire-eaters, ignoring the jugglers and merely nodding to the urchins who were crying out in their treble voices that there was a play toward that very afternoon; that Master Edward Alleyn, no less, was to play Barabbas, the Jew of Malta, penned by that great, unrivalled playwright Christopher Marlowe. He crossed the road, waving aside the bread and ale sellers, smiled briefly at the puppets on their sticks and slipped between the smooth stones of a grey building half hidden in the shadows.

'He'll be on his own in there,' Frizer said, doubling his pace. 'Come on.'

But his companion held him back. 'Don't be a pizzle. Look – catchpoles.'

Skeres was right. As Marlowe slid through the open gate, a pair of large guards in the Queen's livery crossed their halberds and stood grimly, watching the crowd.

'God, you're right,' Frizer said. 'Know what that is, don't you, Nick? Only Her Bloody Majesty's Palace of Whitehall.'

'Hmm,' Skeres nodded. 'Friend Marlowe knows people in high places, don't he?'

'It seems he do.' Frizer looked around him. 'Well, shame to waste a crowd. Got your dice?'

'Does the Archbishop of Canterbury bugger goats? And it's your shout, by the way.'

Kit Marlowe did indeed know people in high places. But it wasn't a person he had come to see today, but a place. Sir Francis Walsingham would be buried tomorrow, at St Paul's in the City, but today his inner sanctum in the corridors of Whitehall might yet provide an answer as to who would send him there. He had flashed the arms of Walsingham to the guards at the gate and from there he knew his way well. Chances were that the strongboxes here would be locked too, as they had been at Barn Elms and at Seething Lane when he had visited. But he was wrong. The strongboxes, like the door to the room itself, were wide open and a young man sat at Walsingham's desk, his face narrow, his eyes large and his hair combed back. He was Marlowe's age or thereabouts, but much smaller and his back was crooked under the dark velvet.

'Yes?' He was surrounded by parchment, quills and an inkwell, for all the world like a Cambridge scholar with vivas looming.

'I was looking for Nicholas Faunt,' Marlowe lied.

'Were you?' The man placed his quill on its rest and leaned back. He seemed almost dwarfed by the chair and the table. 'Who are you?'

'A friend to Her Majesty,' Marlowe said, not looking away from the man's careful, hazel eyes.

'I know that,' the man said, 'or you wouldn't have got past the guards. Specifically.'

Marlowe flicked the Walsingham cypher from his purse and it clattered on Walsingham's desk.

'Walsingham had no son,' the man said, recognizing but not touching the metal. 'Nor any son-in-law . . . at the moment. I must assume, then, that you are either a steward . . .' He looked Marlowe up and down, the large eyes narrowing. He took in the doublet, the buskins, the Colleyweston cloak '. . . for which you are too well dressed. Or . . .'

'Or?'

'Or you are one of Walsingham's people. One of his golden lads. If you know Faunt, I assume you are a projectioner.'

'And what can I assume you are?' Marlowe asked.

'I am not Essex or Ralegh,' the man said.

'What?'

Something like a smile played around the seated man's lips. Suddenly, he stood up and thrust out a hand. 'I am Robert Cecil,' he said. 'The Lord Treasurer's son.'

Marlowe blinked. He knew that Lord Burghley had a son – two in fact – and that Robert was his favourite. He knew that Burghley had been the confidant of the Queen since before he, Marlowe, was born. But what he had not been ready for was the man's height. He barely came up to Marlowe's chest and his bent back gave him the appearance of a toad.

'Christopher Marlowe.' Marlowe took the man's hand and shook it. A strong enough grip, but perhaps not *that* skilled with a blade.

Cecil smiled. '"Let earth and heaven his timeless death deplore,"' he said, '"For both their worths will equal his no more."'

'You know my *Tamburlaine*.' It was Marlowe's turn to smile. 'I am flattered, Sir Robert.'

'Don't be,' Cecil said, sitting down again as soon as he could. 'I have yet to see your *Jew*. I'll reserve judgement. But I must concede, Marlowe, you *do* have a mighty line.'

Marlowe half bowed.

'Why do you want Faunt?'

'Now that Sir Francis is gone . . .'

'Ah, an assignment. Yes, I see.'

'I had assumed that Faunt—'

'Would take over the reins of office?' Cecil finished the sentence for him. 'Yes, I rather think he did too. No, my father has filled that breach. Which means that, de facto, I am your new master, Marlowe.'

'Honoured,' Marlowe said, but he wasn't sure he meant it.

Cecil looked at the man. He could read people like his father could, read them almost as well as Walsingham. But Marlowe . . . that might take a little time. 'That business about Essex and Ralegh,' he said. 'A piece of advice my father gave me. Forget it.'

'Forget what?'

Cecil laughed. Kit Marlowe had no idea what a rarity that was.

'He also told me not to let my sons cross the Alps, lest they learn nothing but pride, blasphemy and atheism. Do you think he's right, Master Marlowe?'

'I have not crossed the Alps, sir,' Marlowe said. 'I cannot know.'

'Hm. And you cannot know who killed Walsingham.'

'I . . .'

Cecil laughed again. Then, suddenly, his face was a mask of seriousness, the eyes liquid, penetrating. He held up a piece of parchment. 'My people intercepted this yesterday,' he said. 'It was printed at Rheims, the English College.'

'The scorpions' nest,' Marlowe nodded. 'Yes, I know it.'

'I know you do,' Cecil spread his arms to the riot of documents cluttering the room. 'I have been doing my homework, since father nudged me in this direction, acquainting myself with Sir Francis's secrets.' He looked at the parchment again. 'They say that the Spymaster died blaspheming, urine pouring forth from his nose and mouth.'

'They *say* that the Pope is God's vicar on earth. They *say* that the Communion bread and wine *becomes* the body and blood of Christ.'

Cecil smiled and nodded. 'Exactly. Arrant nonsense, all of it. Do you believe Walsingham was murdered?'

'It's possible.'

There was a silence between them.

'Tell me, Master Marlowe, you are a scholar of Corpus Christi, are you not? Cambridge?'

'I am.'

'Well, I was at John's, briefly. That makes us enemies, does it not?'

Marlowe smiled. 'If you are a boy with nothing in your head,' he said.

But Cecil wasn't smiling. 'Should you be considering involving yourself in the matter of Walsingham's death, Marlowe, don't; there's a good fellow.'

'Is that an order, sir?' Marlowe felt he had to ask and silently congratulated himself for not leaving even a scintilla of a pause before the 'sir'. Something told him that this man could detect a scintilla at twenty paces and would not forget it, nor forgive.

'Oh, I don't give orders, Master Marlowe,' Cecil said. 'I have people for that. Can you see yourself out?'

Marlowe half bowed and spun on his heel, careful to collect the Walsingham cypher first. At the door, Cecil's voice stopped him. '*Sero sed serio*,' he said. 'England has a new Spymaster now.'

'*Sero sed serio*,' Marlowe repeated in his head. The Cecil motto – 'I sow, but seriously'. Seriously: that Marlowe could believe. But it all depended on exactly what Robert Cecil intended to sow.

The little bookshops along Paternoster Row were busy as usual that morning. The coney-warren lanes that ran between them were full of the rough and tumble of a great city, the draymen and liverymen and guildsmen scuttling like ants under the shadow of the great cathedral.

No one paid much attention to the man who prowled the leather-bound volumes of Master Munday's emporium, tucked into the tightest angle of Amen Corner. He had the air of a scholar about him, his robes of good quality, but fustian for all that. His hair was pulled back behind his ears so that nothing could interfere with the intense concentration he gave to each tome that he pulled from the shelves. Soon, he had amassed quite a little pile, much to the delight of the proprietor, who liked the sound of money as much as the next man. Except that the next man was Kit Marlowe.

'Don't tell me you've room for any more, Dr Johns.'

The scholar spun at the mention of his name. 'Kit!' His eyes widened. 'Kit Marlowe!' And they hugged each other.

'Master Munday,' Marlowe smiled. 'This is Michael Johns, my old Cambridge tutor. Whatever you're charging him for these,' he pointed to the teetering pile, 'halve it, there's a good bookseller.'

'I've got overheads,' Munday quibbled, scrabbling for his spectacles to work out exactly how much he might lose this morning.

Marlowe clapped him carelessly on the shoulder. 'I'm sorry to hear that,' he murmured. 'Dr Henderson, aptly enough at the sign of the Cock in the Strand – I understand he has a sovereign remedy for such cases.'

Munday scowled. He was in no mood for Kit Marlowe today. The man was a menace, always finding a little volume that Munday had underpriced and then haggling him down still further. But doing it on behalf of a third party was too much.

'What brings you to London, Dr Johns?' Marlowe asked, politely. 'If memory serves, you hate the place.'

Johns looked sheepish. 'I do find it rather . . . large,' he said. 'But needs must. These aren't for me; they're for my employer.'

'Wadham?'

Michael Johns was a gentle, circumspect soul. He didn't like discussing his private life, certainly not in the middle of a London bookshop. He led Marlowe towards the window, away from Munday, who could – and did – gossip for England. 'I didn't take the Oxford post in the end, Kit. A Cambridge man like me? No, it wasn't to be. No, I'm now – and don't laugh – the official librarian of His Grace, the Earl of Northumberland.'

Marlowe frowned. 'Somewhere in the north, isn't it? Near Martin Frobisher's Ice Sea?'

Johns flicked the man with his sleeve. 'No, I'm not actually *living* in Northumberland, Kit. His Grace's main library is at Petworth – that's in Sussex, by the way; nowhere near anywhere that Martin Frobisher has been, I'll wager.'

They both laughed.

'His Grace heard I was . . .' The scholar balked at using the dread word 'unemployed'.

'Between opportunities,' Marlowe suggested.

Johns's face brightened. 'Indeed. That I was between opportunities. He has more books than we had at Corpus Christi, and that's including the Parker Library. He needed someone to catalogue and annotate them so – here I am! His Grace is very generous and kindness itself. He is in London on business and has unleashed me, so to speak, on the bookshops.'

'Well, if it's the aristocracy's money,' Marlowe said, 'Master Munday, whatever you're charging for those,' and he pointed to the pile of books again, 'double it.'

Munday's eyes lit up, but the spark died almost at once. If it was the aristocracy's money, he knew he would never see a brass farthing, remind them though he may.

'There are some fascinating works here, Kit,' Johns said, a scholar to his fingertips, never happier than when he had his nose in some intractable Greek.

'If you're done, then,' Marlowe said, 'bring them along and we can talk. There's an ordinary I know around the corner that serves a spice cake like you've never seen before, not even at His Grace's table.'

Marlowe was right. The spice cake was indeed exceptional. He sat back on his chair, idly picking up damp crumbs with a forefinger and licking them off appreciatively. Michael Johns was not a trencherman. Years living on the meagre stipend of a Cambridge tutor had left him frugal, undemanding. Even now he ate at the table of the Earl of Northumberland, he often had to decline whole portions of a meal. He crumbled his cake and pushed it around his plate, picking out the more succulent figs and leaving the rest behind.

'Tell me, Kit, although I am loath to ask it . . . Are you still . . . er . . .?'

'Searching for the Muse? Always.'

'No.' Johns found himself looking around the room, checking that the other diners had no ears. 'No, I mean . . .' his voice dropped to a whisper, '. . . on the Queen's business?'

'Oh, that.' Marlowe's face was suddenly grim. 'You might say so, yes.'

'I heard . . . we all heard . . . about Francis Walsingham.'

The Michael Johns whom Kit Marlowe knew in Cambridge

would not have heard anything about Francis Walsingham. Or any other politician, come to that. He spoke of Aristotle and Plato as if they were old friends, his companions of a mile, but current affairs blew past him like the winds from Muscovy, gusting along the Cambridge streets. Now, though, he moved in different circles.

'Tell me about the wizard earl,' Marlowe said.

Never a nautical man, Johns could nevertheless tell a tack when it had changed and took the hint. 'A fascinating man, Kit; you'd like him.'

'I would?'

'He is a poet, a dreamer. Wears his heart on his sleeve a little, not unlike a certain Secundus Convictus I once knew at Corpus Christi not so long ago. *He* went on to become a famous playwright, I understand.'

'Did he now?' Marlowe chuckled. 'And you had him down for the church?'

'Not for long, I didn't,' Johns said, with a faintly regretful smile. 'But, talking of the wizard earl . . .' He ferreted in the pile of books in the satchel at his feet. 'This might interest you.'

Marlowe took the volume and read, in gilt letters on the spine, '*The History of the Damnable Life and Deserved Death of Doctor John Faustus.*' He shrugged. 'Not one of God's creatures, I assume.'

'Indeed not. I'm delighted to have found that. His Grace has the original German work, but I fear my German is poor at best. Do you . . .?'

'Not a word,' Marlowe confessed.

'Faustus was a scholar and magus, Johannes of Helmstadt, back in the thirties. They say . . .' Johns dipped his head. 'They say he sold his soul to the Devil.'

Marlowe flicked through the pages. 'Belzebub,' he murmured. 'Astaroth. They're all here.'

'I'm not sure you should make light of these things, Kit. There are more things in Heaven and earth than we can even dream of in our philosophy.'

'I'm sure there are,' Marlowe agreed, nodding. 'I was just thinking how this might work on the stage. Here,' he pointed to a page near the book's end, '"And the demons came and took Faustus by the hair, screaming down to the bowels of Hell." That's rattling good stuff. I can probably do something with that. Tom would have to . . . oh, I don't know . . . he could do something with trapdoors. Springs. Smoke . . .' He looked up and almost started in surprise. He had all but forgotten Johns was there. 'I couldn't borrow this, could I, Michael? Say, for a week or two?'

'Well, I . . . what His Grace has never had, he will never miss, I suppose. Please, yes, do borrow it.' He pushed the book a little closer. 'I look forward to seeing what you make of it. But . . . but I will get it back, won't I, Kit?'

'In spades, Michael,' the playwright assured him. 'In spades.'

Marlowe had the rare skill of being able to walk and read at the same time. His boots rang out on the cobbles as he strode, one hand holding the book, the other flinging out to the side, placing players and poetry in the air around him. Urchins and dogs began to gather at his heels and soon he was almost a carnival procession in his own right. He took a sharp left up the rise of Maiden Lane towards the bulk of the Rose, quiet now in the morning sun. Master Sackerson was chatting with someone hanging over his wall, a maidservant beat a mattress out of a window and Kit Marlowe had a play cooking in his head. Apart from the death of Walsingham and the advent of the rather disquieting Robert Cecil, all was well with the world.

A hand appeared in his vision, splayed over the words. He was so lost in thought, he at first simply tried to see around the fingers, but it was no use and, with a sigh, he looked up.

'Master Faunt,' he said, unsurprised. 'Good morning to you.'

'And to you, Master Marlowe,' Faunt said, with a faint smile. He had used most of his social graces on the bear and he was not feeling at his best that morning. He had had a difficult week.

Marlowe decided to let the conversation run in its accepted pattern. Although he loved to turn language on its head, he could tell Faunt was unusually strained. 'What brings you to the Rose? The performance won't be starting . . .'

Faunt waved a hand in irritation and Marlowe took the opportunity this gave him to slam the book closed and stow it away in his satchel. 'I am not here for the performance, Kit, as you well know,' he hissed through gritted teeth. 'I am here to talk to you, about . . .' he looked from side to side, suspicious as ever, '. . . you know who.'

Marlowe could think of at least a round dozen of people who would fit that rather loose description, so opted for looking interested and alert. No doubt more clues would come, but Faunt remained stubbornly silent. 'Well, of course . . .' the poet began slowly, but was still on his own. 'Sir Francis . . .'

'Yes, yes,' Faunt said, impatiently. 'Very sad, I know. We shall not look upon his like again. But . . . Robert Cecil, Kit! What of him?'

The conundrum was solved and with very little work on Marlowe's part. But even so, he wanted to know which way this cat would jump. He thought it likely that Faunt would not be very happy with Cecil's arrival like a cuckoo in the nest, but with Faunt it paid to be sure. Before he could speak, Faunt was back in full flow.

'He came out of nowhere. No one knows him. Did *you* know him, Kit?'

Marlowe shook his head, looking sympathetic.

'He is Burghley's son, I give him that. But not his *eldest* son. That I could have understood . . . except of course that Thomas Cecil is a total idiot when it comes to politics.' Faunt stopped and revisited his last sentence. 'Thomas is a total idiot. Nice enough fellow, but a more foolish one never wore ermine.'

Marlowe gave the idea some thought and, after a second or two, had to agree. 'So, Robert . . .?'

Faunt sighed. 'Political genius, I fear.' He leaned against the wall of the Bear Pit and sighed. 'We won't shake him off in a hurry.'

'It was not exactly easy to pull the wool over Sir Francis's eyes, as I recall,' Marlowe said, soothingly. 'There is no reason to suppose that much will change. We have an overlord. He has,' and he smiled modestly, 'two of the greatest brains in London, no, in England . . .'

'In Europe,' Faunt added, his spirit rising a little.

'Indeed. In Europe. I met him at Westminster,' Marlowe thought it only fair to lay the facts out clearly before Faunt found out and misconstrued. 'Oh, purely by accident, of course.'

'What was he doing?' Faunt kept his voice level.

'He was . . . going through Sir Francis's papers.'

Faunt's nostrils flared and he went a shade of purple unusual in a man of his good health. 'He was . . .?'

'I was there to do the same myself,' Marlowe said quickly, 'and with far less right to do so. If he has become the Spymaster, he needs to know—'

'He could have *asked*,' Faunt said, his face now white with anger. 'He could have *asked me*. The . . . the little . . . imp!'

Marlowe could not help laughing. 'An odd choice of word, you'll excuse me for saying,' he said.

'It's what the Queen calls him. Her imp. Her little man, her pygmy. And worse.'

'He is rather small,' Marlowe said. It was only the truth, after all.

'Small enough to poke and pry, to make trouble.' Faunt heaved a heavy sigh and clapped Marlowe on the shoulder. 'Well, Kit, we will prosper or fall under the imp whether we worry at it or not, I don't doubt. Did you manage to find out anything . . . else?'

Even with only Master Sackerson for company, Faunt was all circumspection.

'The doctor is working on it for me.' Marlowe took his cue from Faunt and spoke in riddles. 'His dark friends are helping and we should soon have word.'

'Words for my ears only,' Faunt reminded him. 'Not for the imp.'

'Of course,' Marlowe assured him. 'When I know, you will know. But no one else.'

'Hmm.' Faunt shoved himself upright from the wall and straightened his hat. 'Can I find you here? Is a play in the wind? I have noticed the bills. Something about a Jew? What did the Master of the Revels think of that?'

'What he always thinks,' laughed Marlowe. 'That we should in fact be putting on solemn readings of the Scriptures. But Henslowe's money works for Jews as well as for Scythian shepherds and so – the play must go on.'

'I may find time to come and see what you have made of

the subject.' Faunt tried to sound as though he didn't care, but he had never missed one of Marlowe's plays since the very first, since the Queen of Carthage had been resurrected in darkest England. He somehow felt he needed to keep an eye on the playwright; deep inside he wondered whether he might one day see himself portrayed up there in the wooden O. *The Tragedy of Nicholas Faunt* – he could see it now.

'You are always welcome, Nicholas, you know that,' Marlowe broke into the man's daydream. 'There will be a ticket at the door, as there always is.'

'Kind,' Faunt murmured. 'Very kind. Well, I must be away. Mistress Faunt is expecting me this afternoon. We are to go on the river, or so I believe.'

'What for?' Marlowe was puzzled. He had never heard Faunt willingly mention his wife; as for doing her bidding – this was not the Nicholas Faunt he knew.

'For leisure, as I understand it.' Faunt looked as though he did anything but. 'In spring, or so I am told, the Thames can be very lovely.' He grabbed a handful of Marlowe's sleeve and pulled him close. 'Kit. We must find something to do. Not only do I want justice for Sir Francis, but . . .' He seemed lost for words and the disconcerting purple colour was creeping back into his cheek.

Marlowe removed his hand from where it was crushing the velvet. 'I understand,' he said, kindly. 'A man can only bear so much leisure.'

Faunt was feeling better. He waved an airy farewell to Marlowe and Master Sackerson and wandered off down Maiden Lane. Perhaps if he were to be late, Mistress Faunt would take to the river without him.

In the shadow of the Rose, two men turned as Marlowe and Faunt said their goodbyes and scurried into the dark of the flats, stored against the wall.

'Could you see anything?' the taller, broader one said.

'Nothing,' the shorter weaselly one replied. 'They're experts, them two. They talk without moving their lips. Like this.' He mumbled a word or two, lips clamped together like a Thames mussel.

'What?' His companion was in no mood for levity.

'Exactly.' The shorter man smiled, showing blackened teeth. 'Exactlerly.' He carefully enunciated every syllable. 'You need to move your mouth to be heard clear. And they don't.'

'You must have had a clue about some of it.'

'Well . . .' the failed lip reader looked up for inspiration, but just saw the grimy backs of old flats. 'One of them . . . Faunt, isn't his name? Yes, well, he said something about imps. You can see that, it's hard to do a pee with your lips shut. See.' He demonstrated, smacking his lips to show his point.

'Ah. Imps. That would be the Devil, then. We can make something of that.' The taller man was interested; they might well have something here. 'Anything else?'

'Jews. I know he said something about the Jews. And the river.' He waited for his friend to speak. He always knew the answer, even when he wasn't sure of the question.

'So . . . Let me see. It seems to *me*,' he was still thinking. 'It seems to *me* that they are planning to raise an imp to throw some Jews into the river.'

His companion was dubious. 'Really? I don't think Master Marlowe and Master Faunt would . . .'

'Look.' The taller man bent down and poked the other man in the chest with a grimy finger. 'Don't come the star-struck stuff with me. Just because Marlowe is a playwright . . .'

'. . . and poet. Don't forget poet.'

'Yes, and poet. Just because he is that, don't think he isn't above drowning some Jews in the river. Remember Bamburgh?'

'Do I ever!'

'Could always be the blood libel. Or . . .'

The small weaselly man leaned forward, his nose almost twitching with anticipation.

'Or . . .' he slapped his thigh with the realization. 'Or, it's a code.'

'A *code*! Of course it is.' His low brow furrowed. 'So we're none the wiser.'

'Not really.' The sigh was heartfelt. 'But you got some practice in and that's never a bad thing.'

They crept out from under the concealing flats.

'I forgot to ask. Have you got any lines in this here play?'

Skeres smiled modestly. 'One.'

'Have you?' Frizer said, impressed. 'What?'

'I'm a extra knight in Act Two. I have to say "Prithee".'

Frizer waited. 'Is that it?'

'Well,' his friend was annoyed. 'Sometimes I says it twice. But I give it a lot of feeling, even when I only says it once.'

'You're not getting a bit stage-struck, are you, Nick?'

'Me?' Skeres was outraged. 'Never.'

'As long as you're not. We've got a job of work to do here, remember. A certain gentleman we know would not be too pleased if he thought we weren't getting on with the job, now would he?'

'I'll remember, I'll remember.' There was a pause. 'My old mother's coming to see me, first night. I got her a seat and everything.'

But Frizer had gone.

SEVEN

I t was nothing he hadn't experienced before. Years ago, when he scurried as a pot boy at the Star in Canterbury, when he rolled back to Corpus Christi with his lads of the Secundus Convictus under a drunken moon, he hadn't known it. Now he did; the footsteps at his back, the shadow on the wall, the whisper on the stair. He could place exactly when all that started – it started the day that Francis Walsingham had found him on the road from Cambridge and Kit Marlowe had never been quite alone ever since.

Now, under the Hog Lane stars, the tenter-grounds white and the windmills groaning, he heard it again, the soft pad of feet, the quiet hiss of breath. The footstep was just a thought behind his own, the breath just a touch more laboured; most men would have missed them in the hum the world makes as it spins, but not Kit Marlowe. He quickened his pace. It was yards yet to his front door, more if he doubled back through the Bedlam gate. But Bedlam was not the way to go; Marlowe had to keep his wits about him tonight. Tonight of all nights. The world, after all, had turned upside down. The Papists said that Francis Walsingham rotted in Hell, the Protestant Hell where all the Antichrists lay – Luther, the madman of Wittenberg; Zwingli, the people's priest; Calvin, the lunatic of Geneva – the Devil had them all. And without Francis Walsingham, as the world was now? What then? What now?

Whoever was following Marlowe was keeping his distance. This was no drunken roisterer, groping his way blindly towards Shoreditch. Nor was it an honest tapster making his way home. Marlowe stopped, stooping briefly to tie his boot, and risked a quick glance to his left. His shadow was tall, well set up and he had stopped too, trying to flatten himself into the timbers of the houses that led to Pietro's garden. The oak was too solid and the doorway too shallow: he stood out like a sore thumb.

Marlowe walked on, striding out again, making for the north. He had seen this ruse before, one used by the coney-catchers all over the city. One behind, one ahead, like the jaws of a coney trap, slamming suddenly on the neck of their hapless prey. But there was no one ahead. The stars were bright and the moon on the wane and Hog Lane was deserted as far as the eye could see.

He walked beyond his front door and heard his follower's footsteps falter. What was this? Did the man know where he lived and had Marlowe's way tonight confused him? The footsteps picked up pace again and, when they appeared to be closing, Marlowe spun suddenly to face him, the dagger gleaming in his hand.

'Ho, sirrah!' he shouted. 'Are you lost?'

'It's me, Master Marlowe,' his shadow said, stopping in his tracks. 'Carter, Dr Dee's man.'

Marlowe's eyes narrowed, but the blade tip stayed steady, aimed at the man's throat. 'Carter,' he nodded, recognizing him. 'What do you want?'

'If I may approach?' Carter asked. He knew about Kit Marlowe, the suddenness of his temper, the speed of his knife.

Marlowe spread his right arm wide but showed no sign of sheathing his weapon. 'Approach away,' he said.

Carter moved slowly, unsure of the man he sought.

'Did the doctor send you?' Marlowe asked.

'No, sir, the lady Jane. Mistress Dee would like a word. In private.'

It was late. And the windows of the little house along the Cheap glowed with the candles of insomnia. Not for nothing had John Dee chosen Elias Carter for his factotum. The man was as close as a coffin and all the long walk through London's tangle of streets, he had told Marlowe precisely nothing. It would be to break a confidence, he said. And that, he would rather die than do. Mistress Dee was in London, that was all he would say, at a little house the magus used from time to time. And she was worried. Worried enough to send for Kit Marlowe.

Jane Dee looked lovelier by candlelight than in the sun. The flames danced in her eyes and shone on her long, chestnut hair.

She was fully dressed and thanked Carter for his trouble before he melted into the darkness of the stair.

'Thank you for coming, Master Marlowe,' she said, offering him a chair. 'It is a Godless hour and you will think me forward.'

'One hour is much like another to me, lady,' he said, 'and why would I think that of the wife of the Queen's magus?'

'You must call me Jane,' she insisted softly, sitting in front of him and staring into his face, 'if you are to help me, as I hope you will.'

He smiled. 'Then you must call me Kit,' he said.

She laughed, a light, musical sound like water over pebbles and the ice of the early morning was broken. Since Madimi had been born, mouth open ready to yell, hands reaching for attention, she, like Marlowe, had been no respecter of hours. She had no air of sleep about her, rather the spark and glitter of a midday sun on leaves. She was still but, nonetheless, the air about her was not. Her laugh died and her face became serious. 'You knew the first Mistress Dee,' she said. 'Helene.'

Marlowe sat up slightly straighter, pulling infinitesimally away from this electric woman. Had she dragged him through the night streets to ask about a dead woman who had aroused her jealousy? 'I did.' His voice was cold.

Jane Dee smiled. She had expected this reaction so she carried on. He would understand soon enough. 'And you know, then, how broken John was by her death.'

'He was,' Marlowe remembered. 'I promised him I would make her live again.'

Her eyes widened. 'Live again?' she repeated. 'I had no idea you were a magus, too.'

It was Marlowe's turn to smile. 'I'm not. Unless you count words magic. I intended – perhaps still intend – to write her for the stage, in one of my plays.'

'John would like that,' she said.

'Forgive me, Jane,' Marlowe asked with a frown. 'I don't see . . .'

She raised a hand. 'Clearly, I didn't know John then,' she said, 'but he has told me how close he came to . . . well, ending his own life. A blackness creeps over him at times, I know. And never more than now.'

'And this has to do with Helene?' he asked her.

'I don't know,' she shrugged. 'No, it can't. But . . . the death of Walsingham. He wrote it in his journal – "The eleventh hour" several times. He has been staring into the scrying stone recently; not idly, as he usually does, as you or I might glance at the page of a book. No, he has been pacing his study at night, sitting hunched over the stone, seeing who knows what in its demon depths. He sees the future, Kit – you know that.'

Marlowe nodded.

'*Octogesimus octavus* – he forewarned of it.'

'The year of the Armada, yes. But it turned out well.'

'It might have done,' Jane nodded, 'but Philip still sits on his throne and how many more galleons will he send against us? You know Rodrigo Lopez?'

'Dr Lopez? The Queen's physician? Not personally, no, but . . . I have heard the name, of course.' Marlowe could recite forwards, backwards and in cipher the entire complement of Her Majesty's household, but there was no need to tell Jane Dee that. 'I believe the late Sir Francis Walsingham consulted him from time to time.'

'John fears him, Kit. "Beware the wolf," the stone told him. The man is a magus of a different kind. He knows the poisons of the hedgerows.'

'Does he, now?'

'The pestilence will come, John says; here, to London. On a scale we have never seen before. There will be crosses on the doors and the graveyards won't be deep enough to hold the dead. They will rise, shrieking, from the ground.'

The playwright in Kit Marlowe listened with envy. This woman should be writing for the stage – no; if it were allowed, she should be *on* the stage. He could almost feel skeletal hands claw his throat. If Philip Henslowe found out about her, she'd never be able to call her soul her own.

'And, Kit.' She grabbed both his hands in hers. 'Promise me you'll stay away from Deptford.'

'Deptford?' he chuckled. 'Wouldn't be seen dead there.'

'Don't mock me, Kit, please,' she said solemnly. 'Don't mock John.'

'Was Deptford in the scrying stone?' Marlowe asked.

'That and much more,' she told him. 'And all this, all John's dark moods, started as soon as you came to him with that damned cup.'

'The poisoned chalice,' Marlowe said. 'I see. If you feel I am to blame, Jane, then I am sorry. But, what can be done?'

'Talk to him, Kit, please. He trusts you, loves you as a true friend. He won't talk to me.'

'Is he at home?' Marlowe asked. 'Winchester?'

'He is to wait on Her Majesty at Placentia in two days. He has lodgings there.'

She was still holding his hands and he shifted so he was holding hers.

'I've never been to Placentia,' he said. He was about to say more, but checked himself. After all, Placentia was just along the river from Deptford.

'Is it safe?' He heard her voice in the darkness.

'Is the world flat?' he chuckled and pulled her to him, untying the thongs of her farthingale.

'Walter,' she scolded him. 'Be serious.'

He looked at her wistfully, her silhouette outlined against the window that overlooked the river. The dawn light gave a dull gleam to the white of his eye, to his teeth bared in his wicked grin. He wrapped a loving arm around her shoulders and turned her to the glass. 'What do you see?' he asked her.

'The river,' she said, 'in the early morning.'

'Ah, but what a river.' He stood behind her, enveloping her in his powerful arms. 'That way,' he pointed with his right hand, 'the Queen's palace of Whitehall and, far beyond it, Hampton Court. That way,' he pointed with his left, 'the Black Deeps and the open sea and the Queen's palace of Placentia.'

'Must she always be with us?' she asked him, her voice quiet and tired. 'Even here?'

He chuckled again and nuzzled her ear, breathing in her fragrance. 'Durham House is mine because the Queen gave it to me, Bess. I have my knighthood because she tapped my shoulder with her rapier blade. I named Virginia in her honour and I am forbidden to leave these shores again by her command. It's the way of it.'

She turned to him, looking into his dark eyes. 'What about me?'

He laughed, not at her, but at the thought that she could even ask it. 'What about you?' he asked. 'You are the love of my life, Bess Throckmorton, but you are bound to Gloriana more tightly even than I am. Good God, woman, you hold her candle as she gets into bed, unwrap her unmentionables. Have you any idea how many men would give their right arm to see what you see every night?'

Bess pulled a disgusted face. 'That *was* rather a long time ago, Walter, dear,' she said. 'And you may be sure that I never looked *too* closely, even then.'

'Aha,' he laughed, 'the Virgin Queen keeps many a mystery under her farthingale.'

'Virgin Queen!' she snorted. 'She's no more a virgin than I am!'

'Precisely,' he said. 'And, talking of which . . .' He pulled her closer and they kissed in the window of Durham House, the Queen's house that looked out over the Queen's river. She checked him. 'What if she ever finds out?' she asked. It was a question which had haunted her for weeks now, ever since she had first melted into his arms.

'You are unattached,' he shrugged, 'as am I. *And* you're an orphan; I can make an honest woman of you.'

She blinked, her eyes suddenly full of tears. 'Are you . . . are you serious?'

'I am *always* serious,' he said. 'How would it feel to be Lady Ralegh, wife of the Great Lucifer?'

She pulled herself away, turning and leaning her head against the cool glass. 'Don't even joke about it,' she whispered. 'We both know that if she ever found out, it would be the end of us both.'

'No,' he said, smiling. 'No . . .'

'She's a jealous old besom,' Bess snapped. 'I've tried to love her, tried to understand her, but I can't. Her teeth are black and rotten. Her paps hang like seaweed on some Godforsaken, gale-wracked coast. Did you know, she's virtually bald?'

He shook his head, stroking her satin-smooth shoulder with

a warm palm. 'Too much information, Mistress Throckmorton,' he said.

'She thinks you – any man, for that matter – is dying for love of her. And she, the Ice Maiden, holds you all off with her coquettish humour. The old crow!' Bess all but stamped her foot.

'Well,' Ralegh led her towards the bed. 'I have been summoned to dine with the old crow on whatever crumbs she wants to feed me – tomorrow, at Placentia. Actually,' he glanced out at the first light of dawn spreading over to the Queen's Wharves and the masts riding at anchor below them, 'make that today. Which gives us, by my old sailor's reckoning and a fair wind, three hours.'

And she squealed as he threw her on to the mattress.

Christopher Marlowe had once been told that every man and woman alive had a season that suited them best and he would always choose the spring. They all had something to be said for them: winter, crisp and invigorating; summer, hot and languid; autumn, with its tint of the fires of Hell and damnation wafting on the air, meat and drink to a poet. But spring was gentle, soft and promising and, although his humour tended to the black, he loved the sound – beneath the hearing and coming as a tantalizing whisper on the breeze – of buds popping. He walked now in Placentia's gardens with John Dee, brushing his hand on the tops of the clipped box hedges to release their acrid scent.

Dee was pleased to see him, but confused. 'How did you know I was here, Kit?' he asked, a furrow deepening on his brow.

Marlowe was in a cleft stick of enormous size and struggled to escape without letting Jane down. 'I . . . I heard it from . . . someone . . .'

Dee laughed. 'Christopher Marlowe,' he said, in mock surprise. 'I do believe you are caught in a lie. Quickly, quickly, let me get to pen and paper; this day must be marked properly.' He looked at his companion, who was as surprised as he; lies were his stock in trade and he had felt his tongue tie itself in a knot without his bidding. Dee brought out his hand from where it was tucked inside his coat and between finger and thumb dangled a small piece of twine, twisted and knotted in an intricate design. 'Don't worry, Kit,' he said, shaking it so that the knots fell out and it hung straight and true. 'My fault entirely. But tell me the truth this time or I will tie the knots tighter and encase it in crystal and you will never lie to man nor beast again.' He glared at him, but his mouth twitched below his scanty moustaches.

Marlowe licked his lips and muttered a few test phrases under his breath. All seemed to be well, but he didn't want to risk a repetition, so he decided on the truth, or what might pass for it. 'I happened to bump into Mistress Dee and she happened to mention you were here.' Even as he spoke, he could tell it wasn't one of his best, but it was better than the last attempt. He looked at Dee and raised an eyebrow.

Dee pursed his lips and let it pass. 'That was good of Jane,' he said, in studied, noncommittal tones. 'But let us set that aside for now. I'm glad we will have this time to talk without interruption. It's hard to know these days if anyone is hiding behind an arras or similar furnishing touch. Out here, we should be safe.'

'Safe from eavesdroppers at least,' Marlowe said. He was always on the lookout for cover adequate to hide an archer or arquebusier skilled enough to kill at a distance and never be found. The unlucky man would hear the pock of the string; the lucky man would go down poleaxed and know no more. 'Nicholas Faunt came and found me at the Rose.'

'Now, *there*'s a place where no one can hide,' Dee said, irony dripping from his tongue.

'Now, don't worry,' Marlowe said, clapping him on the shoulder. 'No one ever eavesdrops on Faunt. At least, they don't do it twice. Master Sackerson was our only witness.'

Dee looked solemn. 'There are men in England,' he said, 'who could speak to the bear and find out all he knows.'

Marlowe looked askance. That really hardly warranted an answer, though he was well aware that Michael Johns was right; there were more things in Heaven and earth than those he knew or even dreamed of.

'Don't look at me like that!' Dee said, a trifle waspishly. 'I've seen it done. Barnaby Salazar had a very convincing conversation with his cat, in front of what I would call an audience of the discerning, myself among them.' He drew himself up and gave himself a little shake, the epitome of outraged dignity.

Marlowe smothered a smile. 'What did he say?'

'Salazar or the cat?'

'Either.'

'Nothing of note, to be sure. But it was interesting to see. The cat seemed to enjoy the experience, which is more than can be said for most animals which cross Salazar's path.' Dee's face clouded for a moment. 'Not the sanest of gentlemen sometimes, Barnaby Salazar, but he has some interesting theories, very interesting.' He wandered off into a brown study and Marlowe left him there for a pace or two.

'But,' the poet said, bringing the magus back gently to the here and now, 'the bear aside, we were not overlooked nor overheard. He was wondering if we had made any headway.'

Dee sighed. 'I know the answer lies somewhere amongst the gentlemen we spoke of.' Even when they were alone with only the bushes for company, Dee was circumspect. 'Within the School of Night, as we sometimes call ourselves; a conceit of Ralegh's, nothing more, but it describes us well, I fancy,' he said, then looked thoughtful. 'Either the answer or the murderer.'

'Or both?'

'Indeed. Or both. Kit, I have been wondering . . .' Dee was never sure what Marlowe's financial standing was. He either lived on fresh air, or being a playwright was a better-paid employment than seemed reasonable to suppose. 'Do you have a man, these days?'

Marlowe was startled. 'A man?'

'Yes, a man. Like Carter, for example.'

'Oh, a *man*. No, I have done in the past, but I find I do nicely with just a maidservant. And now Tom Watson has . . . made alternative arrangements, shall we say . . . perhaps I will keep one in my employ for a little longer than has been usual.'

'We need to move more quickly and relying on you bumping into Mistress Dee accidentally – you never did say where that was, by the way.'

'Hither,' Marlowe said with a shrug. 'Thither.'

'As you say, hither, thither, she spends a lot of time there. So, to make things a little easier for us both, I thought I could lend you Carter.'

'To do what? I dress myself and if a button is awkwardly placed, I can always call for Agnes. She is a mistress of the whitening stone, so my linen is always sparkling.' He shot a cuff to prove his point. 'And she cooks like an angel.'

'You can't send Agnes flying around the country on errands though, can you? Apart from the fact she sounds a flighty piece,' Dee held up his hand as Marlowe drew breath to argue, 'I just can't see her delivering clandestine messages, following a miscreant, fighting for your life. Can you?'

Marlowe had to agree that, multifaceted though Agnes undoubtedly was, those tasks might be beyond her. 'If you insist, Doctor,' he said, a trifle sullenly. 'But there will be none of that sleeping across the doorway, choosing my clothes nonsense.'

'Heaven forefend!' Dee threw up his hands in mock horror. 'He will be there to send wherever you need, to do with whatever you wish. Hither, in a word, or thither indeed. His middle name is discretion and he had a brother in the Merchant Venturers in Prague.'

'Had?'

'Poor man died,' Dee said. 'Carter was very stoic about it. Took it like an Englishman.'

Marlowe was still unconvinced, but if it would calm Dee down a little, then it would be worth it. He nodded. 'Is he here?'

'Yes, in the servants' quarters. When I have seen the Queen, I will send him to you. Are you back to Hog Lane now?'

'I thought I might set off on my travels from here, but, yes, I can go back to Hog Lane. It was in my mind to start with Ralegh, then perhaps . . .'

Raised voices behind them made them turn. There was no anger in the hallooing, just a sense of a giant ego hailing every fellow in his path well met.

'Speak of the Devil and he is bound to appear,' Dee said, quietly and suddenly they were in the maelstrom within which Walter Ralegh travelled.

'Doctor; this is a rare treat!' An apparition in silver half armour strode between the apple trees, the sun flashing on the damascened breastplate and pauldrons.

Dee turned. 'Sir Walter; a rare treat indeed.'

'How's the old girl today?' Ralegh asked when he was close enough to speak softly.

'If you mean Her Majesty,' Dee bridled a little, 'she is very well.'

'Delighted to hear it. Who's this?'

'Sir Walter Ralegh, allow me to introduce Master Christopher Marlowe.'

'Marlowe the playwright?' Ralegh extended a hand, ignoring Marlowe's bow.

'The same, sir,' Marlowe said. 'I'm flattered that you've heard of me.'

'The Great Lucifer not knowing Machiavel?' Ralegh laughed. 'The idea! Tell me, Master Marlowe, was Ned Alleyn your choice for Tamburlaine, or was that Henslowe?'

'He's a fine actor,' Marlowe said, with a carefully noncommittal expression plastered seamlessly across his face.

'Yes.' Ralegh nodded. 'And Alleyn's not bad either.' He nudged Marlowe in the ribs but noticed that the playwright was not smiling. 'You have an audience with Her Majesty? The play's the thing, I'll warrant.'

'No, Sir Walter. I have merely come to chat to my old friend the doctor. He can be a hard man to find and, when I do, I make the most of it.'

'Oh, I see. Well, there it is. Don't suppose you ever wear this stuff, do you, in your line of work?' He patted the steel across his chest.

'I've never found an audience to be *that* unappreciative,' Marlowe said. 'Although, when the day does come, I hope I can rely on you to lend me some old bits of yours.'

Ralegh laughed, but neither Dee nor Marlowe had yet so much as cracked a smile. There was a sudden flutter from under the trees, not yet in bud, and a lute announced the arrival of the Queen's ladies, Bess Throckmorton among them. The men bowed.

'Mistress,' Ralegh called to Bess.

'Sir Walter.' She curtseyed, hiding her face in case she burst out laughing.

The men watched as the ladies skipped away over the lawns of Placentia, the lutenist following at a suitable distance. Ralegh looked up at the great walls of the palace, pale in the spring sunshine. He sighed. 'I expect the Queen intends to bend my ear about the cost of this place. It looks all right from the outside but, trust me, it's falling apart. Could do with some of your magic, Doctor.'

'I think the Queen prefers your magic these days, Walter,' Dee said, his mischievous eyes twinkling.

'Yes,' Ralegh said, but he wasn't smiling now. 'Well,' he patted Marlowe's arm. '"Return with speed, time passeth swift away. Our life is frail and we may die today."' He winked and, tucking his plumed helmet into the crook of his arm, strode after the ladies.

'The Great Lucifer,' Dee murmured when he was out of earshot. 'Take my advice, Kit, and don't cross that one. He doesn't just carry that sword for the look of the thing.'

Marlowe chuckled. 'Anybody who can quote *Tamburlaine* can't be all bad,' he said.

'Don't flatter yourself,' Dee warned. 'Don't forget, that phrase was from Act One, Scene One. He need only have read the first pages.'

Marlowe's eyes widened. 'Now I am even more flattered, Doctor,' he said. 'When the Queen's magus can quote from the work of a cobbler's son, down to the precise page, the world has indeed turned upside down.'

Sometimes, when he was not doing anything else, Marlowe let his mind wander back to when he had been carefree. It was not an easy thing to remember that earlier day, when he was not worrying about his father and where his temper might take him; about the choir school and whether he would pass muster with an unbroken voice for just one more Sunday; that his tutor would once again forgive the unfinished paper, the unlearned text. And all of this was to set aside the worries that today may be the day when Nemesis got the better of Euterpe and finished him off, whether or not he had delivered his pages to Tom Sledd.

As he made his way back from Placentia along the river to

the Rose, his mind could rove wherever it wanted, but to his annoyance it kept coming back to Walter Ralegh. The Great Lucifer would have been delighted at that, of course and not in the slightest bit surprised. To him, it was a natural fact that he was the centre of the world – round or flat, the answer was the same. Walter Ralegh first and last; except that he was never last. The man had been hard to read and that was always a red rag to the bull that was Marlowe's inner sixth sense. He could usually see not just the skull but the innermost thoughts beneath the skin, but with Ralegh, that had been next to impossible. Apart from the fact that he was clearly involved with Bess Throckmorton in a way that would make the Queen froth with rage, he gave little away. He needed watching, that one, and carefully too.

EIGHT

Tom Sledd was worried. He sat cross-legged on the apron of the stage and looked out with sombre face into the groundlings' pit. The smell of slightly spoiled vegetables and slightly soiled groundlings rose up and enveloped him like a mother's arms. He was born to this job; when Ned Sledd had taken him under his wing after he had been abandoned under his cart as a baby, he had been marked with the mark of Thespis and he could never be happy anywhere else. But even so – he was worried.

'Tom? You look worried.' A voice spoke near his knee and he looked down, his eyes slowly adjusting to the dark after looking into the sun which flooded the centre of the pit.

'Kit?' Tom Sledd shielded his eyes for a moment. 'I wasn't expecting you today.'

'Well, you know how it can be. I am a little betwixt and between today. I had to be out at Greenwich and then I need to be on the road. A little visit here seemed not too out of my way. How are the rehearsals going?'

'Well. Very well. First night coming up.'

'I know. But . . .' Marlowe peered up into Sledd's face. 'It's all going well, is it?'

'Yes. Like I said. Well.'

'Then why do you look so worried? It isn't the baby, is it? Meg? They are both in good health.' Marlowe knew that Sledd loved his family above all things, even above the Rose and that was saying something.

'They are blooming, thank you for asking.'

'Then . . .?'

Sled jumped down into the groundlings' pit and stood in the sunbeam, arms spread. 'Where is the disaster, Kit? Where is the leading man with a quinsy? Where is the lad who plays Abigail coming to me with a voice deeper than my own? Where . . .?'

Marlowe laughed. 'Oh, I *see*! When you say things are going well, you mean they are going far too well. If there is no disaster here, then it is still looming.'

'You have, as usual,' Sledd said with a sigh, 'hit the nail upon the head. Once we finally wrung those pages out of Watson, everything went like a dream. Even the walking gentlemen know how to walk – and you know how rare *that* is!'

Marlowe knew. It was quite incredible that when you put a perfectly normal, intelligent person on a stage and asked him to walk its length, he suddenly had the gait of an ostrich with the ague.

'Alleyn knows his lines.' Sledd shared this heresy in a hiss.

'No! What? All of them?'

'Every one. And he doesn't appear to be in love at the moment, either.'

'I would imagine that Mistress Alleyn is glad of that.' Marlowe watched as a smile tweaked the corner of Sledd's mouth.

'Burbage. He's a worry. He hasn't complained at all about not having the lead. Shaxsper has stopped moaning about not being asked to write more pages. Master Henslowe has stopped badgering me to put up the prices . . .'

Marlowe's eyes nearly fell from his head. 'I can see why you are concerned, Tom.'

Sledd laughed at last. 'I know you think I have lost my mind, Kit, and you may well be right. But I only really feel happy when I have things to worry about. And when everything is going well . . . I worry.'

Marlowe spread his arms. 'I would call that task accomplished, Tom,' he said. 'Isn't worrying about nothing worry enough?'

'It will have to do, I suppose.' Sledd kicked a turnip out of his way and under the stage, where it elicited a smothered oath from a carpenter mending a plank. 'Sorry!' Now he could worry about alienating the stagehands.

'I have something to worry you, if you want to hear about it,' Marlowe offered.

'Really?' Sledd's ears pricked up. 'What?'

'It is very rudimentary as yet. It has few characters, no plot as such, but it has special requirements that will make your brain spin. Rainbows. The Devil appearing in the flames of Hell. Automata.' Marlowe sketched it out in the air above his head. 'People will need to fly. To disappear. Tom – it will be a marvel of the age.'

Sledd looked intrigued. 'When will it be ready?'

'I don't know, Tom. I have . . . I have things to do before I begin. But . . . soon, I think. It is knocking at my soul, wanting to be free.' The playwright shook himself and strode out across the pit, making for the door. 'Just some food for thought, Tom. Food for thought until I get back.'

'You'll be here for first night?'

'If I can, Tom. If I can.' He slapped the stage manager on the back as they passed each other in the pit. 'Don't just stand there,' he said. 'Go and make some plans. Flying, don't forget. Flames of Hell. It will be costly, but worth it.'

Marlowe slipped through the wicket gate of the Rose, as he had so many times before, on an echo of Henslowe's voice from above.

'Costly? Did someone say costly?'

He was still smiling when he passed Ned Alleyn at the bottom of Maiden Lane, extricating himself reluctantly from the lissom arms of a Winchester goose of some loveliness. He wore his best swain's expression, quickly stifled on seeing Marlowe. The projectioner felt better for that; Tom Sledd was about to have as much to worry about as he could possibly want, because it was a well-known fact that Alleyn could not keep a word in his head when he was in love.

Marlowe decided to follow his advice to Tom Sledd and to put his worries aside. He could afford to let Walter Ralegh wait a while. The next on Dee's list was Henry Percy, the wizard earl, but Marlowe chose him first because of Michael Johns. The Cambridge man was closeted in the earl's Blackfriars house surrounded by his books when Marlowe found him, but the noble earl himself was at Petworth and that was where Marlowe rode now, Johns at his elbow, on the road from Southwark.

It was a day that was properly spring, with a tang in the air that no one and nothing could miss; a smell of green buds popping, of sap rising, the smell of birdsong and soft breezes. Marlowe inhaled deeply and turned to smile at his old tutor. Johns was never at his happiest on a horse and his brow was furrowed and his lip caught between his teeth with the simple effort of not falling between its hoofs. The poet opened his mouth to speak, then shut it again, the words unspoken.

Johns had not missed it. 'What is it, Kit?' he asked, a tutor's second sense still living under his librarian's clothing.

The poet laughed. 'I was about to say something pithy about the spring, Michael,' he said, 'but I have got into the habit of keeping my poetry to myself, in case Will Shaxsper should be about.'

'Shaxsper?' Johns was puzzled. As they ambled the lanes into Petworth, there wasn't a soul about.

'He's not here now, of course. Or at least, I can't *see* him. But it seems to me sometimes that I can scarcely open my mouth without him being close by. I don't want to give him all my best lines.'

'Can it be that bad?' Johns asked. Despite much evidence to the contrary, the scholar always preferred to think the best of everyone.

'Probably not,' Marlowe admitted. 'And I would imagine his thoughts on spring would tend to veer to the "Hey, nonny nonny" – poor Will; he isn't really very good, though he tries. You must give it to him that he tries.'

Johns extended an arm to a tree which overhung their road and, regretting it instantly, gripped his horse between his knees and hung on for grim death. 'Rough winds,' he declaimed, 'do shake the darling buds of May . . . umm . . . di dum di dum di dum di dum di day.'

'Jot that down when we get to Petworth,' Marlowe advised, 'and send it to Shaxsper. He'll be grateful. Even with the di dum.'

Johns laughed. He hadn't been with Kit for so long in years and with the sun warm on their backs, he could forget for a moment that the man clearly had an ulterior motive. 'Sing something to me, Kit,' he asked.

'Really?' Marlowe looked askance. 'I haven't done much singing lately.'

'All the more reason to do it now, then,' Johns said. He loved music, though he could neither sing nor play. He was like the Pope, or so he had heard. He knew what he liked.

'Something you know? Some Tallis?' Marlowe would have to rack his brain to remember all the words to some of the pieces which had once tripped off his tongue.

'Something new, if you have anything.'

'Hmm . . . let me see. I heard a song in a tavern the other night . . .' Marlowe looked round at Johns, who was blushing. 'It's only a little suggestive, Michael,' he admonished. 'In the ear of the beholder, really. It is written in parts, but I will give it my very best, if you would like to hear it.'

Johns wasn't sure now. He had never taken holy orders, but he had come close and had a monkish air about him, even now. But he nodded, all the same.

Marlowe cleared his throat and hummed a cadence in his chest. Then, he opened his mouth and the voice which, a lifetime ago, or so it seemed, had brought tears to the eyes of a Canterbury congregation, rose to the trees and made the pigeons plunge away, clapping their wings, applause before it was due. '"Fair Phyllis I saw sitting all alone,"' Marlowe carolled, '"Feeding her flocks near to the mountainside . . ."'

Johns smiled to himself and nodded gently to the music. Nothing too untoward so far. He hoped it would stay that way.

Petworth's walls stretched, it seemed, for miles, circling the little village with its sleepy roofs and mellow stone. The deer in the park lifted their heads at the sound of the horses, the bay and the chestnut, taking the gentle rise to the house. The sun sparkled on the lake and all was well with the world. A knot of labourers was sawing timbers under a slope of cedars, the men in their shirtsleeves, sweating and grunting with the effort. They paused as the horsemen trotted nearer and one of them came over. His hair clung to his forehead and his shirt clung to his body as he took a swig from the jug at his hip.

'Michael!' he saluted the librarian. 'Don't tell me you've finished at Blackfriars!'

'Miracles take a little longer, Your Grace.'

The man laughed. 'That they do. Who's this?'

Johns dismounted gratefully, with the air of a scholar far more used to travelling on his own two feet. 'My lord, may I introduce Christopher Marlowe. His Grace, the Earl of Northumberland.'

'Good God!' Percy almost dropped the jug. '*The* Christopher Marlowe?'

Marlowe swung out of the saddle, an altogether more practised horseman and bowed. '*A* Christopher Marlowe, certainly,' he smiled. 'Beyond that, I cannot say.'

Percy laughed and shook his hand. The men were of an age and of a height, the noble lord skinnier, but strong for all that. 'You're Tom Watson's friend.'

Marlowe's face fell a little. He hadn't expected this. 'Ships that pass in the night,' he said.

'Ah, I see.' Percy led Marlowe to a fallen log and they sat down. 'Do I detect a note of disdain?' Percy clicked his fingers and one of the sawyers took the horses' reins from Johns. The tutor-turned-librarian joined them on the rough wood, the scent filling his nostrils in the clean morning air.

'Master Watson lodged with me in London,' Marlowe said, keeping his voice neutral.

'Ah, the women,' Percy nodded, spying the fly in the ointment. 'Got a bit much, eh? Yes, I've noticed he has an eye for the ladies. Titled, below stairs, they're all one to Tom, I fear.'

'He once said to me that if all the women in the world were laid end to end, he wouldn't be at all surprised,' Marlowe said and the earl laughed. Johns allowed himself a smirk, no more. He was still feeling a little rattled by what had happened to Phyllis. 'May I ask . . .?'

'How I know him? Certainly. The man's an outrageous scrounger, as you cannot have failed to notice. He collects patrons as I collect books. Do you know his *Helene Raptae*?'

'The rape of Helen?' Marlowe translated. 'No, but I've heard it often through the bedchamber wall.'

Percy roared with laughter. 'Christopher Marlowe,' he said, slapping the man on the back, 'you're exactly as I imagined you.'

Marlowe looked closely at the wizard earl, wondering for a moment why he spent his time imagining Christopher Marlowe at all.

'Watson dedicated the Helen poem to me a couple of years ago. An odd choice I thought then and still do. But now you're here, you couldn't have a look at it for me, could you? I didn't like to say so to Tom, but it does need some work.'

'I am a playwright, Your Grace.'

'Yes and I'm a sawyer.' He turned and called to one of his men. 'Not a very good one, Nat, though, eh?'

Nat laughed and waved. 'You're coming along, my lord,' he said. 'Be all right in ten or twenty years.'

Percy laughed and turned back to Marlowe. 'Any man who can do what you did for Ovid can surely save Tom Watson's bacon. What do you say? Will you do it?'

'Your Grace, I confess I came at Michael's suggestion to gaze with envy at the rest of your library. I had not thought to be here long.'

'Nonsense. You must stay as long as you please.' He glanced across at the horses. 'No luggage? No man?'

'As I said, sir, I had not intended to stay. I could send for my man and some more linen.'

'Excellent. Come up to the house and we'll make the arrangements. Then,' he stood up and shook Marlowe's hand, 'I want to know how *The Jew of Malta* is going. Tom Watson says he gave you a few pointers.'

Marlowe's smile froze on his lips. 'Yes,' he said. 'I'm sure he does.'

They ate simply that night, by the usual standards of the Petworth kitchens. Percy decided on a whim – and his cook was always ready for any whim that his master could devise – to eat with the men, out in the woods. The thought being master to the deed, there was soon a trail of kitchen servants scurrying to a clearing near the sawpit, carrying tables, plates and knives. A hole was dug, a fire was laid and a hog was soon roasting above it. Bread, salads and *hochepot* to fill the gaps that pork was unequal to were spread across the board and soon the glade was silent except for clashing of plates and chewing.

Michael Johns retired before the *blanc mange* was brought out. Worn out by his unaccustomed ride, he took his leave and retired to his rooms under the eaves. He felt at home there, just a few staircases and a landing or two from the earl's great library, surrounded by parchment and leather and ink; a scholar's paradise.

The Percy wolfhounds were pacing around the glade, snuffling in the undergrowth and growling at unseen prey. The estate workers had melted away, their faces greasy with their master's pork and their bellies fuller than they had been all winter, generous though the Percys were. As dark fell and the embers died down, Marlowe and the wizard earl pushed back their chairs and, whistling to the dogs, they made their way back into the Hall, where a small fire burned in the great fireplace. Over it, carved deep into the stone, were the arms of Northumberland and Poynings, echoed in the embroidered cushions on the earl's favourite chair. The hounds found their usual spots amongst the straw and settled down for the evening, as full of pork as any worker.

The earl had sent the household staff to their beds too and he and Marlowe sat in the warmth of the shifting fire and lit two bright candles to light their talk. The claret served now, after the rough wine in the glade, was the best that Marlowe could remember.

'What made you write about the scourge of God?' Percy asked, suddenly.

'Tamburlaine?' Marlowe accepted the earl's refill of his cup. It was a pleasant change to talk of the writing of his plays, rather than be berated by Tom Sledd for asking for the impossible; though how the stage manager would respond should Marlowe one day set a play in an empty room with two actors talking to each other and scarcely moving, it was hard to imagine. It was hard to imagine how the audience would react too – vegetables would certainly be a feature. He looked up and saw the wizard earl looking expectant. 'I don't know. Perhaps because he was larger than life. He took on the world foursquare and didn't give a tinker's damn about the consequences.'

'A villain, though?' Percy topped up his own wine. 'A rogue?'

'Undoubtedly. They make the best stage characters. Someone I know at the Rose – a friend, I hope I can call him – Will Shaxsper . . . sorry, Will*iam* Shak*espeare* . . . have you heard of him?'

The earl thought for a moment, then shook his head. 'No.'

'No. Well, Will is trying to write something on Henry VI.'

'Who?'

'There you have it,' Marlowe shrugged. 'Two unknowns in as many sentences.'

'You never thought to write anything current?' Percy asked.

'A little more . . . what could I call it . . . cutting edge? Up to our minute, as it were?' He reached for his pipe and pouch. 'Do you drink smoke?'

'I dabble.' Marlowe took the proffered clay and tobacco. 'What do you mean, "current"? "Cutting edge"?'

'Well, topical, you know. Something on the Queen, say . . .'

'That would be treason,' Marlowe said, flatly.

Percy blinked. 'Oh, yes. Yes, of course.'

There was a silence while both men lit their pipes and blew rings to the vaulted ceiling. It looked for a moment as though the wizard earl would start a new tack, discussing the weather, perhaps. But Marlowe wasn't going to let it go. 'Would that bother you, Your Grace? Treason, I mean?'

Percy's eyes narrowed. He believed in omens. To him, the turn of a card, the flight of a bird, the trail of a snail were not chance. It meant something – all of it. If he could only work out *what*. Was Marlowe's arrival chance, after all? An old student of Michael Johns'. An old friend of Tom Watson's. All of it chance. All of it just coincidence. Or was it? He pointed to the heraldry over the fireplace. 'Politics,' he said, the pipe smoke curling around his face, watering his eyes. 'You mentioned Henry the Sixth a moment ago. I don't know anything about him, but one of our claims to fame, among many, I say in all modesty, is that one of my ancestors fought for Hotspur. My family have held the North for centuries, when the Tudors were struggling Welsh gentlemen scratching a living somewhere to the west of Offa's Dyke. When you and I were in our hanging sleeves, Marlowe, there was a rebellion in the North.'

Marlowe nodded. The ripples of that rebellion still unsettled the waters around Walsingham's Whitehall.

'The Percys were banned from Alnwick. Oh, I can come and go as I please. I am welcome at the Court; I have my country estates and my town houses. I sit in the Lords along with the great and the good. I have my books and my deer herds and my laboratory. And, talking of *Tamburlaine*, which I believe is where all this started, I could buy Master Henslowe's theatre ten times over.' He leaned forward. 'What I cannot do, darling of the Muses, is go North. If I so much as show my face in Alnwick, I shall be offering my head to London Bridge.'

'So, you don't approve of the Jezebel?' Marlowe was chancing his arm and he knew it.

Percy leaned back in his chair. A smile broke over his face. 'As long as I have my books and as long as I search for the love of my life, I stay away from all that. Politics and I are but nodding acquaintances, Kit. Like you and Watson, we are ships that pass in the night, eh? Now,' he said, snuffing out his pipe and quaffing the dregs of his claret. 'Come and see my *officina magicae*.'

'Ah, the famous laboratory,' Marlowe sensed that their earlier conversation was at an end. He was glad – he had been rather afraid that he was about to be asked for a critique of Spenser's latest load of rubbish and he really did not want to start *that* conversation. The Queen was a lot of things, but faerie-like was not one of them!

'Just promise me,' Percy said as they reached the door, 'that I am not going to see anything you are about to see in some baldactum play any day soon.'

'Your Grace!' Marlowe feigned outrage. 'I don't *do* baldactum.'

The *officina magicae* was reached through a very ordinary-looking door. Somehow, Marlowe had been expecting some kind of fanfare, some arcane symbols at the very least. He had not known Henry Percy long, but he sensed the thespian manqué not far beneath the skin. The door was perhaps a little heavier than might be expected down in the nether regions of the house, beyond the kitchen, full of muted bustle despite Percy's release of the servants to bed; a hog roast with all the trimmings didn't wash itself up, as Percy was blissfully unaware. The key to the door was hauled up from beneath the earl's jerkin on a long chain, but there was no squeal of wards moving, no skirl of hinges grating as he pushed open the door, touching his candle flame to the sconce just inside.

'Well,' he said, turning around and waving an arm. 'Here it is.' He waited, looking anxiously at Marlowe. 'What do you think of it?'

The first thing that sprang to the poet's mind was that it wasn't how he had imagined it. Although he was aware that Percy had an intellect a man could shave with, he somehow had not expected such order. Bizarre order, it was true, but a place for everything and everything in its place was still apposite, even when the things in question were not immediately identifiable.

On the wall opposite the door were small wooden pigeonholes from floor to lofty ceiling. Some were very tiny indeed, but others housed bigger items – without looking too intently in the wavering candlelight, Marlowe could pick out a lamb, curled up as though asleep. As it had two heads, he assumed this was not the case, but it intrigued him enough to move closer.

He skirted the table in the centre of the room on which rested an astrolabe of complex design. Its foot was embedded in the wax which had dribbled unchecked from a candelabrum hanging on chains from the ceiling and a glacier of the best beeswax joined the table to the wheel above it. A book lay open beside the instrument; Marlowe never passed a book without a cursory glance, but this told him nothing. He had never seen anything like the symbols written there and he realized with some surprise that the book was still being written; a quill was resting between the open leaves and an ink bottle was close by.

He glanced back, to see Percy leaning nonchalantly against the doorjamb, looking proudly at his room and its effect on his guest. Assured that it was still as full of amazement as always, he trod softly, touching his light to all the candles until the last one was lit. The room was now ablaze and nothing was hidden – it was brighter than noon, mostly because each sconce was backed by a system of mirrors and prisms, which threw the light now here, now there.

Marlowe hung back. Although he was desperate to gain as much knowledge as he could in this place – after all, keeping a good cellar and being generally popular with the outside help did not preclude anyone from being a murderer – he did not want to seem to be too keen. He let his eyes roam over the little cells set against the wall. The lamb was, happily, stuffed, but there were jars with beetles still crawling over small-leafed twigs, crystals which took the room's light and threw them into the back of their containing box and, in at least one case, revealed a pair of red, malevolent, though mercifully small eyes peering back. Some cells held books, others parchment rolls. A healthy crop of Jew's Ear sprouted near the ceiling. Something at eye-level caught his eye and he leaned closer. It seemed to be . . . but, could it really be . . .?

The earl was suddenly by his side. He followed his gaze. 'I see you have found my breakfast,' he said, plucking the chicken leg from its hiding place and throwing it to the floor. 'I wondered where that went.'

Without warning, from a floor-level cell much bigger than the others, a mastiff the size of a small pony launched forth on a wave of cacophonous barking and snatched up the meat, swallowing it in one bite. Marlowe was afraid of nothing on God's earth or out of it, but he jumped backwards a good yard and stood, eyes wide, staring at the beast.

'Ignore him,' Percy chuckled. 'He's just an old softie, really. I tend to keep him a little hungry because he is a guard dog but,' he bent down and planted a kiss between the dog's ears, 'I've had him since he was a puppy and he really means no harm. Do you, boy?' The dog wagged his rump ecstatically, somewhat at odds with the volcanic growling in its grizzled throat.

Marlowe nodded at the dog; the nearest it was going to get to any affection from him. He stepped to one side and continued to look at the shelves until his heartbeat steadied and he could trust his voice. The wizard earl, with a final fondle of the dog's ear, came to stand beside him.

'Ah,' he said, proudly. 'I see you are admiring my sun picture.' He pointed to a murky piece of glass. 'I am very close to making permanent pictures of the view from my camera obscura – I have one above the stables – but I have not got it quite. Not quite. But I will. When I speak to the future, as I do from time to time, with my portents . . .' He broke off. 'I didn't ask you, Master Marlowe, but . . . you *do* believe in foretelling the future, of course?'

Marlowe was in another tight spot, not his first that day and he felt it unlikely to be his last. 'Well, of course,' he hedged, 'I *am* a very close friend of Dr Dee.' No more was needed.

Percy leaned in. 'I know the doctor very well myself,' he confided. 'He and I . . . well, perhaps the least said, the soonest mended. But I never saw his laboratory at Mortlake before the fire. That is one of my biggest regrets.'

Marlowe waved an airy hand. 'I saw it,' he said. 'A world of wonders, even beyond my small skill to describe.'

Percy stepped back and caused some consternation for a moment, as the dog's tail was beneath his heel. 'But . . . my dear, dear fellow. I had no idea. The doctor never likes to speak of it, although we all beg him, whenever we meet.'

'We all?'

With a nervous laugh, he said, 'Some friends, just some friends with similar . . . interests. It was near the death of Helene, or so I understand.'

'It was a bad time for him all around,' Marlowe said. 'Though Jane and the children have done much to heal him.'

Percy struck a lovesick pose, leaning on the table, oblivious to the wax and ink. 'Yes,' he said, looking into the middle distance, 'it is a love match, to be sure. Tell me,' he suddenly focused on Marlowe, 'do you know whether he *foresaw* it at all?'

'I only met the lady a few days ago,' Marlowe protested. 'It isn't really a question a gentleman poses.'

'No, no, indeed not,' Percy agreed, quickly. 'But I have here . . . hmm . . .' he ran his fingers across the spines of some small volumes crammed in a niche, 'yes, here it is. I have here a small treatise on scrying for one's future love. Being country charms, dew is heavily represented, as are straws and dog roses and the like, but there is a lot of sense in here. Of course, some of the charms are simple soporifics, poisons even, some of them. But interesting. Very interesting to the man of science.'

Marlowe held out his hand. 'May I borrow it for a while?'

Like any bibliophile, Percy was loath to lend, but let go after a few seconds' delay. 'Of course,' he said. 'As my guest, you are more than welcome. But . . . please tell Master Johns you have it. He keeps a ledger, you know, of which of my books are where. It is the only way.'

Marlowe slipped the small volume inside his doublet. He might mention it to Michael Johns but, on the other hand, he might not. It depended on how useful it might prove. He changed the subject. 'I couldn't help being interested in this book,' he said, pointing to the open ledger on the table.

'Ah,' Percy spun round. 'I keep my notes in here, of my results in my experimentation. At the moment, my main concerns are with the future, as you may have guessed, a man of your discernment, and I keep my findings all written here.'

Marlowe peered down at the book.

'You won't find anything out, Master Marlowe, though you look all night. It is based on the Algonquin tongue, taught to me by Master Hariot, who in his turn learned it from . . . I digress. But it is something I promised not to share, so . . .' and he closed the book firmly, 'I must ask you to look elsewhere for entertainment. My experiments with viscosity, now – let me show you.'

Marlowe had never actually spent an hour watching paint dry before but, like a perfect guest, he did so now. The dog dozed in its kennel. An early bluebottle, lured out by the day's sunshine, settled on the lamb. Petworth slept and finally, his head full of figures, so did the wizard earl. Marlowe covered him gently with a cloak he found hanging on the back of the door, blew out the candles one by one and made his way back to his room and a soft, welcoming bed.

NINE

'*Tenez!*'

Percy's racquet cracked against the ball and the game was on. A gaggle of lovely ladies was watching from the galleries as the earl and the playwright went through their paces. Both men had hung their doublets on a Percy lackey who had done this before. His face and hands were a mass of bruises where the tennis balls had ricocheted off him over time. It was an occupational hazard to be sure, but his family had been faithful to the Percys now for generations and he took it all, literally, on the chin.

The ball thumped on to the penthouse roof and hit the ground near Marlowe's feet. That was one of the best *piqué* serves the Canterbury man had seen; he would have to be on his mettle this morning. He reached to return the service, watching as the ball sailed over the net, slicing against the dedans board and forcing Percy back to return it. Once more, twice, and the point was Marlowe's. There was a flutter of laughter and applause from the ladies.

'Come on, Henry,' one of them called. 'You're walking.'

Percy tried to catch his breath and smile at the same time. It wasn't easy. This man might be the Muses' darling, but he was fire and air as well and all of it was coming Percy's way this morning. Sleeping leaning on his arms on a table in his laboratory was nothing new, but it wasn't the ideal position to adopt for six straight hours just before a tennis bout.

Again, the ball whistled over the net, bouncing off the Percy retainer, who groaned but held his place. This time, it was Marlowe who was caught on the back foot and the earl won the point. Four more times, Percy's serve should have sealed the game, but Marlowe's skill at the chase beat him and the ball's spin gave the playwright the edge.

While they paused for refreshment, quaffing more excellent claret, Michael Johns leaned over from the gallery overhead and beckoned Marlowe to stand closer. 'You *are* going to let him win, Kit, aren't you?' he whispered. 'It would be the polite thing to do.'

'I'm not sure there'll be any "letting" about it,' he wheezed back. 'The man's good.'

'Charles the Eighth, the King of France, died during a game of tennis, you know,' Johns reminded him.

Marlowe looked appalled. '*Now* he tells me,' he hissed, mopping his face with a towel. The ladies were mopping Percy enthusiastically. Petworth was no mean prize.

'Oh, don't worry,' Johns was quick to give scant comfort. 'You're in no danger. He wasn't actually playing. He hit his head on the way in to watch. Those French lintels, eh?'

'Ah.' Marlowe had caught sight of a figure sidling in to the far end of the court, under the shadow of the penthouse. '*Now* I can throw any match you like.'

Carter had arrived and Marlowe needed to have a word with him.

The bout lost, Marlowe took his leave of his host and the ladies and wandered with Carter through the birches that ringed the lake. It was another beautiful spring day, the clouds high and wary of the sun and the ancient pike slid silently under the darkling surface of the waters.

'How long have you been with the doctor now, Carter?' Marlowe asked.

'Since Prague, sir; a Godless place.'

'So I've heard,' Marlowe said. 'Tell me, how much has the doctor confided in you? Am I to give you letters for him, or—'

'There's been murder done, sir; that much I know. Sir Francis Walsingham. I doubt if I can help much on that score. The doctor said I was to give you every assistance. I . . . Down!'

Marlowe felt a thump in his back from Carter's right fist and the next thing he knew he was face down in the undergrowth with Carter on top of him. Both men scrambled to a kneeling position, their daggers in their hands. A crossbow bolt quivered in the trunk of a birch where Marlowe's head had been seconds before.

'There!' Carter shouted. 'Heading for the rushes!'

Marlowe saw him too, no more than a shadow in the trees, crashing through the bracken still dead from last year, a bow slung across his back. The tennis had taken more out of the poet than he realized and Carter was faster, bounding through the undergrowth, batting aside the lower branches that lashed his face in their revenge. Both men knew that the bowman could turn and fire again at any moment, but the chase was on and neither of them stopped to consider that. Now he was in view and had lost the element of surprise, the game was an equal one, give or take a bolt or two through the neck.

'This way!' Marlowe heard Carter shout and saw the man leap the gnarled tree roots that snaked towards the water. Marlowe followed him.

Now they were together, they took stock. The bolt had struck yards behind them on higher ground and the path wound on along the lake's edge. A heron, startled by the noise, crashed up from the reeds in a flap of feathers, eyes bright, beak sharp. But the bowman had vanished before either man had even seen him.

'It seems I owe you my life, Carter,' Marlowe said, extending a hand now that he had sheathed his knife.

'It's nothing, sir,' Carter said. 'Every assistance, remember?' He nodded to the far bank. 'You've made an enemy here,' he said. 'I can't believe that quarrel was aimed at me.'

'I could understand it if the wizard earl had lost the match,' Marlowe chuckled. It helped to laugh at sudden death; it kept the scythes-man in his place.

'He's an odd one, is Henry Percy.'

Marlowe looked at Carter. Most servants wore livery, knew their place, tugged off their caps in the presence of greatness. Clearly, Elias Carter was no ordinary servant. But then, John Dee was no ordinary master.

'How well do you know him?'

Carter sheathed his dagger too and stared into Marlowe's face. 'May I speak freely, sir?' he asked. 'Man to man.'

'Men we are, Carter,' Marlowe shrugged. 'Speak out.'

'The doctor is too trusting,' his man said, making his way back to the high ground. 'You'd think, with his knowledge of the darkness, he'd be more careful.'

'You think Henry Percy is not a man to trust?'

'He is a devotee of the priest of the sun.' Carter's voice was hard, his face grim.

'The priest of the sun?' That sounded familiar, but when a man spent most of his life with actors, many phrases which made no actual sense could sound as familiar as his own name.

Carter checked the stand of birches, not for bowmen but for ears. 'Giordano Bruno,' he said, as though the name burned his lips as it escaped into the mild spring air.

'I remember him!' Marlowe clicked his fingers in recognition. 'Clashed with the authorities in Oxford a few years back. I heard him speak.'

'That's him. I went with the doctor to meet him in Heidelberg. He's as mad as a tree.'

'Believes the planets whirl around the sun.' It was all falling into place now.

'Like I said,' Carter grunted, 'as a tree. The man's a midget, but his views are poison. They'll burn him one day; mark my words.'

'And the wizard earl is a devotee?'

'They all are.'

'All?' Marlowe was learning much today.

'The School of Night is what they call themselves.' Carter stopped walking and turned to the playwright. 'Master Marlowe, can I be frank with you?'

'Please.'

'The doctor is a wonderful man, kind, thoughtful, the best master a man could wish for. I would walk through the fires of Hell for him.'

'As would I,' Marlowe agreed.

'But his . . . what does he call it? *Mathesis*. Heavenly figures. It's all a load of bollocks, you know.'

'Are you sure about that, Carter?'

They walked on and came to the crossbow bolt, embedded in the birch's trunk. Carter wrenched it out, with some difficulty; if it had hit Marlowe it would have killed him for certain. It had come from no great distance and had still had most of its power when it struck the tree. 'As sure as I am that this is a hunting quarrel.' He sniffed the iron head and checked the wooden flights. 'The bow that fired this has a range of a thousand paces. Judging by the depth of it in that tree, I'd say our friend fired from . . . what?' He looked up and sighted along the bolt. 'Two hundred paces?'

Marlowe was a cold steel man himself, hand-to-hand was his milieu, but he could tell that Carter knew whereof he spoke, so he nodded.

'Shall we?' He strode off in the direction of the bolt's trajectory, taking average steps until he reached another birch. Here, he crouched. 'Broken bracken,' he muttered. 'I had hoped for more. The print of a man's shoe, perhaps.'

Marlowe was impressed. 'I can see why the doctor employs you, Carter, whatever you think of his philosophy.'

Carter looked worried. 'That will remain our secret, Master Marlowe, won't it? I wouldn't upset the doctor for all the magick in the world.'

Marlowe laughed. 'Don't worry,' he said. 'I'm good at secrets.'

That evening found Marlowe with Michael Johns in the earl's great library. The glow of the dying sun still lay on the leather spines and the warmth had brought out the aroma of glue, ink and paper, in a fugitive scent that filled the air, to be smelled only by those who loved books. Johns was scratching away with his quill, entering the volumes faithfully into his ledger.

'You won't forget *Eroici Furori*, will you, Michael?' Marlowe was flicking the book's pages through his fingers.

'Where did you get that?' the tutor-turned-librarian asked.

'Up here.' Marlowe was standing on the third rung of a ladder. 'Next to *Every Man His Own* . . .' he peered closer, '. . . *Cordwainer.* I thought that was what it said. Good God, who publishes this stuff?'

'Put it back, Christopher,' Johns tutted. 'It belongs in the Occult section. I haven't got there yet.'

'Dangerous book, this,' Marlowe said, reading the scribbled notes in the margins.

'Cordwaining?' Johns was a little surprised. Marlowe's own father was a shoemaker. Where could be the harm? He supposed the untutored might hit their thumb once in a while, but dangerous?

'The *Eroici*.' Marlowe humoured his old tutor.

'Oh, there are five other Brunos here somewhere. I saw them when I started cataloguing. Arcane. Difficult Latin, too.'

'Have to be,' Marlowe commented. 'The priest of the sun can't risk any Johannes Factotum understanding his views.'

Johns at last put the quill down. He knew his Kit Marlowe, the Canterbury lad with the golden voice and the mighty line. He loved him for what he was. But Kit Marlowe was an over-reacher too. And Michael Johns feared for that. 'Giordano Bruno is an atheist, yes. And the Earl of Northumberland has his books in his library. What of it? He's got a copy of your *Ovid* here too and, though I don't know how he got it, your *Tamburlaine* text. I haven't found *The Jew of Malta* yet, but it's only a matter of time. Oh, and don't forget that book on Johannes Faustus you've taken a shine to. Where is all this leading?'

Marlowe closed the book with a smile and looked at Johns. The man was an innocent, never abroad unless he had to be and the ways of the world were strange to him. But Carter was right. They would burn Giordano Bruno one day. And perhaps they would burn those who owned his books or had even read them.

'Where it's leading me,' Marlowe said, putting the book back beside its strange bedfellow, 'is a little visit to His Grace's armoury. I hear it's one of the finest in the country.'

It was. There was still enough light through the oriel window of Petworth for Marlowe to find exactly what he was looking for. The armour for the tilt made by Peffenhauser of Augsburg left him cold. Impressive as the Helmschmid harnesses were and the row of halberds with the Percy crests, it was the ballistae that Marlowe had come for. Even here, Percy's books took pride of place. A well-thumbed copy of Nicolo Tartaglia's *Inventions* lay alongside fowling pieces by the dozen. But it was not black powder that filled Marlowe's mind this gilded evening. It was the whine and whistle of a crossbow quarrel and the thud it made when it hit a tree – or a man.

There, mounted on a wall, were thirty or forty crossbows, enough to start a small war. They were French, German, English and . . .

'That one's Chinese.'

Marlowe turned at the words. Henry Percy stood there, a lantern in his hand against the gathering dusk.

'It repeats, fires ten bolts one after the other. Ingenious, isn't it?'

'Undoubtedly,' Marlowe nodded. For the life of him, he couldn't see how the thing worked.

'What are you doing here?' Percy asked. His voice was chilly, enough to offset the lingering warmth of the day.

'Forgive me, Your Grace.' Marlowe crossed to him, into his pool of light. 'Your armoury is almost as famous as your library. I just couldn't resist.'

'You could have *asked*, Marlowe,' Percy said. 'But come, let me show you my pride and joy. Over here, the finest of our English suits for the field and tilt. Made in Greenwich, every one.'

'Fascinating,' Marlowe smiled and walked away from the rows of crossbows, any one of which could have been used earlier that day in the attempt to kill him.

Marlowe had not been keen to take on Carter as his manservant. He had tried it once before, but it hadn't been all it was meant to be; in fact, it had not been like having a manservant at all, more like being tethered to a snake of uncertain loyalties. But Carter turned out to be an excellent servant: there when necessary; quiet when quiet was needed; a witty conversationalist when a little company was required. He was as adept with a goffering iron as Agnes and not inept with a needle either. Saving Marlowe's life was the cherry on top.

Henry Percy was a gentleman by nature as well as by birth and if he was a little put out by Marlowe's prowl in the armoury, it would have been a keen observer of human behaviour who would spot it. He was also rather taken by one of the lady guests who looked a lot like his first wife, or so his prognosticative bone told him and when Henry Percy smelled love in the air, he really did not want any spare men around. Especially when that spare man looked like an angel, who might have a touch of the Devil in him, and had a way with words which would charm the very birds from the trees.

At breakfast, Percy had turned to him, a lovesick glint in his eye. 'Do I remember your saying that you could not stop long?' he asked, rhetorically. 'I do feel most ill at ease, my dear fellow, for detaining you. I have sent a message to your man; I believe he is packing as we speak. Oh,' he held lightly on to Marlowe's arm as he made to rise, 'please, do not rush. Finish your oatmeal first, please.' His smile was tight and small. 'The cook would be mortified to see a full bowl returned to the kitchen, whatever the reason.' And with that, he had turned away and said no more.

Carter waited at the foot of the sweeping stairs, both horses saddled, bags slung ready for the off. Marlowe was about to mount when the great door swung open and Michael Johns appeared, ink-stained and distraught at the top of the flight.

'Kit!' he called. Then, thinking of his position in the household, 'Master Marlowe!'

Marlowe turned. He had not meant to hurt his tutor's feelings but he had forgotten him entirely. 'Master Johns,' he said, taking up the ethos of the morning. 'I would have come to say farewell, but . . .' he gestured to Carter, 'my man here had the horses ready and my bay is skittish, as you know.'

'Your man?' Johns was confused. 'I didn't know . . .'

Marlowe grabbed for the scholar's inky hand and squeezed it. 'He came on later,' he said. 'He had business in town.' He winked slightly and forced a smile. 'I don't know whether you have met; Carter is his name.'

Johns sketched a salute to Carter, who nodded gravely in return. 'But . . . Kit,' he whispered. 'Why are you going now? I thought you were getting on so well with His Grace.'

'Well enough,' Marlowe said, 'until he found me in his armoury. But since part of his armoury had almost found me, I thought I had every right. He disagreed. So, before the social niceties are forgotten, I must be away. That settles the why. As for the where – I expect Carter knows.'

Johns boggled. '*Carter* knows? You let your *manservant* tell you where to go? Kit . . .'

Marlowe squeezed his hand again. 'Michael, calm yourself,' he said. 'All will be well.' Tom Sledd popped into his mind and he smiled. 'Don't worry so much. Go back to your cataloguing.

Let us both do what we do best.' He turned and bounded down the steps and sprang on to his horse. Carter wheeled his mount and together they trotted down the great drive to the lane which ran along the endless wall that bordered the Northumberland estates. The spring morning was cool and the dew had damped down the dust, cushioning it beneath the horses' hoofs.

Carter bided his time before speaking. 'A nervous gentleman? What's his name? Johns, I think, is it?' Living cheek by jowl with Dee and his motley household had made Carter something of an expert on nervous disorders.

Marlowe mulled the thought over. 'Unschooled in the ways of the world, certainly. Michael Johns is really too trusting to be loose among anyone but scholars like himself. But needs must when the Devil drives, Carter. In Petworth's library, he is as near to heaven as any man should ever get on this earth. If I know him, he will have forgotten about us already.'

Carter gave him an old-fashioned look. For someone so intelligent, his new master, as he tried to think of him, was very foolish, as all great minds are. Michael Johns would never forget Christopher Marlowe, if he lived to be a hundred.

'So,' Marlowe said, after another companionable silence, 'where to now?'

Carter gave him another look. He had expected to be rather more of the manservant, rather less of the master in this partnership. 'I don't have the list, Master Marlowe,' he said.

'Yes, you do,' Marlowe laughed. 'I somehow don't see the doctor sending you off will they, nil they into the blue without some guidance. So, again, where to now?'

Timing was important in this kind of situation, as Carter knew only too well. John Dee had taken a day to school him in the ways of Christopher Marlowe and even then had only scratched the surface. But if he had taught Carter one thing only, it was to know when he had pushed him far enough.

'I had thought perhaps Master Salazar. His home is on the way back to London from here, so we will waste little time if he proves to be elsewhere.'

'I know little of him,' Marlowe said. 'In fact, it could be said that I know nothing of him. You?'

'He has visited the doctor from time to time. An unusual

gentleman, I think it fair to say. He . . . they say he is fond of animals.' Carter didn't like lying but saw no point in always telling the strictest truth.

'That's a pleasant trait,' Marlowe said. 'Does he keep a zoo? Lap dogs? A bear?' It pleased him to think that Master Sackerson might have kindred spirits somewhere, even though destined never to meet.

'I am not sure quite what or how many they may be,' Carter said. 'I have just heard tell he has a menagerie, of sorts.'

Marlowe had never had much affinity with animals and dogs in particular had never really been a favourite of his, nor he of theirs. A menagerie sounded not so bad, though. A menagerie suggested cages, a measurable distance between them and him. 'But that can't be all there is to the man, surely? Somehow, I cannot imagine the doctor having much in common with a menagerie-keeper.'

'I really cannot say more, sir. Perhaps if we wait to see if Master Salazar is at home.' Carter looked dead ahead and closed his mouth tightly. Sometimes it was better to say too little than too much and this was, in his humble opinion, certainly one of those times.

TEN

Barnaby Salazar's house looked almost normal in the pearly spring light of that early afternoon. It was closeted behind a high yew hedge and a path of silvery shingle led from the wicket gate to the front door, which was of oak, grey and gnarled in its natural state. Marlowe would not have been surprised to see a green shoot pulsing from the boards; there was a feeling of suppressed power to it, that it was almost daring the visitor to knock. The knocker, centre and at eyelevel, was unassuming. He had expected – hoped for – something more elaborate, more arcane, but except for the fact that the house was of a fairly substantial size, it felt like a country cottage. It belonged in a clearing, surrounded by toadstools and hanging vines. He tapped the knocker and stood back.

Carter had opted – with barely concealed alacrity – to stay in the lane with the horses. Marlowe had agreed readily, but Carter had been ready to argue his case. If a man unsettled John Dee, it was not for nothing; Carter was not ready to see what Dee had seen and which had kept him sleepless five nights in a row.

The door creaked open slowly. Marlowe was impressed; Dee had taught him years before that nothing impresses like a nicely creaking door if a man sets out to be a magus. He had also taught him that a creaking door is more difficult to create than one that opens on hinges smooth as silk. From a narrow crack between door and jamb, an eye peered out and looked Marlowe up and down, with no little disapproval.

'Yes?' The voice belonging to the eye was croaking and slow, as though not often used.

Marlowe swept a bow. 'Good afternoon.' He would have added a salutation but realized as he spoke that he had no idea whether he was addressing man or woman. 'Good afternoon,' he said again. 'I would speak with Master Salazar; is he at home?'

With no preamble, the door was closed again, the creak, which had risen up the scale on opening, now running down in a cadence of sharps and flats. Marlowe stood up. He was unsure quite what this might mean. Was Salazar not at home? Was it, as he had no idea other than Carter's directions to tell him, not even Salazar's house? He waited in indecision and was about to turn and leave when the door opened, this time silently, as though hinged in velvet.

The man in the open doorway was as unlike Marlowe's imaginings as it was possible for anyone to be. His age was difficult to determine, but was probably between forty and fifty. His hair was jet black but heavily laced with grey and sprang back from a high forehead in a mass of springy curls, oiled to perfection. His beard was trimmed with exquisite precision around a mouth which was just the pleasant side of petulant. His skin was smooth and unlined, his frame spare and trim and yet, despite the trimmings of middle age, he stood as if he was in some discomfort, every joint tense, every limb stiff.

'Master Salazar?' Marlowe ventured. This was not the owner of the doubting eye. That had been pale and rheumy; this man's eyes were the richest brown, sparkling and alive. It would be his luck, Marlowe thought with his usual cynicism, if this was the manservant and the eye belonged to Salazar. But no – this time his luck held.

'Indeed.' The man sketched a small bow. 'I am Barnaby Salazar. And you are . . .?'

'Christopher Marlowe. I—'

'Not *the* Christopher Marlowe? The playwright? The poet?' The man appeared to be charmed.

'Yes, but today I . . .'

'Well, come in, come in,' he said, stepping to one side and extending a hand into the hall. 'Forgive Jorge for his inhospitable welcome. We have so few guests here that he forgets himself. And he is . . .' he dropped his voice, '. . . Portuguese.' He set his lips and gave a knowing nod, as if that explained everything.

Marlowe had never knowingly met a Portuguese person before, although he had looked down the business end of a Spanish cannon or two, so he couldn't judge whether Jorge was a typical example. But it seemed the best thing to just smile knowingly and step in.

Carter, looking through the dense yew branches, saw Marlowe disappear inside; he fingered an imaginary rosary and muttered the Nicene Creed under his breath. He could fill time with Hail Marys until his new master re-emerged. If he re-emerged.

The hall was dark after the garden but not too dark to see. Jorge lurked in the background and was reluctant to come nearer, like a sulky child. Salazar sent him back to his kitchen with a stream of what Marlowe had to assume was Portuguese and then led Marlowe into a room which ran the entire back of the house, overlooking a little garden, laid out in knots and, further off, the rolling fields towards London. The glass in the windows was in small panes, but in an intricate design, which Marlowe had never seen before. It was like a rainbow which catches the eye and then is gone, only to reappear when the watcher looks away. It was almost hypnotic and Marlowe had difficulty sometimes in looking through rather than at it. He blinked and tried again.

From behind him, Salazar laughed. 'I see you are admiring my window, Master Marlowe,' he said. 'It is from a design by Sir Thomas Hariot. It represents . . . tell me, are you a mathematician amongst your many talents?'

'Sadly, no.' Marlowe saw no need to lie. 'Numbers and I only get on in the most tangential of ways. Which is to say, I scarcely understand them at all.'

'But ciphers? Surely, a wordsmith like yourself can appreciate a cipher?'

'I enjoy a conundrum or two,' Marlowe agreed, his eyes drawn again and again towards the window.

'Then mathematics should not be a mystery,' Salazar said, with the zeal of an adept. 'If you think of each number simply being a symbol, as letters are in words, then . . .' He saw the look on Marlowe's face. This was an argument he had heard before, from Thomas Phelippes and others in Walsingham's stable. It had cut no ice then and cut none now. Salazar smiled and gave in gracefully. 'It represents something rather wonderful, if you are of a mathematical bent,' he said. 'And it is a comfort to me, when my own work is not going too well.' He eased his wrists in his cuff and winced a little.

Marlowe had not expected this to be so easy. 'Your work?' he said. 'I would be interested to hear something of it. I have just come from Petworth and heard of what you are achieving here from His Grace.'

Salazar's eyebrows rose up his forehead like two leaping jaguars, black and lissom. 'You did? I had no idea that I had made such an impression on Henry. You flatter me.' He stood there, looking very pleased with himself, then recovered his manners. 'Please, take a seat for a moment. Jorge has gone to prepare a small repast for us. At this hour, I usually enjoy a glass of Madeira and a *pastel de nata* or two. I hope you will join me.'

It had been a while since breakfast and, although Carter had brought a loaf of bread and some cheese with him for the journey, Marlowe was suddenly hungry. Assuming of course, he thought to himself, that a *pastel de nata* was actually food. 'I would be delighted,' he said and sat at one end of a sumptuous couch, his back firmly to the window.

Salazar sat facing him, crouched like a raven on a small stool in the inglenook. 'Do tell me, Master Marlowe,' he said, 'for I am agog. What part of my work did Henry speak of?' He hugged his knees and looked expectant.

Marlowe gave a laugh and played for time. 'We were in mixed company, Master Salazar,' he said. 'He did not go into detail, for fear of pressing the intellect of the ladies beyond its natural limit.' As he said this heresy, he thought of his sisters back in Canterbury, who had minds like razors fresh from the strop. He apologized to them silently; they need never know.

Salazar nodded wisely. 'Henry is a gentleman in every way,' he said. 'So thoughtful. And an excellent host. You were staying with him, you say.'

'I was. A brief stay, but wonderfully stimulating.' Marlowe was not sure whether the next piece of information should be shared, but nothing ventured, nothing gained. 'He showed me his *officina magicae* – his laboratory, as Dr Dee calls it.' He didn't add that his book of hedge magic still resided in the pack across his horse's rump.

Salazar sat up straight and looked at Marlowe in admiration. 'His laboratory! You must have been a very honoured guest, Master Marlowe. Few are shown around his laboratory.' He chuckled. 'You met his hound?'

Marlowe went a little pale at the memory. 'I did. A very spectacular animal.'

'A masterly summing up, Master Marlowe, if I may compliment you thus. When I met it, I nearly lost my bowels, I don't mind telling you. And I have dogs of my own, none too friendly some of them. But Cerberus . . .'

Marlowe was not surprised to hear its name.

'. . . he is built of different clay. When we have had our bite to eat, I will show you *my* laboratory.'

That solved one problem – *pastel de nata* was food.

The door swung open and Jorge entered with a silver tray between trembling hands. The Venetian glasses on it rang and chimed as they knocked together and the pile of *pastel de nata* on the silver platter rocked and trembled. The man seemed so infirm that Marlowe got up to help him, but all he got for his pains was a glower that would have turned milk.

'Oh, don't try and help him, Master Marlowe,' cautioned Salazar. 'He prefers to do things for himself. He gets quite testy if you treat him as though he were old.'

The rheumy eye was turned again on Marlowe and again the poet felt that he was being tested and found very wanting. The tray eventually found its home on a small, intricately carved table by Salazar's knee and Jorge lurched off again, slamming the door behind him, his only way to show his displeasure at the temerity of the popinjay here to keep his master from his work.

Salazar poured the Madeira and delicately placed one of the pastries on to a small pewter plate and passed it with a glass to Marlowe. 'These should be just for Easter,' Salazar said, helping himself. 'But they are far too good to just eat for a few days a year. You are familiar?'

Marlowe shook his head. He had rather expected something rather more appetizing than this small morsel with the blackened top. When Agnes turned out something looking like this, it usually meant tears and promises to do better next time. He swallowed hard and bit into . . . heaven. Beneath the burned offering was a bliss of custard, flavoured with orange and molasses. The pastry was a mere wrapping for the joy within and disappeared in the warmth of the mouth as if it had never been. He realized he had closed his eyes; when he opened them, it was to see Salazar convulsed in silent mirth.

'I will never tire of seeing an Englishman meet his first *pastel de nata*,' Salazar said, wiping his eyes with a lawn handkerchief. 'The reaction is always the same.'

Marlowe licked his lips to gather the random crumbs which had escaped and held out his plate for more. He was almost speechless with pleasure. 'I don't believe I have ever eaten anything so exquisite,' he mumbled, his mouth already full.

'We Portuguese are proud of our ugly little beauties,' Salazar said with a smile. 'Personally, I am fond of them not just because of their taste, which is of course like angels' breath, but because of the beauty which is so much more than skin deep. Who would think, to look at one of these, what pleasures lie within. It is a philosophy which drives my work. When you have eaten your fill, I will show you my laboratory and you will see.'

Marlowe looked anxiously across at the tray, counting silently to see how many more of the small wonders were still left.

'The appetite of the young always amazes me,' Salazar said. 'When I was your age, I could eat a dozen of these at a sitting. Now, five is my limit. But, Master Marlowe, I will call Jorge and he will make a new batch, for your journey. How would that be?'

Marlowe suddenly felt like a greedy schoolboy and stopped eating. This was not why he was here, although, as reasons went, the tarts were quite convincing. He swallowed the one he was in the middle of and resolutely put his plate aside, brushing crumbs from his fingers. 'No, Master Salazar, though thank you. I would love to see your laboratory now, if you would be so kind.'

Salazar quaffed the dregs of his Madeira and stood up. 'Certainly, as long as you are sure.' He looked down at the tray. 'Just one more left, look.'

Marlowe shook his head.

'Perhaps later. This way,' he pointed to a door Marlowe had not noticed before at the far end of the room. 'My laboratory is through here.'

Going ahead, he pushed the door open and to Marlowe's surprise, they were outside in a small walled garden. In one corner, a brick building had been constructed, half leaning on the wall but with a soaring roof, rising to a point in the centre. There seemed to be no windows, but the chimney dribbled smoke; the only sign of life. Salazar caught Marlowe's dubious look.

'It doesn't look much,' he said, 'but it is full of wonders. At least, I hope you will find it so.' He reached inside the breast of his doublet and pulled out a small key. The keyhole it fitted was so small it was invisible in the grain of the wood and opening the door seemed almost in itself an act of sleight of hand. Just inside the door, a candle was burning in a covered lantern and Salazar reached in and lit a spill, which he used to light more in sconces around the walls, much after the arrangement in Percy's secret room; but without the mirrors and crystals the light was altogether dimmer.

Marlowe, standing behind Salazar, could at first see almost nothing, but he didn't need the sense of sight. The smell that rollicked and rampaged out of the doorway was almost visible in its intensity. He had smelt all of its components before, just never all at once. There was a threat of Master Sackerson, of the mice in the wainscoting, of the sharp smell of a fox that had marked his trail on a frosty night. There was the smell of blood, too, of death and, hard and shrill above them all, the smell of fear. He stepped back, his hackles rising in sympathy.

Salazar looked over his shoulder as he pinched out the taper and put it back on the shelf. He did not share his laboratory with many people, but he had been struck at how often they hung back, often refusing to enter at all. 'Come along in, Master Marlowe,' he encouraged. 'You won't be able to see much from outside.'

'I apologize, Master Salazar,' Marlowe said, trying to breathe through his mouth as much as possible, to minimize the smell. It reminded him of the dyeing houses which sprang up wherever the Huguenot weavers of his childhood set up shop along the

Stour; the stench of urine made his eyes water. 'I am finding the smell a little . . . bracing.'

Salazar spread his nostrils and breathed in extravagantly. 'Smell?' He inhaled again. 'No, I don't really detect anything, Master Marlowe. Perhaps I have become used to it. Take a deep breath outside if it bothers you and I can show you around.'

'I can manage, Master Salazar, please don't trouble yourself.' Marlowe stepped into the room and then became aware of something else; the sounds which came from every dark corner, of shuffling, snuffling, of breathing like the sigh of the stars in their courses. 'This is your . . . menagerie?'

'My laboratory,' corrected Salazar, the fanatic's gleam coming into his eye. It was hard to reconcile him with the man dishing out pastries and Madeira moments before, just yards away. He stepped into the middle of the room, deftly closing a ledger open on the table as he did so. 'Here about us, Master Marlowe, is my Work. My Life's Work. Come, come nearer.' He beckoned and Marlowe stepped into a nightmare.

No one had ever been able to accuse Marlowe of being soft-hearted to God's creatures; if anything, he was oblivious most of the time. But there was something in the eyes that glowed from the backs of the cages that filled three walls of this prison that spoke to him, as if they were human. They cried out for his help, for his understanding. One and one only of Salazar's captives sat at the front of the cage: a small capuchin monkey, its hands, so like his own, gripping the bars. It looked him full in the eyes and bared its teeth in the parody of an ingratiating smile. To all intents and purposes, it looked like any other creature any nobleman might have in his private menagerie, except that into its chest, someone – and it had to be Salazar – had carved an arcane symbol and had shaved the skin around it. The scar showed livid, puckered and raw, and the little monkey touched it from time to time, wincing when the pain was still there.

Salazar approached the cage and stroked the little creature's head. It didn't flinch from his touch but rather leaned in to the caress. Marlowe could not hide his surprise. 'You are wondering, Master Marlowe, I have no doubt, how it is that this animal does not fear me. And the answer is simple.' The magician's eyes glowed almost as brightly as those within the cages. 'He knows that his pain has a reason. That, with his pain, he can bring me closer to my goal. And I suffer myself, Master Marlowe, as often as I can. But a man has only so much blood in him, after all. I can only sacrifice myself when I am strong enough. And when I am not,' the entire room seemed to hold its breath, 'I must have help.' He turned his hot, fanatic's eyes on Marlowe, who could think of nothing in reply. Salazar scratched the little monkey's head with a sharp nail and it whimpered in pleasure. 'I must have help,' he whispered and leaned on the cage front, his eyes closed.

Carefully, quietly, Marlowe trod gently backwards towards the doorway and it was only when he felt the mossy bricks beneath his feet that he ran.

Marlowe erupted out of Salazar's front door like a cork from a shaken bottle and was out in the lane in less time than a wink. But of Elias Carter, there was no sign. The horses were quietly cropping the grass on the side of the road and the sound of their strong teeth tearing at the clumps was a taste of normality that Marlowe was eager to embrace. He stood with his arm over his saddle, patting the dusty neck of his bay. Where was Carter? In normal circumstances, his absence wouldn't have rattled him at all, but with the charnel-house smell of Salazar's laboratory still at the back of his nose and the unearthly silence of the animals in their cages filling his head, he needed Carter to be where he left him; otherwise, he might be anywhere. He leaned against his horse's neck and felt the sun-warmed bristle of its clipped mane, smelled the sweat and road-dust, breathing it in as though it were the costliest perfume. He closed his eyes and tried to banish for a while what he had seen.

Suddenly, his head snapped up and he was alert; he could hear voices, distant voices. If it was Salazar or even Jorge, he would have to choose between being politic and polite, blaming a sudden rush of blood to the head or calling for the watch to have them locked up for their own protection. He had let down his guard in this strange place. His first reaction had been one of extreme caution, but he had been seduced by pastry and wine. Not for the first time, perhaps not for the last, but it had been unwise, no matter how he looked at it. His smile was rueful as he realized that at least there was one good thing in all of this. He would not have to explain himself to Francis Walsingham, God rest his soul, if soul or God there should be.

The voices were not coming any closer and they sounded friendly, if not downright jovial. Keeping his horse as cover, he peered about him and finally decided on the direction; he was more than a little relieved to realize that the sound was coming not from the house behind him but from a small stand of trees a little further off down the lane. With his hand on the hilt of his dagger, he started off in the direction of the voices, but before he had taken many cat-like steps, three men suddenly emerged, one of them Carter. As the manservant saw Marlowe, he held up a hand in greeting and turned to the other two with words of farewell.

They turned sharply and went off down the lane with a swaggering gait that reminded Marlowe of someone; he couldn't quite place it, but he knew enough actors to be familiar with that self-satisfied strut. He shook his head and waited for Carter to reach him.

'I'm sorry, Master Marlowe,' Carter said, coming up to him at a trot. 'I didn't expect you to be so quick.'

'Nor did I,' Marlowe agreed, but was still rather displeased; Carter was meant to be his eyes and ears, not disappearing to play in the woods with cronies like some schoolboy. 'Who were those men and why did you leave the spot? I might have needed you.'

Carter looked crestfallen. 'I do apologize, most heartily, Master Marlowe,' he said. 'I was sitting here, waiting, as we agreed, when those two men called me from the wood.'

'And you went?' Marlowe was aghast. This man was supposed to be watching his back and yet he hardly seemed able to watch his own.

'I . . .' Carter's mother had once told him, long ago, that if he could say nothing sensible, it was better to say nothing at all. She had also told him that the moon was made of green cheese, so he picked and chose as to which of her wise saws to believe in. The former seemed to have some merit, so he shut his mouth.

'Who were they?'

Carter shrugged.

'What did they want?'

He had an answer to this one. 'They had a flask . . .'

'They wanted to share their drink with you. Any ideas as to why they might feel so generous?'

Carter hadn't really thought that one through. The flask had looked rather dirty and the alcohol smelled like something from a drain, so he had not partaken anyway. The further he was away from the two, the stranger the whole thing seemed. One minute he had been saying his invisible rosary, the next he was hobnobbing with a couple of . . . what? Cutpurses, to be sure. Marlowe had saved him from a fate which, if not worse than death, could actually have been death itself. He could not explain all this to Marlowe, so contented himself with a murmured apology.

'We'll say no more about it,' Marlowe said, springing up into the saddle using the grass bank as a mounting stool. 'If we see them on the road, we may investigate further, but for now, perhaps we can just take it as a lesson learned with no bones broken.'

Carter bit back his natural tendency to tell him that, as a whippersnapper, he had no right to teach his grandmother to suck eggs. He knew he had had a narrow escape, in more than one way, so decided to simply play the humble manservant for as long as the cap fitted. He also mounted, checked that the bags and baggage were still present and correct and, with a click of the tongue, urged his horse round and back on to the road to London.

ELEVEN

Marlowe had walked along the Strand many times, past the great houses mellow in their stone. The Convent Garden stretched to his left, a convent no longer but the homes of the squatters and the dispossessed. He wondered how long it would be before the property men moved in, evicting the crawling things without ceremony or redress. To his right had once stood old John of Gaunt's palace of the Savoy, but the peasants had torn it down in the hurling time before the Marleys had settled in Canterbury and the ghost of time-honoured Lancaster wandered there no more.

The increasingly necessary Elias Carter had arranged this meeting. Sir Walter Ralegh was at home at Durham House along the river that morning and he would be pleased to receive a poet after his own heart.

No one answered the heavy iron knocker that Marlowe rapped against the sturdy oak, but the door gave on its latch and he stepped inside. The hall was cool after the glare of the Strand sunshine and a curious smell hit Marlowe's nostrils, still cringing a little after Salazar's onslaught. In a dark corner, crated in rough wood and sacking, stood bales of dark leaves, dried and curling. Tobacco. It had to be. From the orchards of the Americas. A globe stood in another corner, inscribed with curious symbols. Leviathans crashed through the flowing waters and mermaids sat on the rocks where the lost land of Lyonesse stretched beyond the Lizard. In the third corner, the silver half armour that Ralegh wore as the captain of the Queen's Guard stood on its frame, glowing in the half light from the open door that stood in the last corner.

'Hello?' Marlowe called, but all he heard was his own voice echoing back, muffled by the arras on the walls. This was odd. A man like Ralegh had people around him all the time, as far as the eye could see. Where were they? Especially on a day when the master was expecting guests.

Marlowe crossed the hall and walked through the open door. A corridor with Dutch tiles on the floor stretched ahead, leading to another door. 'Hello?' There had to be *somebody* in. Through the warp of the coloured glass, he could see a figure in the orchard. Actually, two figures, standing close.

'Sir Walter?' Marlowe stepped off the terrace on to the close-cropped grass. Ralegh spun at the sound of his name, revealing an extremely flustered lady, whose breasts had spilled out of her bodice. Crimson with embarrassment where seconds before she had been rosy with lust, she was hauling down her farthingale. Ralegh, in the meantime, was fumbling with his codpiece. It was all a little too little. A little too late.

'Damn you to Hell, sir! What do you mean . . . Marlowe? Is that you?'

'Sir Walter,' Marlowe thought it best to bow in the circumstances. At the very least, it stopped the necessity to find somewhere else to look. 'If this is a bad time . . .'

There was a commotion to Marlowe's left and a knot of Ralegh's staff arrived, as flustered as their master. 'My apologies, Sir Walter,' one of them muttered. 'He barged his way in.'

'I beg your pardon?' Marlowe, who had never needed to barge his way in to anywhere in his life, faced the man down.

'Swords, Scranton. Now!' Ralegh barked. 'Spanish School, Marlowe? Italian? It's all one to me. All one to you?'

'Spanish . . .? No, there's no need . . .'

Ralegh, suitably attired again, strode across the grass until his nose was inches from Marlowe's. 'When a man is caught with his Venetians down, he can go one of two ways,' he hissed. 'He can turn crimson and mumble his apologies. Or . . .' he suddenly lashed out with his right hand, slapping Marlowe across the face, 'he can call his discomfiter out. True, you are far enough below me in rank to be the shit on my shoes, but I am known for my magnanimity.'

Marlowe's hand was on the hilt of his dagger as his vision reeled from the blow. Ralegh saw the movement and stepped back out of harm's reach. '*You* may wrestle with knives in alleyways, pizzle,' he snarled. 'A gentleman uses a sword.'

Scranton came bustling out over the lawn with two rapiers half hidden under a cloak. 'Either of these,' Ralegh said, unlacing his doublet, 'would buy a dozen plays from you. Take your pick.'

'Sir Walter . . .' Marlowe checked himself. He was as much of a hothead as the Devon man, but he had not come to pick a fight.

'Choose!' Ralegh shouted.

Marlowe looked at the weapons again, one Italian, the craftsmanship of Milan, one Spanish, the cutting edge of Toledo. He snatched the one nearest to him. Ralegh snorted and took the other one, bending the sprung blade and extending both his sword arm and his right leg, balancing himself in readiness.

'Walter,' the lady spoke for the first time. She crossed to him, turning her back on Marlowe so that he couldn't see her face. 'If you know this man, let it go. Isn't it embarrassing enough, without . . . you don't know how good he is.'

'Please,' Ralegh chuckled. 'He's Kit Marlowe, the son of a Canterbury cobbler. I'm amazed he knows which end to hold that thing.'

Marlowe was going through none of the elaborate Italian moves that Ralegh was using. He calmly passed his dagger to Scranton and stood facing Ralegh.

'Gentlemen,' Scranton cleared his throat. 'Come to the point.'

Both of them, their doublets dropped, their lawn sleeves rolled, closed so that the tips of their blades touched. Scranton took hold of each and steadied them. 'A fight to the finish, Sir Walter?' he asked.

'You know there's no other kind, Scranton,' Ralegh said. 'To the finish, Marlowe?'

This was insanity and Marlowe knew it. But men died every day in affairs of honour like this: a chance remark, a careless slur; even a glance could set blades clashing. And many was the mother's son who would not be coming home tomorrow. Against that, the Queen's command to shorten the length of rapier blades at court looked rather feeble.

'Walter.' The lady spoke again, loudly now and with eyes filled with tears. 'For the love of God!'

'For the love of you, Bess,' Ralegh smiled. 'Get on with it, Scranton.'

'*En garde!*' the flunkey growled, throwing both sword points into the air and stepping back. Both men locked their free arms behind their backs and bent their knees, their blades scraping together as they moved. Ralegh blinked first, his blade licking under Marlowe's and probing for his ribs. The Canterbury man was faster, parrying and regaining his footing on the still dewy grass.

'Stop them, Scranton,' Bess all but screamed. 'They'll kill each other!'

Scranton ignored her, arms folded, watching the play of the swords. Ralegh drove Marlowe back, his attack fast and furious. The playwright scythed left and right, parrying for his life. Ralegh paused. 'Your defence is fine,' he conceded. 'What is that school? Not the Italian, I'll wager.'

'The Kentish school,' Marlowe told him, 'with just a hint of Cambridge and the smock alleys.' He hacked and slashed in return and it was Ralegh's turn to pull back.

'Good!' the courtier hissed through clenched teeth, winded by the exertion of the last few passes, 'but I prefer the School of Night.' He tossed the rapier to his left hand and lunged. The blade tip slashed Marlowe's arm and blood spurted in an arc, crimson spattering the whiteness of his shirt.

'A hit!' Scranton called and the two men came to the *en garde* again.

'First blood, Marlowe,' Ralegh said. 'I am satisfied.' He saluted the man, kissing his sword hilt.

'But I am not,' Marlowe growled. 'To the finish, you said. To the finish it is.'

He sprang to the attack again. He had to be careful now. He could use his left hand too, for his dagger, but he would never trust his sword to it. Ralegh had proved that he was deadly with either; better not give him time to use that ploy again. The steel rang in the quiet garden along the Strand. Lawyers along the road, black-caped and on their way to the Temple, smiled to themselves. Swords meant death, injury at least. The sound of coin in the morning and they loved it. Ralegh was retreating steadily now and Marlowe had turned the attack, driving him towards the apple trees, green with their new leaves. *Quarte. Sixte. Quarte* again. Damn. Ralegh cursed under his breath; the man *was* good and he'd have his work cut out now. Whoever

said that age and experience would always beat youth and
enthusiasm had not been thinking of a fencing bout to the death,
Ralegh was certain.

Marlowe's point caught him high on the left shoulder and
Ralegh reeled. His skin ripped like a pear; he barged forward
to lock hilts with the playwright while he caught his breath
and bled all over him. There was a sob from Bess Throckmorton,
one that racked her body. She had to turn away; she could not
bear to look. Yet, she had to look.

'A hit!' Scranton shouted. He looked as shocked as Bess. He
couldn't remember when he'd last seen his master bested on
the piste. The points slid together again.

'Now,' Marlowe said, 'match blood. Now I am satisfied.'

'The Hell you are!' Ralegh snarled. 'It isn't finished 'til it's
finished. *En garde!*'

'Madame,' Marlowe braced himself for the next pass. 'May
I at least know who it is that I am to die for this morning?'

Bess looked at Ralegh, her face a mask of tears. He was
shaking his head but she spoke anyway. 'I am Bess Throckmorton,
Her Majesty's maid of honour. The daughter of Nicholas
Throckmorton.'

'I see.' Marlowe saluted her with his sword, kissing the
coiling quillons of the hilt. 'A matter of honour, indeed.'

Ralegh's blade hissed past his right ear, taking a lock of
hair with it. Marlowe parried and riposted suddenly, his blade
probing between Ralegh's quillons, grazing his hand. The
Devon man's boot came up, thudding into Marlowe's ribs and
the pair grappled together, hair flying, teeth bared as they
wrestled. Marlowe kicked the sword out of Ralegh's hand and
the courtier scrabbled after it, lashing out with his feet in an
attempt to trip the playwright up. He stumbled but didn't fall
and the blades clashed again. At close quarters, as the hilts
locked for the umpteenth time, Ralegh thrust his thumb into
Marlowe's eye socket. The Canterbury man drove his head
forward, his skull cracking Ralegh's nose and he fell back
hard. His vision swam, what with the tears and the concussion
and his guard was down.

'In the name of God!' Scranton shouted, rushing towards
Marlowe whose sword was raised.

Ralegh had dropped to one knee. He held his sword out to the side, hauling his shirt aside with his other hand. 'Finish it, Marlowe,' he muttered. There was blood in his mouth and one tooth, at least, was loose.

Marlowe was having difficulty seeing out of his gouged eye and there were at least two Great Lucifers kneeling at his feet.

'No!' Bess Throckmorton's scream shook windows all along the Strand. She was suddenly at Marlowe's side, gripping his arm and blinking through her tears; she looked into his face. 'He is the love of my life,' she sobbed. 'I will give you anything.'

He looked at her, the earnest, pleading face, beautiful even when slick with tears. Bess had cried without holding anything back and her eyes were red and swollen, her lashes clotted together and her lip trembled. She held his gaze and he crumbled. In any event, his eye hurt, his arm hurt, his legs felt like lead and his lungs were wheezing like old bellows. 'I suspect that Sir Walter would not give me the time of day,' he gasped.

Ralegh laughed, losing his balance and landing on his haunches. 'On the contrary,' he said, through swollen lips. 'I have all the time in the world for a man who can fight me to a standstill. But the bout's not done. Finish it, Marlowe.'

'No,' Marlowe threw the sword down. 'Now, it is finished.'

Everyone in the orchard breathed a sigh of relief, not least Scranton, who clapped his hands and sent the terrified servants for water, towels and bandages.

Bess Throckmorton looked at Marlowe and mouthed a silent 'Thank you.' Then she pulled up her skirts that had been dragging in the dew and marched over to the slumped frame of Ralegh. 'As for you, Walter Ralegh,' she actually stamped her foot. 'I never want to see you again.' She spun on her heel and made for the house.

Marlowe did his best to walk normally and sat down next to Ralegh. 'I'm sorry,' he said, looking at the lady's disappearing back, 'if I have been the unwitting cause . . .'

'Oh, it's nothing,' Ralegh smiled, although the movement cost him dearly. 'What's today? Wednesday, is it? She'll sulk until Friday, then I'll turn up at Placentia suitably bandaged and her heart will melt. It's happened before.' He frowned at Marlowe – another expensive gesture in terms of pain, 'but never because of another swordsman. What did you say you wanted?'

'Well,' Marlowe's whole body was beginning to stiffen and there was no sign yet of Scranton's ministering angels. 'I had thought to talk poetry, one Muse to another, as it were, but something you said during the bout rather intrigued me.'

'Oh, what was that?' Ralegh extended a careful leg; he had dancer's legs, the Queen was wont to remark, rather unsettlingly and he wanted to make sure it was all right.

'Just before you broke every law in the duelling book and changed hands . . .'

Ralegh chuckled and immediately wished he hadn't. 'Sorry about that,' he said. 'Needs must. I had to do something desperate.'

'Just before that, you mentioned the School of Night. What's that, if I may ask?'

An odd look flickered over Ralegh's bruised and battered face. He looked the poet up and down and liked what he saw, except that the man was younger and no doubt handsome, should you like that kind of thing. 'How long have you got?' he asked.

'If I may, Carter,' Marlowe was more than a little testy the next morning. 'A brief word?'

'Master Marlowe,' Carter looked startled. 'If I may say so, sir, you look . . . terrible.'

'You should see me from my side,' the playwright muttered. He had spent a comfortable night, in fact, in Sir Walter Ralegh's second-best bed, replete with Sir Walter Ralegh's excellent food and more than a little mellow with Sir Walter Ralegh's exotic wines. He had also had the most fascinating evening he could remember for a long time. He and the Devon courtier were kindred spirits, poets with fire in their blood and a longing for more than the tired old world could give them. Even so, Marlowe's eye was bruised and swollen and blood still seeped from the gash to his forearm, when he forgot himself and moved too quickly.

'You could have something to do with that, Carter.' Marlowe looked levelly at the man. 'Me looking terrible, I mean.'

'Sir?'

'I thought you told me Sir Walter was ready to receive visitors.'

'That's what he told me.'

'He almost received the last rites. I found him in . . . shall we say . . . in a delicate position.'

'Against a tree?'

'What?' Did this man see the same visions as the magus? 'It is how he likes it, so I'm told,' Carter shrugged. 'Keeps him in touch with nature and such. Don't suppose it does much for the lady in question.'

'There are those,' Marlowe reminded the man, 'who say a lady is never in question. Wait a minute.' He paused in his stride along the Strand. 'Have you been here all night?'

'Yes, sir, outside Sir Walter's gate.'

'Why?'

'I have my orders, Master Marlowe,' Carter said straight-faced, 'from the doctor. I can't keep you in my sight all the time, but I'll never be far away.'

'So, let me understand you: Ralegh expressly told you he'd be expecting me.'

'Expressly,' Carter said.

'Odd, that.'

Carter stopped and faced the man. 'What Ralegh says and what Ralegh does is as different from white king to black bishop. It's his way and you're lucky to walk away from it. Tell me, are we any nearer to who killed Sir Francis Walsingham?'

Marlowe sighed. 'Not this side of the second coming,' he said.

The carriage jolted to a halt in the busy throng along Candlewick Street. Nicholas Faunt would have ignored it, but he saw the Queen's arms of '*Semper eadem*' emblazoned on the door and he stopped walking. The coachman touched his cap, steadying the whinnying greys in their harness, bracing his feet on the board.

Faunt looked inside as the door swung open. He climbed

aboard and sat opposite the carriage's single occupant. 'I don't usually accept lifts from strange men,' he said, with no expression, 'but in your case, Sir Robert, I'll make an exception.'

'Damn good of you, Faunt,' the new Spymaster tapped the roof with his silver cane top and the greys lurched forward. 'Going my way?'

'That very much depends on where you're going,' Faunt said. He didn't like Robert Cecil. The man had robbed him of the Spymaster's job and was treading on toes in all directions. A pity the nurse who had dropped him as a child hadn't done a more final job.

'*Quo vadis?*' Cecil was looking out of the window as the carriage swung right along Fish Street, making for the bridge. He answered his own question before Faunt could so much as open his mouth. 'You're going to the Rose. Marlowe's new play. So am I.'

'I hadn't you down for a playgoer,' Faunt arched an eyebrow.

'Oh, I'm not. Our Puritan friends see them as inventions of the Devil, don't they? Cesspits of filth and lewd behaviour. Well, that's pushing it a bit, don't you think? Even so, I always bring a dozen handkerchiefs to wipe the seat down, just in case. No, it's just that this particular one is written by Marlowe.'

Faunt looked at the broad sweep of the forehead, the shrewd mouth, the rheumy hazel eyes. 'You *do* know he's on our side, don't you?' he asked.

'Is he?' Cecil counted. 'I envy you, Faunt. How comforting it must be to be so certain, so assured. Look there,' he pointed out of the window as the river slipped by, the ships bobbing black on the silver sparkle of the water. 'The heads.'

Faunt looked. Three of them jutted above the stone parapet, their hair blowing in the wind, their jaws all but rotted through. He couldn't hear the teeth rattling this far below, what with the creak of the wheels and the snorting of the horses, the hiss of the water speeding past the bridge stanchions, but he knew the eyes had long gone, prizes for the ravens of the Tower.

'James Morgan,' Cecil said wistfully. 'George Barnard. Roger Talbot.'

'I know,' Faunt said. 'I put two of them there, in a manner of speaking.'

'Yes,' Cecil sighed. 'No one doubts *your* ability, Faunt. Sir Francis always spoke most highly of you. My point is that those three were certain once, assured. Certain we wouldn't discover their treason, assured in their loyalty to the anti-Christ. And yet, look at them now.'

'But Marlowe—'

'Is an overreacher,' Cecil cut in. 'They say he sups with the Devil.'

Faunt laughed. 'Then I hope Belzebub is using a long spoon. Marlowe is a playwright,' he said. 'He will sup with whoever buys his verses. Or pays to see them on the boards.'

Cecil sighed again. 'All right,' he muttered. 'I can take a hint. Your seat at the Rose is on me.'

'So, how come you're a knight, again?' Ingram Frizer hissed in the darkness of the wings.

'Superior bearing, I suppose,' Nicholas Skeres shrugged, remembering to hold his chin high. Whoever had made his costume had skimped on the hemming and the stiffened hessian was as sharp as a knife. He looked down at his friend, bending with care. 'That's why you're a carpenter.'

'That Henslowe's a bloody idiot. Couldn't cast a shadow, he couldn't.'

'Ssshh!' Tom Sledd's irritated command brought an instant silence to the wings.

Centre-stage, Ned Alleyn as Barabbas was having trouble with his daughter Abigail. She wasn't obsequious enough for Alleyn's liking and anyway, her voice kept dipping to that of a tenor. Monstrous as his ego was, he had leapt at the chance to play the lead in Marlowe's latest, but he hadn't reckoned on having to be so old. A slight peppering of silver at the temples was one thing; going on stage as grey as a badger did nothing for his god-like looks. He longed to be Tamburlaine again.

'No, Abigail,' Frizer and Skeres heard Alleyn thunder, with rather more fire than the scene merited. 'Things past recovery are hardly cured with exclamations. Be silent, daughter . . .'

'He really doesn't like her, does he?' Skeres observed out of the corner of his mouth.

'Er . . . you *do* know she's a man, don't you, Nick?' Frizer felt he ought to ask.

'Of course I do,' Skeres said, ducking out of sight to avoid Tom Sledd's wrathful stare. He rested against the woodwork, making the streets of Valletta wobble a little. 'So, where are we with Marlowe, then? What do we tell His Nibs?'

'Well,' Frizer closed to him, ignoring the play for a moment. 'First, he goes to Blackfriars . . .'

'. . . where he meets up with that old tutor of his, that cove from Cambridge. Michaels.'

'Johns.'

'Like I said, that's him.'

'Then . . . if memory serves, he makes for Petworth.'

Skeres had a sudden thought. 'Hey, he *will* cover the cost of those horses, won't he? Only, they don't come cheap, you know.'

'Yes, he's good for it.'

'And while Marlowe's there—'

'He plays tennis.'

'Never mind that. What about the crossbow thing, eh? I nearly shat myself.'

'Whoever it was wasn't aiming at you, Nick,' Frizer pointed out, one eye on the action.

'No, but all the same . . .'

'Then we goes to that foreigner's place . . .'

'Out of which Marlowe shot like all the devils in Hell were on his tail.'

'That cove of his, Carter. He didn't give much away, did he?'

'Bugger me sideways.' Frizer was looking past the actors now, into the dusk of the theatre. 'He's here.'

'Who?'

'Him.'

'Never!'

'Are you two actually in this play or not?' Tom Sledd hissed in Skeres' ear. 'Only this is Act Two, Scene Two and that's the bloody Senate House out there. See.' He shook the sheaf of papers in his hand. 'It says, *if* you can read, "Ferneze, Martin del Bosco, *knights* and officers. Get out there and be a bloody knight, for God's sake.'

Skeres scuttled on to the stage, notably lagging behind the others. He stood there, open-mouthed. Rehearsals had been different. All sorts of people had been coming and going, walking across the O, chatting. Musicians had been warming up, with hautboys and sackbuts. Ned Alleyn had been signing autographs and showing a whole gaggle of Winchester geese his extensive repertoire, often in broad daylight in the open. But *this!* This was different. Four hundred faces faced him. Eight hundred eyes, give or take, burned into his soul. Ferneze and Martin del Bosco were in earnest conversation, but nobody was looking at them, or listening to them. Instead, they were all looking at Nicholas Skeres, waiting for his one line.

So frozen was he that he didn't see the aged woman in the groundling mob near the stage nudge a large man standing next to her. She was beaming broadly. 'That's my Nick, that is,' everyone but Skeres heard her say.

Marlowe and Tom Sledd leaned against the wall of the Bear Pit, a flagon of wine between them. The silence after the roar of the crowd was almost a living thing and even Master Sackerson's usual evening snufflings had abated to just the occasional snort as he fell momentarily asleep over his dinner.

'So,' Sledd finally said.

'So, indeed, Tom,' Marlowe agreed, leaning over for more wine.

'They liked it, I think.'

'They seemed to, certainly.'

The two looked into the middle distance, at the sun just going down between the chimney pots. Audiences were hard to read. Some who had seemed in raptures had then gone home and told all of their friends to go and roll in dung rather than go to the latest at the Rose. Other audiences, which had seemed to be crammed with Puritan killjoys scowling in silence, had subsequently run through the streets yelling the Rose's wares. You really could not tell. So it was useless to speculate. And yet . . .

'It was a full house, at any rate,' Sledd said. 'I see Faunt was there.'

Marlowe smiled. 'Good old Nicholas,' he said. 'He always comes and usually denies it.'

'He was sitting with some little cove, I don't know who he is. Needed a cushion, or so I was told.'

'A cushion? The Rose has cushions?'

'A guinea,' Sledd said with a smile. 'I didn't know we had them either and I certainly didn't know how much they cost. But Master Henslowe had it on his list and so . . . there you are. The gent paid up, as good as gold.'

'Henslowe doesn't miss a trick,' Marlowe agreed. 'He was pleased, was he, with the house?'

'I heard him singing,' Sledd remarked.

'Oh. *That* pleased. I've only heard him do that once before.'

'Twice,' Sledd corrected him. 'Once when he counted up the total for *Tamburlaine*, do you remember? We did an extra day on the run and everyone went mad for it. Performances almost round the clock. Alleyn couldn't speak at the end, had to more or less mime that final act.'

'And the other time?' Marlowe had to know.

'When Mistress H went to stay with her mother. She was gone three months.'

'I do remember that,' Marlowe said, thinking back. 'I don't remember the singing, but I do remember the bonus he gave everyone.'

'And took back in the next pay,' Sledd said. 'But the thought was there.' He looked sideways at Marlowe. 'Do you mind if I ask you a question?'

'No.'

'That wasn't the question.' Tom Sledd had known Marlowe a long time.

'Fair enough. I don't mind if you ask me *another* question. I just don't promise that I will answer it.'

'Who is that?'

Marlowe looked around. 'That what?'

'That man at the bottom of the lane. I've seen him around and now he seems to be leading your horse.'

Marlowe stood up straight and peered into the growing dusk, to where he could just make out Carter, silhouetted against the beams of a lantern shining out of the windows of the inn on the opposite side of the road.

'Ah. That would be Carter,' he hedged.

Sledd looked closer. 'I don't see a cart.'

'No, not *a* Carter. Just Carter. He's . . . he's my manservant.'

Sledd almost fell into the pit. '*Manservant!* Hold on, Kit. We don't know if this play is going to go that well – not yet, anyway.'

Marlowe scratched his head and looked a little shamefaced. It was easier to be labelled a spendthrift than a spy. 'Well . . . I fancied spoiling myself a little.'

'But you hated having a manservant before. What was his name? Windmill, was it?'

'Windlass,' Marlowe corrected him. 'Jack Windlass. And he wasn't a manservant, not really.'

'You're right there,' Sledd agreed. 'I never saw your linen so creased. But . . . even so, Kit. A *manservant*.'

'I'm just trying him out,' Marlowe said, to bring the conversation to a close. 'He's on one month's approval.'

'I wager you won't keep him,' Sledd said, smugly.

'I won't take you up on that, Tom,' Marlowe said, flinging his cloak over his shoulder and finishing up his wine. 'But I have to go. Tell everyone well done. Except . . . what was wrong with that knight in Act Two? He looked like something poleaxed. Either get him acting lessons or replace him, would you?'

TWELVE

Carter was trying to look inconspicuous, to give him credit where it was due, but sitting on one horse and leading another, it was tricky to say the least. Marlowe decided to give him the benefit of the doubt, however, and simply mounted his bay.

'Are we going anywhere in particular, Carter?' he asked him. He should be carousing with the cast, but this was hardly his first 'first performance' and there would always be another, after all.

'The doctor has been in touch, Master Marlowe,' Carter said. 'He has spoken to . . . two gentlemen . . . and they would be pleased to meet with you tonight.'

'As pleased as Ralegh?' Marlowe could bear a grudge as well as the next man.

'I did apologize for that,' Carter said, a little testily. 'I had been led to believe . . .'

Marlowe flapped a hand at him. 'Yes, yes, we'll take that as read, shall we? But if it is *two* gentlemen this time, I need to know they are expecting me. One disgruntled scientist was bad enough; two might be the death of me.'

'I have seen the note, Master Marlowe,' Carter said, somewhat on his dignity. 'I have it here if you want to look at it.' He reached into his saddlebag and rummaged.

'No, Carter, I believe you. But, surely you can see I am a little chary of just marching in to someone's garden again. It wasn't a pretty sight last time, I can tell you. In fact, when you next see me the wrong side of a glass or two, ask me for a private fact about Walter Ralegh; for now, I will just say his reputation with the ladies is not necessarily well-earned.'

Carter looked intrigued, but there was a job to do; scurrilous details about the size of Walter Ralegh's personal equipment could wait until another day. 'I believe the gentlemen in question are in one case happily married and in the other, not much of a one for the ladies. I think you will be able to enter their presence with impunity.'

Marlowe was unconvinced, but as he always expected the unexpected, nothing much had changed; he would go in with his hand on his dagger hilt and the eyes in the back of his head well and truly open. 'You are being very circumspect, Carter. Are we going somewhere near or somewhere far?'

'We need to follow the river west for quite a way,' Carter said. 'We could hire a waterman, but I thought you might prefer to ride and of course the journey is shorter – there are some meanders we can cut out. It is a fine night and the gentlemen are not expecting us early.'

'Riding will suit me very well,' Marlowe said. He needed to clear his head of the smell of the crowd. 'Where are we going, exactly?'

'We are heading to Syon House.'

Marlowe thought for a moment. 'Not Henry Percy again, surely? I heard he is renting the place, though why he needs yet more great houses it is hard to imagine,' he said. 'I somehow suspect I have blotted my copybook with him.'

Carter chuckled. 'You are well schooled in who owns what, Master Marlowe,' he said. 'I expect that goes with your employment.'

'Employment?' Marlowe was startled. Just what had Dee told his man?

'As playwright, sir, as poet.' Carter could not be disconcerted. 'A man needs to know where the patrons are to be found, after all. But, no, it is not His Grace. Nor his brother. Sir Thomas Hariot has a suite of rooms there and he is one of the gentlemen we go to see tonight.'

Marlowe racked his brain; he couldn't remember whether they had met or if he had heard anything about the man. Somehow potatoes crossed his mind, but, surely, a man could not justly be judged because he looked like a potato, if that was indeed the link. 'And the other?'

'Now, this gentleman I know you know. Ferdinando Stanley, Lord Strange.'

'I have met Lord Strange on many occasions,' Marlowe conceded. What theatrical man had not? 'Is he keeping well, these days?'

Carter shrugged. 'I did not enquire as to His Lordship's health, I confess,' he said. 'Why? Has he been unwell?'

'He thinks so,' Marlowe chuckled. 'He is very . . . how can I put it . . . he watches the skies more often than the earth, he thinks more about the poison that could be in his food than the taste of it. Every black cat that crosses his path is an omen and it often proves his worth; any man who watches the skies so much is bound to fall over a black cat in the dark every once in a while.'

'Ah. I understand. In that case, I believe he is well.'

'Good.' Marlowe liked Strange. He took a little getting used to, if only because the mole on his forehead sometimes seemed to be looking at a person more intently than his eyes were, but once over that hurdle, he was diverting company and as sharp as a tack. Keeping him off talking theatre shop was the main thing; some of his Men had played at the Rose and rumour had it that he was trying to poach Richard Burbage. Only Burbage and Strange thought that Henslowe would mind.

The men rode in silence along the darkening lanes and now and then were alongside the Thames. Sometimes they were riding on the banks, the water gliding slick and fast almost at their feet. Other times they were out of sight of it but could still hear the slap of the water against piers and jetties. But most of the time it was a distant rumour to their left, the smell of the foreshore and the cry of the occasional water-bird late home to its nest the only clue that the country's greatest waterway was just a stone's throw away. Before too long, the small town of Braynford was ahead, lights in some windows showing where weavers and spinners sat up late to complete their tasks. A bakery's chimney belched smoke and from an alehouse came the sound of raucous laughter.

Marlowe enjoyed being out at night. The darkness and the steady plod of the horses' hoofs lulled him and his mind could wander where it would. Carter was a good companion; schooled by Dee, he did not chatter or gossip but simply kept pace, half

a horse's length behind and to the side of the road, from where
danger might come.

Usually after a first performance, the playwright's mind
would be full of what could be done to improve it. There
would always be something that would need to be cut, embel-
lished, recast. But tonight, as for many days and nights
before, his head was spinning with the possibilities of the
story of Faustus, the magus who conjured the devil. Let Tom
Sledd worry about the how – Marlowe was the man to tell
the story so that no one who saw it would sleep again. He
would raise the hackles. He would chill the blood. For if not
him, then who?

Carter watched his new master's back as he rode. Over the
years, he had found that a man's soul rode on his back. If he
were vulnerable, uncertain, vicious, unpredictable, all of that
was in the set of his shoulders, the angle of his head. In Marlowe
he saw everything, in much the same way as, it was said, the
world was in a grain of sand. Where the hair curled on his neck,
there was the choirboy. His back, straight and strong, was that
of a man who would brook no argument. The curl of the ear,
the flash of the eye, as the head turned constantly this way and
that, bespoke of the poet and playwright, the man for whom
every sound and sight was grist to his mill. And the right hand,
curled loosely on the saddle at the small of his back, a heartbeat
away from the dagger's hilt, told of a man whose guard was
never down, who never rested. He couldn't see the lover, but
all men were allowed some secrets.

Marlowe's horse kicked a stone and something unknown
skittered through the hedgerow and the spell was broken.

'Not long now, Master Marlowe,' Carter said and on they
rode.

Ned Alleyn had already gone, whisked into the Southwark night
by his favourite Winchester goose, whose friend tagged along
as a spare. The night had been merry, the players of *The Jew*
still hearing the groundlings' applause rattling in their ears and
the ale at the Mermaid flowed like water. The first round, unusually, had been on Henslowe; after that, it was every tippler for
himself.

'He's got a new one, Will.' Tom Sledd was slurring a little
by now; the brew had made him expansive but, at the same time,
confidential.

'Who? What?' Shaxsper prided himself on being a moderately
intelligent man, but riddles were for University Wits and he
wasn't one of those.

'Kit. Kit's got a new play.'

Shaxsper grabbed the stage manager's sleeve. 'Tell me it's
not Henry the Sixth.'

'Who?' Sledd frowned, trying to focus. 'Oh, God, no . . .
um, I mean, no. I can't say too much of course, but . . .' he
checked the revellers to left and right, '. . . there's been nothing
like it before on the English stage, believe me.'

'That good?' Shaxsper was unconsciously grinding his teeth.
One day, he knew, his day would come. But not yet; not as
long as Marlowe was the Muses' darling and the London
riff-raff flocked to see him.

'Better,' Sledd confided, nodding at his tankard in a compla-
cent way for far longer than the riposte warranted, in that way
drunk stage managers have.

There was a roar of laughter as Nick Skeres slid off his stool
and lay on the tavern floor, helpless with ale and mirth.

'Pity he didn't do that on stage,' Sledd grunted.

'What's it about?' Shaxsper asked.

'What?' It was Sledd's turn to be obtuse.

'Marlowe's new play.' Shaxsper might not be a successful
playwright yet, but he could follow a plot.

'Tom Sledd!' A harpy shriek shattered a moment already
loud with merriment.

'Oh, God . . .' Sledd moaned before a very large woman
hauled him off his stool and hugged him with a grip Master
Sackerson would have envied.

'Look at you,' she held him at arm's length momentarily,
before burying him again in her pillowing bosom. Flinging him
away from her once more so she could get a really good look at
him, she cried, 'You're so . . . growed up!'

'Yes.' He grinned sheepishly.

'Not still playing the maid, I'll wager.' She nudged him with
an elbow that could have broken a less nimble man's ribs.

Before he could answer, she reached down and patted his codpiece. 'No, not with a block and tackle like that. Still in the theatre, though, eh?'

'Yes.' Sledd did his best to extricate himself. 'Yes, still at the . . . Curtain. Look, Maggie!' He gripped her sleeve and pointed into the jostling crowd. 'Isn't that Richard Burbage over there?'

She screamed and threw her arms wide. 'Dick Burbage!' she roared and crashed through the throng.

'What was *that*?' an alarmed Shaxsper asked as Sledd straightened his doublet and sat back down.

'Maggie Tupper.' Sledd took refuge in his ale cup. 'She likes actors.'

'Hasn't seen you for a while, I gather, if she remembers you playing the girlies.'

'Last Thursday,' Sledd said, keeping his head down as Richard Burbage was valiantly trying to defend himself in the far corner. 'We have exactly the same conversation most weeks. Mad as a tree, that one. She'll be looking for spots in the palm of her hand next. Where were we?' He tried to focus.

'Marlowe's new play.'

'Ah, yes, well . . .'

But Shaxsper was to learn no more. Not tonight. The doors crashed back, all three of them simultaneously and armed men broke through the crowd, shoving people aside, slapping one or two around the head with the flat of their halberds and forming a ring in the centre of the room.

'Now, look here . . .' the Mermaid's host emerged from behind his counter, a spiked cudgel cradled in his arms.

'You.' A captain in the Queen's livery snapped at him, clicking his fingers. 'Owen, isn't it? You keep this stews?'

The landlord straightened. 'I am Andrew Owen,' he said, 'and I own the Mermaid. What of it?'

The captain turned to face the man. Everyone had fallen silent now and Richard Burbage took the opportunity to extricate himself from mad Maggie. His attempt to leave was less successful, however, because two very large men blocked the nearest door. 'You keep a bawdy house . . .' the captain said.

'The Hell I do,' Owen spat back. 'I—'

'A bawdy house full of Papists.'

'Now you've gone too far,' Owen growled, but his half-step forward ended in him toppling over, overturning a table as he went down, pole-axed.

The captain kicked the still-recumbent Skeres. 'Take him,' he muttered and the hapless gentleman, scarcely walking at all, was lifted bodily and carried towards the door.

'Just a minute . . .' Ingram Frizer slammed down his tankard and squared up to the captain. He barely reached his ruff.

'Him too,' the captain murmured and Frizer's knife was whisked out of his belt and he was catapulted towards the door.

'Search them,' the captain bellowed and his men went to work. Doublets were ripped open, purses emptied. There were shouts from the men and screams from the women, all except Maggie, who was smiling benignly as a guard carried out his captain's orders with a zealousness that he hoped would lead to promotion.

'Do you mind!' Shaxsper was on his feet, butting aside a guard's probing fingers.

'You!' the captain snapped. 'Where are you from?'

'Blackfriars,' Shaxsper told him.

It was the actor-playwright's turn to feel the intensity of the captain's gaze. 'If I'd wanted a comedian, I'd have sent for Will Kemp. Where are you from originally?'

'Warwickshire.' Shaxsper stood half a head taller.

'Warwickshire?' the captain said with a slow grin. 'Hear that, lads? Warwickshire. There are more Papists in that Godforsaken county than there are hairs on my head. Take him.'

'You can't do that!' Tom Sledd had sobered up, as men will when their lives are on the edge.

The captain grinned again. 'See that?' he pointed to the Tudor rose embroidered on his doublet. 'That says I can. Now,' he frowned, 'you're no Warwickshire Pope-lover, not by your accent anyway.'

'That's right,' Sledd said. 'I'm local, me. London through and through.' He too looked at the captain's ruff. 'What are you going to do about it?'

The captain just nodded and somebody else did something

about it. There was a thud and – for Tom Sledd – the world went black.

The great Italianate front of Syon House rose above the trees as the horsemen turned into the sweeping drive through the park. The Queen probably didn't even know she owned this gorgeous building; surely, if she did, she would live here and not Placentia, with all its inconveniences, draughts and ghosts. The river was unpolluted by the hordes of London, the park was full of grazing cattle, sheep and deer, all now sheltering under the spreading trees scattered across the well-cropped grass. In short, it was a little Paradise. As they came nearer to the house, a shape detached itself from a tree. The man stepped forward, his hat pulled low, his cloak swept over one shoulder.

'Hold hard, gentlemen!' The voice was harsh, its age and accent impossible to even guess. 'What is your business?'

Marlowe leaned forward. 'We are here to see Thomas Hariot,' he said.

'*Just* Master Hariot?' the man checked.

'My apologies,' Marlowe gushed. 'We are of course also here to see Lord Strange, Lord Strange.'

'Do you have a stammer, sir?' the cloaked man asked, 'in that you say Lord Strange twice.'

Marlowe straightened up. 'By no means, my lord, but the night is growing chilly and I am sure the gentlemen would rather be abed before dawn. I know I would and my man and I have a long, cold ride ahead of us before we can retire.'

'I am sure . . .' The man coughed and resumed in his lower, assumed register. 'I am sure that Master Hariot will be glad to give you lodgings,' he said. 'But, I ask again, why do you say Lord Strange twice?'

Marlowe leaned forward and tweaked the hat off the man's head. 'Because I would not be so ill-mannered as to leave out your name and title, my lord,' he said, with a laugh.

Ferdinando Strange doubled over, slapping his knees with delight. 'I thought I could fool you, Kit,' he said. 'I made sure my disguise was complete.'

'Nothing can disguise those northern cadences,' Marlowe

told him. 'You live under bigger skies; you have lost the sound of the city. But . . .' he wagged his head, deciding, 'apart from that, you had me fooled. How about you, Carter?'

Carter quickly agreed. 'Oh, yes, sir,' he said. 'I was fooled as well. I had you for a common footpad.'

'Did you?' Strange was delighted. 'A footpad? That was my intention!'

Carter shrugged. 'Then you were a marvel at it, sir,' he said, his voice without inflection. Not only had he noticed him leaning against his tree from yards back, but he also had him for Lord Strange from the first second. But the man seemed pleasant enough, for a landed idiot with a strange sense of fun. He could have had a knife between his ribs, had Carter been of a less phlegmatic bent.

Strange looked up at Marlowe, his eyes aglow in the moonlight. 'I'll just walk alongside, up to the house. Thomas's rooms are around the back, in the old stable. You would never find them on your own.'

'In the stable. I was expecting something more—'

'Palatial. I know.' Strange had his hand on Marlowe's stirrup leather. 'He did have rooms in the house at first, but there were complaints. From the house staff. Speaking for myself, I would have ignored them.'

Carter bridled quietly, all to himself in the darkness to the rear.

'They could always be replaced, of course. But . . . well, the house is leased from the Queen and there was . . . damage.'

Marlowe's heart fell. His nostrils filled against their will with the stench of Salazar's cages, his ears were bombarded by the bay of Percy's hound.

'Nothing a coat of distemper wouldn't fix, but you know how fussy these comptrollers can be. Something about Chinese silk . . . well, I don't know the details, but the long and the short of it is, he has the old stable block and he seems happy there. Poor Thomas; he has never really cared too much for his surroundings, as you probably know.'

'Do you spend much time here?' Marlowe asked.

'Here? Good Heavens, no. I don't come south at all if I don't have to and certainly not here. Wringing wet, the whole suite of rooms. It plays havoc with my chest. As you know, I can't be too careful.'

They turned into the stable yard and Marlowe was saved from having to listen to a recitation of Lord Strange's ailments. A door stood open and silhouetted against its golden light stood a man who did not in fact look anything like a potato. Thomas Hariot raised an arm in a languid wave and disappeared into the room behind him.

'That's Thomas,' Strange said, somewhat superfluously. 'You can tether the horse here . . . er . . .'

'Carter,' said Carter.

'That's right. Wait here. I'm afraid the staff have retired for the night, but there is a niche there in the wall, should you need shelter.'

Marlowe cast an uneasy look in Carter's direction. The man knew his place, it was true, but whether he considered his place was a niche in the wall of a stable yard was entirely another matter. But his man nodded and led the horses over to the rail, as meekly as anyone could wish. Marlowe had a feeling he would pay for this later, but time enough for that when it happened. He followed Strange, who was just disappearing through the lighted doorway.

Inside, the room was warm and bright, with candelabra and a roaring fire. The walls were hung with sin-soft velvet and it was not possible to tell which was glass and which daub. Marlowe exhaled with relief. No smell save that of dripping beeswax and mulling wine. No sound save that of the muttering fire and the guttering candles. He smiled and walked swiftly across a beautiful Turkey carpet, his hand extended in greeting.

'Master Hariot,' he said. 'I have heard so much about your work. Thank you for seeing me, especially at such a late hour.'

Hariot's eyes swivelled from side to side. 'You've heard about my work?' he said. 'What have you heard? Ferdinando, what has he heard?'

Strange moved nearer and patted the man's arm reassuringly. 'I think Master Marlowe was just being civil, Thomas,' he said. 'Master Marlowe is known for his gilded tongue. Poet, you know. Playwright.'

Hariot's eyes stopped flickering and he looked more closely at Marlowe. 'Playwright, you say?' he said to Strange. 'And poet, yes,' Marlowe said. 'I have been to see the Earl of Northumberland. He told me of your language skills. That is all I have heard, really.' Hariot's eyes lit up. 'My Algonquin, yes.' Then he flapped a hand impatiently. 'But, I have mastered that. I am on to new pursuits.' Again, his eyes flickered. 'But . . . the world is not yet ready, Master Marlowe. Not ready. Tell me,' he leaned forward excitedly. 'Do you know numbers?'

Marlowe was puzzled. Surely, everyone knew a number when they saw one. Perhaps some people had favourites, for all he knew. He smiled and hoped that would do.

'Surely!' Hariot said, drawing back and looking amazed. 'A poet must know number. If only to work out rhythm, rhyme. Di dum di dum di dum di dum di dum. That kind of thing.'

'Oh, I *see*! Yes, poets do need to be able to count. Not for rhyme so much. I like my verse blank whenever I can make it so. But rhythm, yes, indeed. In that respect, I know numbers. Pentameters take me all the way up to five.'

Hariot looked doubtful but, even so, walked over to the wall behind him and whipped back the curtain. The plaster behind was as black as the velvet which had covered it and was covered with chalk scribbles, numbers, letters, arcane symbols, all tumbled together. There were signs that some parts had been roughly erased and written over. In other places, heavy underlining emphasized a point which only Hariot had ever understood. 'Do you see it?' he cried. 'Elegant in its simplicity, is it not?'

Marlowe drew a breath to speak, but then discovered that he actually had nothing to say, so let it out again, slowly.

'In daylight, perhaps,' Strange jumped in with an excuse which might pass muster. 'In this candlelight, the eyes play tricks, or at least I find it so.' He leaned towards Marlowe and lowered his voice. 'It is a calculation of the dimensions of the planets. Heresy, of course, in many ways I am sure. But Thomas is certain that . . .'

'What's that?' Hariot was leaning in. 'Ferdinando, you know that of all things I most abhor *whispering*.'

'I was just explaining to Master Marlowe,' Strange said quickly, 'how complex I find your calculations.'

Hariot laughed condescendingly. 'Yes, I am afraid you do, Ferdinando. If it isn't hedge magic, you are not interested, I know.' He suddenly stopped and raised a finger. 'Hark! *Nutomon gokgkhoko! Nomihtu mgeyu nipawset*, or at least I have always noticed that, have you Master Marlowe, or perhaps in town you do not hear the owl, whether the moon is red or no?'

'I am often in the country,' Marlowe said, 'but I confess I know little about the ways of the owl.'

'It gives me the shivers,' Hariot said, confidentially. 'The owl, the fatal bellman, as I call him. Although, *gokgkhoko* fits the bill quite well, I always think.' He looked at the blank faces. 'Forgive me. I forget that not everyone is familiar with the Passamaquoddy dialect of Algonquin. I must remember to use the mother tongue in company.'

Marlowe and Strange had adopted the expression often seen on the face of a mad doctor when consulting with a rich patient who is nevertheless completely, though pleasantly, demented: half nursemaid, half gaoler.

Hariot, enlivened by his brief burst of native speech, rubbed his hands together. 'But, Master Marlowe, I feel sure you did not come here tonight to see my scrawls and hear my nonsense. Why *are* you here, indeed?'

'I . . . I am writing a play, Master Hariot,' Marlowe said, thinking on his feet. 'I am in mind to have a philosopher as my main hero, a man of stature, of brain, of supreme intellect. Here seemed to be the obvious place to come.'

Hariot drew himself up. 'I cannot but agree with you, Master Marlowe,' he said, proudly. 'You have come not just to the *right* place, but to the *only* place. Let me talk you through some more of my calculations. But, first, a drink to keep out the night chill.' He ladled out a generous amount of mulling wine from the flagon on the hearth and handed the steaming goblet over. 'Do you have a manservant with you?' He raised a questioning eyebrow.

'Why, yes, I have.' Marlowe was surprised that Hariot could be so down to earth.

'Here is something for him, then,' Hariot said, scraping at

142 M. J. Trow

the ashes of the fire with a small shovel. 'Here, take it to him in a cloth. Careful, it's hot.' Seeing Marlowe's puzzled expression, he explained. 'It's a potato, baked in the ashes. Quite delicious and very sustaining, on a chill evening.'

Marlowe took it. 'Thank you.' There seemed little else to say. 'I'll . . . I'll just take it out to him, if you'll excuse me?'

As he left the warmth and light and walked out into the cold, dark stable yard, he heard Hariot say, 'What a delightful person Master Marlowe is. And to be writing a scientist as hero – he is very prescient, Ferdinando. Our day will come.'

Carter was curled up in his cloak in the niche and had encouraged one of the horses to stand close to warm him up a bit. He looked suspiciously under its neck at the approaching footsteps. 'Master Marlowe?' he said. 'Done so soon?'

'No,' Marlowe said. 'Our host has sent you . . . a . . . hot potato.'

'A potato?' Carter was dubious. 'For what reason?'

'To eat, I assume. He has cooked it in the embers. It is said to be delicious.'

'Who says?'

'Just Hariot, as far as I can tell. I have seen them at dinners, but I do confess they have never taken my fancy. But, here, take it. You can keep your hands warm on it, if you don't eat it.'

Carter sniffed it dubiously. 'It doesn't *smell* poisonous,' he said.

'The best poisons don't smell,' a voice said behind Marlowe and made both men jump.

Marlowe spun round, hand on his dagger hilt. Lord Strange stood there, looking shifty.

'I can't stay out here,' he hissed, speaking quickly. 'Hariot is the most suspicious man I know. All I want to say, Marlowe, is that I have sent some of the poison from the dregs in Walsingham's cup to my man who checks my food. He has sent word that he has isolated the agent and will let me know more in a day or so. I couldn't say anything more in there; the walls have ears, as we know.' He seemed to remember Carter suddenly. 'Oh, is your man . . .?'

'Totally,' Marlowe reassured him and grabbed him by the arm. 'Well, let's not linger. Just let me know as soon as you do.'

'I will.'

As they scurried across the stable yard, he turned back to the shadowed niche. 'Enjoy your potato,' he said.

'Thank you, Master Marlowe.' Carter's tone had never been more sardonic. 'I shall certainly try.'

Hariot was at the doorway, looking out anxiously. They quickened their pace and were soon back in the mathematician's number-strewn womb, learning more than they needed to know about the music of the spheres and why they played it.

THIRTEEN

'Kit! Kit! Thank God!'

'Will?' Marlowe had seen some apparitions in his time, if only courtesy of Tom Sledd's genius with smoke and mirrors on the stage, but Will Shaxsper that morning at the Rose took some beating. 'That must have been some party. Sorry I missed it.'

'No, you're not,' Shaxsper said. 'I mean, you won't be. Tom's been arrested. Not to mention Jenkins and a couple of the walking gentlemen.'

'Arrested?' Marlowe frowned. 'At the Mermaid? Nobody's been arrested there since old Jack Cade went on the rampage that time. Owen wouldn't stand for it.'

'I'm not sure Owen will last the day,' Shaxsper said. His large forehead was purple, with an ugly gash across his brows that was already blacking both his eyes. 'Come to think of it, I'm not sure I will.'

'What happened?' Marlowe helped the Warwickshire man to a chair and poured him a fortified wine.

'One minute we were having a quiet drink. Alleyn had gone, so had Henslowe. Suddenly, all Hell broke loose. The Queen's men.'

'The Queen's men?' Marlowe repeated. 'What, off duty, you mean? Lads' night out?'

'No, no. Bloody well *on* duty. Armed to the teeth. They were looking for Papists.'

'Papists?'

'Damn it, Marlowe!' Shaxsper roared and immediately wished he hadn't. 'Do you have to repeat everything I say?' He cradled his head in his hands and screwed up his eyes, wincing when it pulled the newly developed bruises and threatened to make his world of pain a whole lot harsher.

'I am sorry,' Marlowe said, patting a bit of Shaxsper that

looked moderately uninjured and trying to look contrite. 'Tom's no Papist.'

'Neither am I,' Shaxsper said. It wasn't necessary for Marlowe to delve deeper into that. 'Nor, as far as I know, is Jenkins.'

'Jenkins . . .' Marlowe looked vague. 'I don't . . .'

'Martin del Bosco, Vice Admiral of Spain. God damn it, you wrote the bloody play!'

'Oh, yes, of course. Jenkins.'

Shaxsper took several deep breaths. 'I'm sorry, Kit. It's all been a bit . . . trying, to be honest. They'd have taken me too, but I got away in the alley outside the Mermaid. You know Mad Maggie?'

'Sadly, yes.'

'I won't have a word said against the woman. She saved my life last night. Got between me and two soldiers.'

'It's where she's happiest,' Marlowe commented.

'What's it all about?' Shaxsper asked.

'I don't know.' Marlowe stood up. 'But I know a man who does.'

The ravens flapped and called to each other along the boughs over the curtain wall that bent with their weight. Their nests, the rough-hewn twigs bought from Southwark and the woods to the east, were half hidden by the spring's leaves and their greedy young kept up their starving cacophony, no matter who strode far below them. It didn't do to dwell too closely on what morsels the parents might be bringing back to fill those gaping beaks; eyes would have probably been the least stomach-churning option, but there were no new heads on the bridge today.

One man walked heedlessly below the nestlings' chorus that Friday: Christopher Marlowe, Master of Arts from the University of Cambridge, playwright extraordinary of the Rose and one of Her Majesty's projectioners. He jumped the puddles at the river gate and nodded at the Queen's guard, who recognized him and let him pass. He was a young man in a hurry and he knew that gold would not gain him admittance behind these walls. The Compter, the Bridewell, Whittington's College;

he knew them all and had bought his way in and out of them at various times since he had come to London. If a man knew a city's gaols, he knew a city's heart and so it was with Marlowe. But not here: this was the Tower, many a man's grave – and woman's too. The Queen's gold cut no ice on Tower Hill. But the Queen's axe cut necks – that much was certain.

Richard Topcliffe, Knight of the Shire and carrier-out of the Queen's least savoury business, sat at his whetstone as the sparks flew from the blade he lovingly worked on. Marlowe crept in to the man's courtyard and stood silently watching the torturer royal.

'Who the Devil are you?' Topcliffe snarled when he saw him. He had been miles away in his head, hunting Papists in the maelstrom of his dreams, listening to the scream of steel and controlling it all with the merest pressure of his foot.

'Christopher Marlowe,' Marlowe said. 'I work for Walsingham.'

'Worked, sonny,' Topcliffe corrected him. 'The Spymaster's dead.'

'Our loss, Master Topcliffe.'

The torturer stopped his wheel. 'Do you know me?'

'I know of you,' Marlowe moved for the first time and sat cross-legged on a bench. 'Your name often crops up when two or three Catholics are gathered together.'

'In their company a lot, are you?' Topcliffe asked, arching an eyebrow, 'Catholics?'

'No more than you, I shouldn't wonder,' Marlowe said. 'Except that when I'm with them, they're still alive and kicking.'

Topcliffe chuckled. He liked a man with gallows humour. 'So are they with me,' he said. 'At first, at least. I tell them how much kicking they're allowed to do. Did Sir Robert send you?'

'Sir Robert?'

'Cecil,' Topcliffe said. 'Our new master. Or yours, anyway. I recognize no mistress than the Queen, God bless her.'

'Amen,' Marlowe murmured. It wasn't a word he used often. 'In a manner of speaking,' he went on, 'you have a suspected Papist here, one Thomas Sledd.'

'I do?' Topcliffe smiled and reached for his pipe.

'You do. Cecil had him arrested on suspicion yesterday, at

the Mermaid. That was a mistake. Sledd is to be released into my custody.'

'Sledd.' Topcliffe put the pipe down and reached for a thick sheaf of papers. 'Yesterday, you say? The Mermaid?'

Marlowe nodded.

'Where's Master Robert's writ?' Topcliffe asked, suddenly suspicious.

Marlowe laughed, an odd sound in this corner of the Tower, where the sun rarely shone. 'Come, come, Master Topcliffe, you and I have been in this business too long to worry about such niceties. Writs lead men to the rack, paper hangs them. I am mindful of Babington and his crew.'

'Point taken.' The rack-master lit his tobacco, his eyes watering briefly as the smoke filled them. 'But you must appreciate I will need something.'

'My word?' Marlowe offered.

Topcliffe laughed. This was a less odd sound, because he often did that in the deepest bowels of the building. He was a man who enjoyed his work. 'The word of a projectioner? You'll have to do a great deal better than that, Master Marlowe.'

'You drive a hard bargain, rack-master,' Marlowe sighed and reached inside his doublet. He passed the parchment to Topcliffe, who took it, read it and frowned.

'This is a deed,' he said, 'for the Rose Theatre and Bear Pit, Southwark.'

'I could provide you with the house receipts,' Marlowe said. 'Philip Henslowe is richer than God. All that could be yours.'

'In exchange for one Papist?' Topcliffe screwed his face up.

'One *alleged* Papist,' Marlowe corrected him.

'What's he to you that you should offer me half of Southwark?'

'To me, nothing, but the man's a stage manager, Henslowe's right hand. He couldn't function without him.'

Topcliffe tapped the tempting offer on the palm of his left hand. He put the pipe down. 'Plays,' he said, 'are the invention of the Devil. I hope *you* don't go to the theatre, Marlowe.'

'Never crossed the portals of one,' Marlowe said, cheerily.

'So, no,' Topcliffe passed the bill back. 'No deal.'

Marlowe sighed. 'All right,' he said. 'I tried. Here.' He passed the rack-master a second piece of paper. Topcliffe read it, noted the Cecil crest, the motto, the spidery handwriting, the signature.

'If you had this all along, why all the other nonsense?' he asked.

Marlowe smiled. 'Let me shake your hand, sir,' he said. Topcliffe took it.

'I am proud to make the acquaintance of a true patriot.'

Topcliffe guffawed suddenly, letting Marlowe's hand go. 'This was a test, wasn't it? To see what my price might be.'

Marlowe nodded. 'We all have our thirty pieces of silver,' he said. 'Sir Robert wanted to be sure.'

'He did?'

Marlowe shrugged. 'Clearly, he couldn't tell you. He's a new broom, man, sweeping out the frowsty corners of Walsingham's regime. He's got to know who he can trust. That's where I come in. Testing the waters, so to speak. He'll be pleased to hear you're as pure as the driven snow . . . er, I'm not mixing too many metaphors for you, am I? Now, Sledd . . .'

'Ah, yes, the stage manager. He's a feisty little shit and no mistake. I had to teach him a few manners this morning.'

'Yes.' Marlowe nodded understandingly. 'Not a morning person, Henslowe tells me. Why was he rounded up, exactly?'

'All part of Sir Robert's master plan. Hound the bastards out, smash the priest holes, light the bonfires. I'll do the rest. But you knew that, surely. New broom and all that?'

'Ah, Master Topcliffe, you and I are merely cogs in the machine, aren't we? The little ratchets that operate your rack. He tells you one thing, me another. Keeps us guessing. Sir Francis did the same.'

'He did,' Topcliffe said, nodding. 'I miss him already. Can you keep a secret, Marlowe?'

'Was Nicholas Udall a pederast?'

'All right, then,' Topcliffe nodded. 'Between you and me.' He leaned forward, careful not to let the pipe set his beard alight. '*That*'s why Cecil's sending his heavies hither and yon. He wants to know who killed Walsingham.'

'You think Walsingham was murdered?' Marlowe feigned innocence.

'Don't you?' Topcliffe spread his arms. 'Oh, if he was a

prelate or a lawyer or even a doctor of physic, I'd say, yes, it was his time and God called him. But he was a Privy Councillor, by God, and the Queen's Spymaster. Such men don't just die in their beds. Any more than you will, Marlowe. Any more than I will.'

'So what does Cecil intend to do? Arrest half of London?'

'*All* of London if he has to. He knows how many Papists still lurk in this great country of ours. He has lists – I've seen them. Men, women, even children. This is a war, Marlowe, you know that. The King of Spain has put a price on the Queen's head, has sent an Armada against us. We must be firm. We must be resolute.'

'Indeed,' Marlowe said solemnly. 'But . . . Sledd.'

'Yes. There are bound to be some mistakes along the way. Gilbert!'

A thickset oaf clattered into the yard and tugged his forelock.

'Thomas Sledd,' Topcliffe said. 'Cell Eight. Bring him here.'

'I'm not sure he can walk, sir.'

'Drag him, then. I know nothing about the theatre, Marlowe. Can stage managers still function flat on their backs?'

'We'll have to see.' Marlowe's smile was tight. Depending on how Tom Sledd looked, he could still slide his dagger blade across the rack-master's throat. They'd cheer that in Rome and Douai more loudly than they cheered the death of Walsingham.

'A cup of wine,' Topcliffe suggested, 'while we wait.'

'Delighted,' Marlowe said. Drinking with this sadist turned his stomach, but needs must or Tom Sledd would never see the sky again. It was two cups later that Gilbert dragged a shambling wreck into the yard.

'K . . .' Sledd tried to say something when he saw Marlowe.

The projectioner was faster and slapped him hard across the face. Weak as he was with Topcliffe's ministrations of the morning, Sledd almost fell over. 'Speak when you're spoken to, sirrah!' Marlowe snapped. 'You may not be a Papist, but you work in one of their Hell-holes. I have instructions to cure you of that.' He pushed Sledd roughly ahead of him and passed the empty cup to Topcliffe. 'It's been an education, Master Topcliffe,' he said. 'Thank you.'

'Glad to have been of service,' the rack-master beamed and

watched as Marlowe kicked the stumbling, silent Sledd ahead of him. When they had gone, he refilled his pipe and took up the curved blade he had been sharpening. 'Gilbert,' he murmured out of the corner of his mouth. 'Take yourself on a little ride. Get to Hatfield and crave an audience with Sir Robert Cecil. Tell him I've just had a visit from Marlowe the playwright and he's sprung one Thomas Sledd using forged papers. Do that for me, there's a good fellow.'

Meg Sledd was used to seeing very little of her husband, depending on the state of the play of the moment and so she hadn't been worried when he didn't come home the night before. When the play was newly in rehearsals, she hardly saw him. When it was newly in production, she hardly saw him. When it was nearly at the end of the run and the next one was in read-through, she hardly saw him. But the bits in between – they were heaven. She ran to her Tom, giving him her shoulder to lean on and, although she was an inferior crutch to Marlowe and Sledd had to take most of his weight himself, he put his arm around her shoulder and let her lead him away.

Marlowe felt a little superfluous but stayed where he was, just inside the door of the Sledds' little house on Bankside. They had carefully chosen where to live, with Sledd wanting to be within sight of his beloved Rose and Meg wanting somewhere where they could forget about the theatre, just once in a while. Bankside had seemed an obvious choice and, allowing for the fact that the river mud only smelled like an ill-kept charnel house at the very lowest of tides, it was a charming little place. Meg had made it nice, with pieces of green glazed pottery from her mother's kitchen to make her feel at home and chairs pulled up to the fire. On this late spring morning, the fire was low, just enough to boil the pot for the baby's gruel and for the soup which bubbled forever on the back hook. Meg had made this house a home and Marlowe looked around with something akin to regret. This and more could be his, *should* be his, but something in him had always kept him from committing to anyone; his heart, his soul would always be in love with words. There was no room for anyone else. But still . . .

A screech broke the fire-ticking silence and Marlowe spun round. What was it? Was it Meg? Had Tom breathed his last, in the little truckle bed in the back room? He was still deciding which way to run when the screech came again, but this time from over his head. And this time, it ended in a gurgle of laughter. Marlowe's heart descended from his mouth and he sagged into a chair. He had forgotten. The Sledds were now three – baby Olympia was making her presence felt upstairs. Marlowe was proud that Tom and Meg had chosen a name from *Tamburlaine* for the child, but would never know the fights they had had over it. Little Olympia, when in later years she jibbed at her name, would have to be grateful that her mother had overturned her father's first choice of Zenocrate.

Marlowe popped his head around the door into the scullery, where Tom Sledd lay in the small bed in the alcove which actually belonged to their little maid of all work, who was watching with big eyes from near to the back door.

'I think Olympia . . .' he said, pointing behind him.

'Yes,' Meg snapped, all efficiency in her worry. 'Go and see to her, Amy, do. Her crying is disturbing her father, can't you see?'

It was hard to see what Tom Sledd might be thinking. His face was a mass of cuts and bruises and both eyes were closed now. Meg was carefully sponging away the worst of the caked blood, but it was a slow process. Marlowe had checked his fingers and limbs as they had made their careful way from the Tower and he was as sure as he could be that nothing was broken. Careful mother that she was, she had a cupboard full of tinctures and unguents, to soothe whatever part of Olympia might be causing problems. Marlowe moved nearer to the bed and was almost overcome with the stench.

'Meg?' he said. 'What is that?'

She looked up and smiled. 'I've got used to the smell.' She gave the sponge a sniff. 'It's very simple; my mother used it on all of us when we were little. It's some vinegar, some rosemary, some . . . do you know, I can't remember everything that's in it. I know there is some clarified lard in there somewhere. Some arsenic.' She saw Marlowe's horrified expression. 'Not much. Just a pinch in a big batch. It's good for the skin.'

Marlowe looked a little askance at the cupboard full of bottles and boxes. 'Does everything you have in there contain poison?' he asked.

'Poison?' She was horrified. 'There isn't enough poison in there to kill a mouse! A little arsenic here, a little belladonna there, but nothing dangerous, Master Marlowe.' She was high on her dignity. 'I have Olympia to think of.'

'Of course, Meg. I didn't mean to imply . . .' Marlowe shook himself free of the thought. 'I was . . . elsewhere.' He leaned nearer, ignoring the smell. Yes, she was right – there was definitely lard in there somewhere. 'Tom?'

The man on the bed turned his head infinitesimally towards him.

'Tom, I have to go now. I know you are in the safest hands. I'll go to the Rose, tell them you are . . . at home.' He couldn't bring himself to say that the man was well. He was a liar by trade, but not by inclination. 'Don't worry.'

This time, Sledd rolled his head from side to side and the slits of his eyes glittered.

'That's easy for you to say,' Meg said, testily. 'But I know you mean well. If you go, he will calm down. Don't let any of those mumming idiots come round bothering him.' Sledd made some incoherent noises and she turned to him sharply. 'Yes, I daresay,' she said. She had honed her ear on Olympia's prattle and could find words in any mumble. 'I daresay the play's the thing, but not for you, it's not. Not today or tomorrow.' She looked at Marlowe. 'Tell them I'll let them know.'

'Wine, Sir Robert?' Richard Topcliffe was at his most obsequious when confronted with raw power. For good, for ill, the Cecils ruled England now and it was as well to rise within the orbit of the stars.

'It is a *little* early for me, Richard,' the diminutive Spymaster looked up at the sharp angles of the Tower's parapets, but no sun shone there.

'Of course, of course. Thank you for coming so promptly.'

'Pardon?'

'My man, Gilbert . . . He must have made good time in getting to Hatfield.'

'He may indeed,' Cecil said, sitting down uninvited. 'But I was at Whitehall last night.'

'Oh.' Topcliffe was momentarily thrown. 'So you're not here about Marlowe?'

Cecil looked at him oddly. 'In a roundabout way, I am. You've got two prisoners here – er . . . Skeres and Frizer. Fetch them.'

'At once, Sir Robert.' And he was gone.

Cecil had never enquired too deeply into the mechanics of murder. Walsingham had set the wheels of the Queen's justice in motion and Topcliffe kept them assiduously oiled. The Queen's imp took the opportunity of the rack-master's absence to acquaint himself with the tools of his trade. The great iron loop that was Skeffington's gyves rested on a wooden frame in the corner of this room, where many a Papist had screamed his last and told all sorts of lies just to make the pain stop. The gyves were adjusted with a set of ratchets that tightened, crushing a man's lungs and snapping his ribs. There were blades without number around the room, lying glistening with oil in soft, clean straw, ready for the day. Cecil tried on an iron glove and noticed the screws at the side which, in Topcliffe's experienced hands, would reduce the Spymaster's fingers to bloody pulp. But it was the rack that had pride of place. Dark stains dribbled over the varnished oak and the hemp that held its moving parts in place was as sharp as razors. Gingerly, Cecil ran his index finger over the surface, the wood worn smooth, the rope new and taut.

'Skere and Frizers, Sir Robert,' Topcliffe announced suddenly, making the Spymaster jump at great risk to life and limb.

'That's Skeres,' Skeres corrected him, 'with an "s".'

'You can have mine, Nick,' Frizer told him. He felt Topcliffe's right hand across the back of his head for his insolence. 'With or without an "s", pizzle,' the rack-master snarled, 'hold your tongue.'

'Gentlemen,' Cecil nodded to them.

'Sir Robert,' Frizer hobbled forward, his ankles heavy with Topcliffe's chains. 'Are we glad to see you!'

Cecil ignored him and beckoned Topcliffe to join him at the far side of the room. 'Marlowe,' he whispered. 'What's all this about . . . your man, Gilbert?'

'He was here, Sir Robert, yesterday. Showed me a writ of yours – forged, of course – for the release of Thomas Sledd. I pretended not to know who he was – Marlowe, I mean.'

Cecil frowned. 'This Sledd; what do we know?'

'What did we know of Gerald Campion until his true Papist colours emerged?'

'You think Sledd is a Jesuit?' Cecil felt obliged to ask.

'No, sir, he *claims* to be a stage manager at the Rose, but that's halfway to Hell in itself, isn't it?'

'No doubt, no doubt,' Cecil murmured. 'Master Topcliffe, could you leave us for a moment? When I have done, strike these men's irons and release them.'

Topcliffe frowned. Letting three of his vermin go was not his idea of fulfilling his duty or keeping the Queen safe. His menagerie would soon be empty at this rate. 'Certainly, sir,' he said. 'And Jenkins?'

'Who?'

'Actor from the Rose,' Topcliffe told him.

Cecil shrugged. 'Do what you like with him.'

Topcliffe's morning suddenly brightened and he strode off to break the good news to the man who had had the bad luck to be playing a Vice Admiral of Spain.

'I'm sorry about this,' Cecil said, finding a chair as quickly as he could so that he didn't have to look up at Skeres or Frizer. 'I thought it best to have you both rounded up as suspects so that you can go about your business as heroes.' He glanced at the rack. 'You know the sort of thing I mean. "They could not break me", et cetera, et cetera.'

'Oh, yes.' Skeres tapped the side of his nose. 'I get you, sir. As soon as you took us on, I said to Ing, I said, "We'll be all right with Sir Robert," I said. Didn't I, Ing?'

Frizer looked less than bowled over with bonhomie. He had been knocked unconscious, fettered (for which he had paid) and left to lie in the filth of the Tower. Food? He could barely remember what that was.

'Marlowe.' Cecil talked directly to him. 'What of him?'

'We've followed him everywhere, sir,' Frizer said. 'Even got ourselves in Henslowe's company at the Rose.'

Cecil nodded. He had thought he recognized the most wooden knight on the stage.

'He went to Petworth.'

'The wizard earl,' Cecil said softly.

'Then to Sendmarsh.'

'Sendmarsh?' Cecil had to think for a moment, but although he had not been Spymaster for long, he had been training for it for many a long year. 'Sendmarsh? That . . .' he clicked his fingers. 'Got it! Salazar.'

Skeres opened his mouth to continue the list, but Frizer was faster. 'Then he went to Durham House, in the Strand.'

'The Great Lucifer,' Cecil murmured.

'Then, and this is where we, sort of, had to part company with him, he went off with his man. We don't know quite where. He crossed the river and went west.'

'I thought I heard him say Zion,' Skeres added, 'but that might just be the play we're in. All those trumpets and tabours and things – they play havoc with your ears.'

Cecil rewarded him with a sharp glance. Could he be stupid or was he merely hiding behind it? It was never easy to tell. But he had the clue he needed. 'Syon,' he said. 'Thomas Hariot.' A dark smile crept over his face. 'Gentlemen, you have done well. Friend Marlowe keeps an odd company indeed. If the Devil cast his net . . .' He rummaged in his purse and scattered silver coins on the scarred table in front of him. 'For your pains,' he said.

'Thank you, sir,' Skeres grovelled. 'Er . . . what should we do now?'

Cecil stood up. 'You are walking gentlemen, aren't you, at the Rose?'

'We are, sir,' Frizer said.

'One of us,' Skeres glowered, 'has a speaking part.'

'Continue to walk, then,' Cecil smiled. 'But far enough behind Marlowe that he is not aware of you. But, as for speaking, don't. Not to him, anyway.'

FOURTEEN

Midday. Spring was being kind and there was real warmth in the sun that said that summer was not far behind. Marlowe sat in the window seat at his house in Hog Lane, looking out on to the tiny patch of trimmed box that he presumed to call a garden. Agnes had spread some linen out to dry on the hedges and the smell of lavender and lye crept in through the casement, which was open just the merest crack. A bird was singing its heart out in a tree on the edge of the garden and Marlowe closed his eyes to listen to it more closely. He had been brought up to the sound of birdsong, but he was ashamed to say that he had no idea which bird it was that was pouring liquid gold from its throat into the warm air. He leaned his head back on the transom and let his mind drift. He tried to remember the last time he had been here, at peace, in his own house, with nothing but silence and birdsong to surround him. The sounds of the road outside swam in and out of his consciousness until they had gone altogether. Then the bird. Then . . . he slept.

'Kit! Kit! Wake up!'

He woke with a jerk that told him he had not been asleep for long. His head bumped on the window, his foot had gone to sleep and there was a face he knew inches from his, hissing at him. He focused on the large, worried eyes, the mole like a third eye on the forehead.

'Lord Strange,' he blurred through dry lips. 'How can I help you?'

'Kit, where have you *been*? I've been here twice already trying to find you.'

'Oh, around. About. The Tower. The Rose. All the usual places, thorough brush, thorough briar.' He suddenly realized the import of Strange's presence in his room. 'Have you news for me? The poison?'

'Yes!' Lord Stanley was triumphant and waved a small wad

of parchment in the air in front of Marlowe's eyes. 'Here it is, by fast horse from Derby.'

Marlowe reached for it, but the other man snatched it away. 'Not so fast, Master Marlowe. I need to explain first. My man – who, as I have told you, I entrust with all my food testing – is by name one Silas Beaucheek. He is a chemist of some local repute, but you will not have heard of him here in London, I am sure. He had little to go on, so has had to cut some corners. As a general rule, if he finds a noxious substance, he makes sure of his diagnosis by feeding it to mice, rats and so on.'

Marlowe thought of Salazar and shivered.

'But with so little, he has come to his conclusion by chemical means only. So,' he stepped back as Marlowe made another lunge for the paper, 'you must bear that in mind. This is almost certainly correct, but Silas refuses to say it is definitely so. He says I am not to tell you unless you agree with that proviso. He brought the news himself, although he is not accustomed to riding so far and so fast. It has made him a little testy, but his reports are always accurate, I stake my life on it.'

'Give me the paper,' Marlowe said, through clenched teeth.

'Do you *agree*?' Strange insisted.

'Yes, yes, I agree.' Marlowe looked very young, with sleep still filling his eyes and anticipation transfiguring his face. 'So, give me the paper.'

With a smile, Strange handed it over and watched as Marlowe unwrapped it.

'Latin. Impressive. Let me see . . . hmm . . .' Marlowe looked up and met Strange's eyes, watching him for his reaction. 'More than one agent?'

The man nodded. 'Cunning devil, don't you think?'

'Cunning. Evil. It doesn't really matter which. One of these I recognize of course. The other . . . wait a minute and it will come to me.'

Ferdinando Strange was hopping up and down with the stress of it all. He shook Marlowe by the arm. 'Come man, surely. It is obvious.' He pursed his lips and mimed with Marlowe the syllables of the Latin name. 'Still nothing? Kit, you disappoint me.'

'*Solanum. Solanum.* That's deadly nightshade, isn't it?'

'Oh, so close!' Strange had now clasped his hands under his chin and the knuckles were showing white with the effort of not blurting out the answer. 'It is the same family, though you wouldn't think that at first. It has to come into flower to see the similarity.'

'Into flower. So, it doesn't usually flower?' Marlowe could feel the answer tantalizing him at the tip of his tongue. 'So . . . not a garden plant. Is it . . .' the light dawned in his eye. 'Can that be right? Potato?'

Strange clapped his hands. 'Yes! Potato.' He suddenly looked very solemn. 'I said to Silas, were they safe to eat? I do sometimes have them on my table though, truth to tell, I don't find them very tasty. He told me that treated properly, they were harmless, but if allowed to become green, to *mature* if you will, they can be deadly. And, of course, like their cousin belladonna, the berries are poisonous, although in the normal way of cultivation, the plant is destroyed long before that stage, to get at the tubers.'

'And the poison is easy to extract?'

'It doesn't need extraction in the accepted sense, although Silas says that the dregs contained a concentrate. The other agent, the nicotine, is simply won, of course, from the dottle of a pipe. All it would need for the poisoner to extract it would be for him to drink smoke for a day or so and then empty the tar from the pipe. A good pipeful could kill a roomful of lusty men in minutes.'

'But Sir Francis lingered,' Marlowe pointed out.

'Indeed. I asked Silas about that and he said he couldn't be sure, of course, that these were the only two poisons used. It could be that many were employed, in minute doses such as we have here, all having a cumulative effect. In a man old and tired like Sir Francis, eventually they would take their lethal toll.'

'Isn't that all a little . . . inexact, though?' Marlowe pondered. 'Poisoners usually look for the quick result. Especially if it is to stop someone's mouth.'

'True.' Strange was an expert on the ways of the poisoner, since he saw one lurking behind every tree, behind every arras. 'But there are other reasons for poisoning someone. Hatred. Wickedness.'

'True.' Marlowe sighed. 'Thank Master Beaucheek for me.

It has both answered a question and posed many more.' He smiled as he heard Agnes come back from marketing, slamming the door behind her and humming as she came. 'Would you like to share a platter with me? Freshly marketed.'
Strange looked askance. 'Potato?'
'By no means.'
'Do you drink smoke?'
'Rarely.'
Strange smiled. 'Then I should be delighted!'

A small fire crackled in the centre of the half-circle created by the tall-backed chairs. There were seven of them, their backs upright and carved with the rampant lions of John Dee's family. The magus had been dreading this for days, ever since Marlowe had first suggested it. He had every faith in the Muses' darling, Machiavel, who moved in ways as mysterious as his own, but this . . . all the men who were about to fill these chairs were his friends; more, they were the finest, most inquisitive minds in Europe, perhaps the world. No good could come of an evening like this, but the Queen's magus knew in his heart of hearts that he had caused it. It might be Marlowe's finger that would point accusingly in the next hour, but it was Dee's suggestion that had prompted it.

Hariot arrived first, his bright eyes glittering in the broad face, his hair thin and lank under the scholar's cap. He carried a satchel with him that Dee knew was full of scribbled numbers, written forward and back in a mad symmetry that only he understood. Percy was next, dusty from the Sussex roads around Petworth. There was a love poem beating out a refrain in his head and the face of a girl he had just met floated tantalizingly in his vision. He loved her voice, though he had heard it but fleetingly and it drowned out the inane babblings of Hariot and the hostly mumblings of John Dee. Ferdinando Stanley had been at his town house when the doctor's letter had arrived; these meetings were becoming very regular, but Strange knew that Dee never called them lightly. There was always method in his madness. Ralegh swept in in his glittering finery, jewels at his throat and in his earlobes. He had left his sword at Durham House but the dagger was never far away, should his honour be slighted. 'Urgent', the doctor's message had said: that was good enough for him.

'I don't wish to be rude, John,' Hariot said as they all took their places, 'but why are we here?'

Dee glanced out of the window. Night had well and truly fallen and his own reflection wobbled back at him through the latticed panes. 'Well . . .'

There was a crash and the door flew open, Barnaby Salazar scurrying through it. 'Sorry I'm late, dears.'

Ralegh muttered to Strange, 'I *do* wish he wouldn't call us that. It's so . . .'

'Overseas?' suggested Strange.

'Bit of a disaster on the domestic front.' Salazar was hauling off his cap and cloak, throwing them to one of Dee's minions. 'Old Jorge died tonight.'

'Who?' Ralegh thought he had to ask.

'Jorge, my steward,' Salazar took the hot toddy another minion offered him and quaffed it back. 'Ah, nectar. Thank you, John. Just what the doctor ordered, eh? I must admit, it came as something of a shock. Oh, he wasn't in the first flush, I'll grant you that, but when a man you have known almost all your life just dwindles and is dead in days, it hits hard. Mistress Jorge is distraught, of course.'

'Mistress Jorge?' Strange frowned. 'Doesn't she have a name?'

'Oh, I expect so.' Salazar caught Strange's disapproving look. 'Oh, come on, now, Ferdinando. You and I are too busy peering into the secrets of the universe to keep track of our servants' names. So, John,' he took a vacant chair, 'what's the order of business?'

Dee cleared his throat and looked around them all. The hairs on the back of his neck stood on end as he remembered that one of them might be a murderer. 'The order of business, gentlemen,' he said, in the rich, powerful voice that often silenced the Queen's court: 'Allow me to introduce . . .' and he clapped his hands. Another door opened and two men strode into the room – Kit Marlowe and his man, Carter.

'What's the meaning of this?' Ralegh asked first, but it was a question on everyone's lips.

Dee sighed and crept towards a chair. 'I'll let Master Marlowe explain.'

Marlowe's genius had filled stages before and his words daily held hundreds in their power. But he had rarely been at the centre of the wooden O himself. Not that this was a baldactum play. This would be a performance like no other. 'Thank you, lords and gentlemen, for coming tonight and at such short notice. I'll not detain you long. Your Grace,' he turned to Percy, 'how do you know me?'

Percy frowned. 'You are the Muses' darling,' he said. 'The most famous playwright and poet in England.'

'But, specifically,' Marlowe said. 'How did we meet?'

'Er . . . you came as a friend of my librarian, Michael Johns, as I understood it to see my books.'

'Sir Walter?' Marlowe turned to him.

'You wanted to talk poetry. As you know, I dabble.' That was it. Clearly, Ralegh had no intention of mentioning a duel fought over the honour of Bess Throckmorton.

'Master Hariot?'

'Um . . . you were looking for a character for a new play, a philosopher. I was flattered, of course . . .'

'Master Salazar?'

'Damned if I know,' the man shrugged. 'Unless it was to sample my country's culinary delights.'

'What of me, Kit?' Strange asked. 'After all, I was just a guest of Hariot's. Why am I here tonight?'

'Patience, my lord,' Marlowe said. 'Hell is empty and all the devils are here. Gentlemen,' he turned to face them all, 'I have been less than truthful. The Earl of Northumberland was kind enough to call me the most famous playwright in England, but tonight I wear another hat.'

The only sound in the room was the occasional crack of a log or a crumble of shifting ash.

'I am what is commonly called a projectioner and I work for Francis Walsingham.'

Only the fire responded while they all looked at each other. Only Dee was unsurprised.

'So,' Ralegh, as usual, spoke first. 'You will know that the doctor here has asked us to bend our minds to that, the assumption being that Walsingham was murdered.'

'That is not an assumption, Sir Walter, that is now a fact. Lord Strange's chemist, a man well versed in finding out poisons in small samples, has isolated the source of the Spymaster's last illness, in the dregs of his cup, though he suspects that the poison had been administered at least twice before the fatal dose. This was no accident. Although the agents can be made from easily obtainable ingredients, it cannot be a normal constituent of any food. No – Sir Francis was deliberately done to death.'

A ripple of astonishment ran around the room. Those who still held goblets pushed them away. It was Strange who articulated what they were all feeling. 'Kit,' he said softly. 'You have your man here with you. Before we go further, I should like to invite mine to this presence. I'd feel more comfortable were he at my back.'

'I'd echo that,' Percy said, suddenly feeling uneasy.

'Marlowe?' Dee looked at the man.

'Very well,' he said. 'I have no objection.'

'Carter,' Dee said. 'Go to the kitchen, will you and bring these gentlemen's people? Although,' he waited until Carter had gone, 'I am not sure we need witnesses to this.'

'Oh, I am sure we do,' Hariot said and sat back, folding his arms.

'Seven chairs,' Percy said, looking around the room. 'And six of us. Who is the seventh for? You, Marlowe?'

'No, Your Grace,' Marlowe said solemnly. 'Call it a theatrical fancy of mine. In the next few moments, the seventh seat will be occupied by Francis Walsingham's murderer.'

The uproar threatened to drown out Marlowe's voice and he waited until Carter came back with the others, liveried servants, the loyal and true who fetched and carried for the great and good in that room. When the hubbub had died down, Marlowe faced them all, standing behind the seventh chair. Each of the seated gentlemen had his servant standing behind him, Carter taking his rightful place behind Dee.

'You are the School of Night,' Marlowe began.

'How the Devil—?' but Ralegh never finished his sentence.

'I told you, Sir Walter,' Marlowe cut in. 'I am a projectioner. How did I know about the School of Night? You gave the name, Dr Dee the essence. And anyway, it's my job to know. One of you in this room killed the Queen's Spymaster. I intend to find out who.'

'I've had enough of this,' Salazar said, already on his feet, his manservant stepping back to let him pass.

'Stay where you are, sir!' Dee bellowed. No one was going to break the half-circle tonight. Salazar slunk back to his chair and his man took up his position behind him, hands folded lightly together in the small of his back, eyes fixed on an indeterminate point near the ceiling.

'John Dee,' Marlowe said, turning to face him. 'The Queen's magus. I know your powers, Dr Dee. I have seen them myself. You twist men's minds, tie their tongues and throw magic dust in their eyes. Smoke and mirrors? Maybe. But my man Tom Sledd at the Rose can do as much, with light and sound. No, your magic is real and a blacker art never existed. If anyone could slip poison into Walsingham's drink or his food, it is you.'

Dee could hardly believe what he was hearing. Marlowe had asked him to set up this meeting and he had told him why. One of the others had killed Walsingham, not the magus himself. How dare he? 'What was my motive?' Dee asked archly, sitting upright and feeling Carter stiffen behind him.

Marlowe's dark eyes flashed fire briefly and he smiled. He clapped his hands once, twice, a flutter. 'Bravo, Doctor,' he said. 'A sharper mind never graced England. You are the Queen's magus. Walsingham was the Queen's Spymaster. You both worship the same woman. There would be no gain in murdering a fellow patriot.'

'What of me?' Ralegh asked. 'I worship the Queen too.'

Marlowe turned to him. 'Indeed you do, Sir Walter,' he said. 'All you have is because of her and you have been known to lie like a dog outside her chamber in your pretty armour, keeping her safe.'

Ralegh shrugged. 'It was my pleasure,' he said.

'Unfortunately, as I have all too much reason to know, Bess Throckmorton is your pleasure too, isn't she?'

Ralegh turned crimson, but said nothing.

'And if the Queen were to find out, your days would not be long in the land. There would be no more expeditions to the New World, no more fat profits from your estates, no more openings at court, if I may use that term in the circumstances.' Strange let out a laugh. 'Back to Bess Throckmorton again,' he said, under his breath. He acknowledged Marlowe as a true genius with words, yet again.

Ralegh was on his feet, his dagger glinting in his hand. 'You'll take that back, Strange,' he said, gravel in his voice.

'Walter!' Dee chided. 'Not now, for God's sake. Sit down.'

'I don't think God interests Sir Walter very much,' Marlowe said, 'because he doesn't believe there is a God.'

A sudden silence filled the room, chill despite the fire. Both Strange and his man crossed themselves. Ralegh's dagger tip pointed to Marlowe. 'I thought it was you who dared God out of His Heaven,' he said. '"Moses was but a conjuror and John the Baptist was a bedfellow to Jesus." I am quoting you there, Marlowe, am I not?'

The playwright-projectioner smiled. 'I have often been misquoted, Sir Walter,' he said.

'Ralegh.' Dee's voice was full of command and the privateer who listened to no one did as he had been told and sat down.

'Why would you kill Walsingham?' Marlowe was like a terrier with a rat in its jaws. 'Because if I know about Bess Throckmorton, I'm damned sure the Spymaster did. Dead men tell no tales, do they? *And* you visited Walsingham on the day he died.'

'This is nonsense, Marlowe,' Percy said. 'You can't just accuse people like this. Some of us are peers of the realm.'

'Peers of the realm,' Marlowe took up the theme, 'who rebel against the Queen.'

'C-careful, Marlowe.' Percy wagged a finger. He was a poet and a dreamer, but he was also a man of honour and the Percys had a long history. His old stammer had come back with the tension of it all.

'Your father hated Lord Burghley,' Marlowe did not need to remind the company, 'and wanted to return the church – how did the minutes of the Privy Council have it – "to the time of the late King Henry"? In that King's time, men who

did not accept the monarch as governor of the church went
to the block. Your family lands have been cut to what you
must regard as penury. How many tenant estates did you
have in the North? Two hundred? Three hundred?' He leaned
nearer to the wizard earl. 'What better way to hamper the
Jezebel of England than to cut off Walsingham, her right hand?
I doubt the Queen's imp spends many nights of sweet slumber
with you on the prowl.'

'Are you including me in this, Kit?' Strange asked. He alone
of the School of Night had ridden the roads with Marlowe.
Lord Strange's Men were travelling actors and Marlowe had,
briefly, travelled with them. The poet turned to the nobleman,
sadly, inevitably. He was so far steeped in accusations now, he
could never turn back.

'Poisons, my lord, the ways of the hedgerows,' he said. 'Who
in this room knows more of their properties than you? Lord
Percy may think he has a knowledge, but compared to yours,
he knows nothing. You come from a family of Northern earls
and – for this alone – Master Topcliffe would rack you and
Francis Walsingham would have had you hanged, drawn
and quartered – you follow Rome.'

There was another silence, but Strange was unruffled. 'I
found the poisons for you,' he said. 'My man Beaucheek . . .'

'. . . Is, for all I know, a figment of your imagination. Are
you taunting me with your superior knowledge, or have you
given me the wrong agents altogether?'

'You forget to point out that I fear witches, Kit,' Strange
said.

'As King of England, you need fear no toothless crone, my
lord. Just take care that your imp can be trusted.'

'King of England?' Hariot spoke for the first time. 'Did I
miss something?'

'You can't hide behind your screen of numbers for ever,
Master Hariot, or your gibberish tongues from the savages of
the West. If Lord Strange here were so disposed, he could
assume the mantle of leader of a good many discontented lords
– the wizard earl here among them.'

'A revolution?' Hariot blinked. 'Overthrowing the Queen?'

'It wouldn't be the first time,' Marlowe pointed out.

'What of me, then?' Hariot persisted. 'If you have convinced yourself that Walsingham was murdered as part of a rebellion against the Queen, how do I fit in?'

Marlowe smiled. 'Count the chairs, mathematician. How many do you see?'

'Seven.' Hariot didn't have to look.

'Seven.' Marlowe nodded. 'The number of the planets in the sky. Except that you see more, don't you?'

'I beg your pardon?' Hariot was flustered. For a moment he thought his heart had stopped.

'Your perspective trunk, the one you hide so carefully in your laboratory. It magnifies the Heavens, doesn't it? Shows you stars that the rest of us have never dreamed of. Tell me, Master Hariot, you have built machines to navigate at sea, could you build a craft that could reach the moon?'

'Don't be ridiculous, Marlowe!' Hariot snapped. 'That's impossible.'

'Ah, but the trying of it,' Marlowe beamed. 'The *challenge.* That's what moves you, isn't it? What sets your blood racing. *Could* it be done? Could you find a way of getting past the most careful, best-protected man in England and kill him secretly, to the extent that most men would say he died of natural causes? That's something you couldn't resist, could you? All it would take is a nod from Percy here, or Strange or Ralegh. You're just a cog, a mere factotum.'

'I've heard enough.' Ralegh was on his feet and making for the door, his man behind him. 'John,' he paused at the door. 'Next time you call a meeting, I want your word that this upstart won't be involved. And as for you, Marlowe,' he turned to face his accuser, 'I'm letting you live tonight because I owe you a debt of honour. I consider that debt collected. Should we meet again, it will go ill with you.'

'I owe you nothing, Marlowe.' Percy was following Ralegh to the door, his man in tow. 'C-consider my warning the same as Sir Walter's.' And he left.

Ferdinando Strange was next. He closed to Marlowe. 'There'll be no more Lord Strange's Men, Kit, not for you. It'll be hard, but I'll find another playwright from somewhere. And I daresay he will do.'

Hariot left without a word, anxious to get home to move his machinery to somewhere safe before the world got to hear of it. Salazar had already gone, slipping out silently in Ralegh's turbulent wake. In the end, only three of them stood there – Carter, Marlowe and Dee.

'I fear you've made some enemies tonight, Kit,' the magus said sadly, staring into the fire's dying embers.

'And lost some friends,' Marlowe said. 'And for what?' He threw his arms wide. 'I really thought it would work, that I would twist their nerves to such a height that one of them would give something away.'

Dee shook his head. 'I didn't want to pour cold water on it,' he said. 'I want Walsingham's murderer caught as much as you do. But a projectioner standing in a room accusing suspects of murder and expecting a result? There's no science in that. And no magic, either. Carter, go with Master Marlowe and watch his back. There are lessons taught by the School of Night it is better none of us experience.'

'I'm sorry, Dr Dee,' Marlowe said. 'Not just for wasting your time, but for the things I said. I'll make it up to you, I promise.'

Dee smiled and nodded sadly, shaking the man's hand as he left. With Carter close behind him, Marlowe made for the stairs and the door. The night was old now and the gentleman's carriages had gone. All except one. Its owner sat inside, his feet on the step, the door open.

'You didn't get round to me, Master Marlowe,' Salazar said.

'Time ran out,' Marlowe said, 'along with Ralegh and the rest.'

'So you don't want to talk to me, then?'

Marlowe looked up at Salazar's man on his perch, the reins slack in his hands. 'There seems little point now,' he said and started walking, Carter at his elbow.

'That's a shame,' Salazar said, raising his voice so Marlowe should miss nothing. 'Because there is one man in this great country of ours who can solve this little conundrum of yours.'

Marlowe stopped and half turned. 'Oh, who's that?'

'Walsingham.' Salazar got up and climbed fully into the carriage, turning and patting the seat beside him. 'Francis Walsingham. Come and see.'

Marlowe hesitated and Carter leaned forward and whispered in his ear. 'Wait here – I will fetch the doctor. This sounds like something he would want to witness.'

Marlowe nodded and put one foot up on the step of the carriage, keeping the other firmly planted on the cobbles. 'Walsingham?' he said. 'How can he help us now? His body lies in Paul's.'

A wild light came into Salazar's eye and he dropped his voice to a whisper. 'Do not speak of it, Master Marlowe. The spirits are everywhere. If he gets wind of it – he may not come.'

'I see.' Marlowe had seen many things he could not explain, but somehow he found it hard to imagine a spectral Walsingham floating above his head, listening in. When he had been alive, he had had people for that; there was no reason to suppose anything would have changed now. 'Master Salazar, I must be honest with you. Carter has gone back to fetch Doctor Dee.'

Salazar looked mutinous. 'The Queen's magus. I do not know whether the spirits will come with him there.'

Marlowe laughed. 'But the doctor raises spirits as a matter of course.'

'Yes,' Salazar agreed with a sneer. 'But his methods . . . I spit on them.'

'If you must,' a voice said from the doorway suddenly open behind Marlowe, spilling light into the street. 'I did hear tell that . . . bodily fluids are an important part of your rituals, Master Salazar. And, of course, if that works for you, who am I to gainsay it?' Dee pushed Marlowe into the carriage from behind. 'Budge up, Kit. There is room for one more inside. Carter,' he spoke over his shoulder, 'stay here and watch the house for me. I feel uneasy tonight, I don't know quite why.' He gave Salazar a dazzling smile from the depths of his wispy beard. 'A goose stepping on my grave, perhaps.'

'Perhaps.' Salazar was clearly not happy to have the magus in the company, but there was little he could do. He settled back in the now rather cramped seat and rapped on the roof of the carriage with his cane. With a lurch, they were on their way.

Carter stood with his back to the door and watched them go, rattling along the Cheap. He had been Dee's right-hand man ever since he had entered his service in Prague. It seemed a lifetime ago and yet, in other ways, just yesterday. Marlowe he could take or leave, but Dee he would take care of until his last breath. He turned to go in, torn between obedience and the call of his heart, to find the door open and Jane Dee standing there, in nightgown and shawl, clutching the woollen wrap close around her.

'Elias.'

'Mistress.'

'Was that the master? Where has he gone?'

'I don't know, Mistress. With Master Salazar and Master Marlowe.'

'And you are still here because . . .?'

'Because I was told to look after the house, Mistress. You and the house.'

Jane pushed him out of the door. 'For the love of God, Elias,' she said. 'Don't do as the master tells you. Keep him safe. That's what we pay you for, isn't it? This road is straight for a good half-mile, with no turnings that a carriage could take. If you run, you'll catch them easily.'

Carter stood looking down at her upturned face, angry, worried.

'Don't just stand there, idiot man. Run!'

And Carter ran. For his life and the life of Doctor John Dee.

Marlowe attempted some small talk in the crowded carriage. He had no idea where they were going or how long it would take and the animosity between the two other men threatened to poison the air.

'I was sorry to hear of Jorge's . . . passing.' He knew how careful he would have to be with the choice of words. Salazar was probably not comfortable with death as a concept, as he considered it at best temporary, at worst a minor inconvenience.

'Thank you,' Salazar said, automatically. 'I shall miss him. In fact, Master Marlowe, it may interest you to know that you were the last person to enjoy his famous *pastel de nata*. Their like will not be seen or tasted again.'

Marlowe smiled reminiscently. 'They were delicious,' he said. 'A local speciality, I assume?'

'Of Sendmarsh?' Dee was surprised. 'Does Sendmarsh have a cuisine of its own?'

'No,' Salazar was testy. 'Portugal. My homeland and Jorge's. Mistress Jorge is English and doesn't have the skill. The secret is in . . .' he laughed. 'But like so many secrets, to tell it is to make it secret no longer.' He smiled sadly. 'Poor Jorge. He did love his *pastel*.' He sighed and his chin dropped on to his chest.

Jorge's death seemed to colour the air in the carriage and the men were silent until the horses were pulled in with a jerk and the driver banged on the roof. 'We're here,' they heard him call.

Salazar was annoyed. 'When will that man learn what the word "quiet" means? He may as well have banged a drum. However, hopefully no harm done. Out you get, gentlemen, but . . .' he put a finger to his lips, 'no more noise, if you please.'

They stepped out into almost total darkness. The man on the box was putting out the carriage lights and there were no buildings nearby showing so much as a candle. As their eyes adjusted, they saw the bulk of something huge and tall looming between them and the stars, but there was no obvious sign to show them where they were.

Carter, coming up behind them, saw the lights go out and heard his master say, 'Where in the name of God are we, Salazar? You can't just take us where you will without letting us know.'

'Ssh,' Salazar hissed. Carter crouched low and kept silent. 'We are at St Barnabas' Church,' he said. 'A small conceit, being so near to my own name, that is all. The location scarcely matters. But now we are here, please follow me, gentlemen.' He reached behind him into the carriage and pulled a small bag from under the seat. 'But, don't forget. Silence. From now on, not a word.'

Marlowe and Dee exchanged glances in the dark, the gleam of starlight shining on an eye being their only contact. Salazar squeezed past and went round the side of the building, with the sure step of practice. Marlowe and Dee followed, the poet with his hand outstretched, the magus hanging on to his sleeve. Feeling each pace with a tapping toe, they found their way around the corner and Salazar was nowhere to be seen.

'Down here!' A voice hissed from near their feet. 'Take care. There is a rail, but it is loose. Come down. I can light a candle then.'

Marlowe went first, one foot at a time and after eight uneven, crumbling steps, found himself in an underground room, a large one from the feel of the air, a crypt by its smell. Dee joined him, stumbling a little on the last step and uttering a smothered oath.

'Doctor!' Salazar was angry now. 'Silence. Silence, though Hell itself should yawn in your face. There is too much at stake to lose it all for the sake of a stubbed toe.'

There was silence for a while as Salazar rummaged in his bag, finally there was the scrape of a flint and a candle flame grew steadily to light their surroundings.

The crypt was low and wide, with coffins piled up on all sides. In the middle was a stone tomb, with one side gaping and on it Salazar had rested the candle, which was, as Marlowe had half expected, made of black wax. Without speaking, Salazar motioned Marlowe to stand at one corner of the tomb, Dee to the other, so that the three of them made a narrow triangle, with Salazar at the apex. Muttering under his breath, he laid out his requirements, touching some to his lips, some to his heart and some, again not unexpectedly, to a part of himself below the tomb. Dee risked a glance at Marlowe and was reassured by the cynical gleam in the playwright's eye.

Carter, crouched on the top step, out of the candle's gleam, bent down to see what he could. He thought that, *in extremis*, he would be able to save his master. Marlowe was young enough and fit enough to stir for himself.

The muttering went on and Dee began to feel the cold from the dirt floor seeping through his shoes. He had not changed into boots before he came out; if Jane ever discovered that he had come out in his house shoes, there would be the Devil to pay. As this domestic detail went through Dee's mind, he could hardly suppress a smile. If he could keep this link with reality strong, he and Marlowe may well survive this night. This idiot in front of him, posturing with his bell, book, candle and whatever else he had brought with him, could kill them all. Dee would be the first to admit that most of what he did was mere charlatanry, but that small, small iota that was not; it needed a man stronger than Salazar to contain it, that he knew. And he could hear the air thick with the chittering of beings locked too long out of the world of men. If a door was opened . . . Dee closed his eyes and thought of Jane, of Madimi and of his poor old, cold feet. It would keep him in the here and now. Jane. Madimi. Feet. He chanted it under his breath and the chittering grew quieter, though it didn't go away.

Marlowe watched Salazar with less trepidation. Despite the light from under his chin giving his face shadows that did not belong there, turning his eyes into fathomless holes and his mouth into the entrance to Hell, Marlowe could still see the genial host, dispensing cakes and wine. The rituals he was muttering his way through clearly meant a lot to him; his concentration was deep and total. He bowed, kissed, patted and postured with his salt and his wine and his stolen bits of the Host. If belief could raise the dead, Francis Walsingham would be walking in any minute; but there had to be more than belief, surely, or every beggar would ride.

The candle guttered and Salazar's mutterings grew in volume and coherence. He flung some salt into the air and momentarily the flame flared blue. Dee smiled to himself. Simple chemistry and one of his favourite effects for the naïve; this time, perhaps more aptly, *from* the naïve. Surely, Salazar could not think that they would be impressed by such simple hedge magic?

With a dramatic gesture, Salazar shot back his sleeve and exposed his forearm, livid white in the candlelight. He picked up a horn-handled knife from the table and passed it through the flame, dipped it in the salt and then the wine. As Marlowe and Dee held their breath, he dragged the tip slowly across his arm, splitting the old scars which lay there like some macabre spider's web against the skin. The blood welled like rubies deep in a mine, showing themselves in the light of a miner's lamp and coalesced to form a black mirror on the magician's arm. Dee smiled again and nodded his approval. A ring of oil on the arm would hold the blood; a clever trick, but not one he himself employed. He had no love for knives nor wish for scars.

Salazar bent at the knees and brought his arm down straight on to the top of the tomb, the obscene mirror bellying and shimmering with the movement. Salazar muttered some more, then his voice came high-pitched and insistent. Dee looked up, his eyes fluttering over the dark ceiling. Marlowe saw the movement and risked a glance to his right. The magus was watching something that the playwright could not see and he held out his hand to the old man, who took it in an iron grip. The buzzing ceased and he looked back at Salazar, but closed his ears to what he was intoning.

Marlowe listened, aware of the touch of his friend on his right hand, the harsh stone beneath the palm of his left, where he pressed down. Salazar was shrieking now, in a voice higher than any human should be able to reach. It was the sound of a knife on a whetstone, of a wet finger down glass, of a nail on a slate. It pierced the ear and went straight to the hairs on the back of the neck. There was no breath in it, just a cry to the Heavens and what they had shielded behind the stars.

At the point where the cry became all but unbearable, it stopped. With a sob, Salazar bent down and sucked up the globe of blood into his mouth and, raising his head, blew a red mist into the air. Marlowe and Dee stepped back a pace in unison, not breaking their grip. On his stair, Carter poised to strike.

In the air, a face that Marlowe and Dee knew well hung, looking sadly at them. The eyes opened, looked beyond them into nothing and then the whole thing faded away. Salazar cried out once more and slumped to the tomb's top in a swoon. The silence after the screaming was palpable, broken after a few seconds by Carter's thundering feet on the stair.

'What was that, Master?' he asked, uncertain of his voice.

'That?' Dee said, in a voice not quite his own. 'Magic, Elias. Just a bit of magic.'

And, leaving Salazar slumped where he had fallen, they felt their way up the stairs.

FIFTEEN

Christopher Marlowe had been more tired than this, many times in his short life. He could think back to when he was singing in the Good Friday vigil, when all the choristers felt ready to drop by the time the altar cloth was stripped and they all scattered in silence, in honour of the Last Supper. Hokum and claptrap he now would call it, but at the time, almost overwhelming for a small boy who was bone tired and emotional. He had been exhausted many a night climbing over the wall at Corpus Christi, hardly able to put one drunken foot before another as he dodged the proctors on the prowl. He had been tired, cold and in fear of his life often when on his dark work for Walsingham. But now, he closed his eyes and swayed as the sleep almost took him; now he felt that if he slept, he would surely die.

A door slammed somewhere on the edge of oblivion and he opened his eyes and squared his shoulders. He was Kit Marlowe, the Muses' darling. He did not sleep. Not in Philip Henslowe's office, anyway, and not when he needed to beg a favour.

Henslowe slid into his chair on the other side of his counting table. 'Master Marlowe,' he said, rubbing his hands together. He had left the takings for the week in the safekeeping of his Lombard friends and he was feeling in a mood to love all of his fellow men, even actors and especially playwrights. 'How may I help you?' His face suddenly froze as a thought occurred to him. 'Although I am not at the moment in a position to advance . . .'

'I am not here for money,' Marlowe said. 'Do you take me for an actor?'

Henslowe laughed a little too loudly with relief. 'Then . . .?' He spread his arms in query.

'I do need a favour and it may cost a little . . . only a little . . . money. But it will greatly enhance your standing

and may even result in . . .' Marlowe dropped his voice,
'. . . enhancement.'

Henslowe looked dubious.

'Personal enhancement, if you understand me.'

Henslowe's eyebrows reached his hairline, a more difficult
trick these days than heretofore. 'You mean . . .' he dropped
his voice to below even a whisper, '. . . a title?'

Marlowe nodded, a finger alongside his nose.

Henslowe sat back, careful not to crush the invisible ermine
or knock his coronet askew. 'So, this favour,' he said, lacing his
fingers across a paunch grown suddenly a touch more baronial.

'It's not anything hard,' Marlowe said, speaking fast so that
Henslowe wouldn't see the catch until it was too late. 'I have
been writing a play in my spare moments . . .'

'You have spare moments?' Henslowe was already wondering
where this was going to go. It was a well-known fact that
Marlowe never slept and even so he took on more than most
sets of twins.

Marlowe's tone was airy. 'A few. I have written . . . let us
call it the bare bones . . . of a new play, but I doubt that Sir
Edmund Tilney would let it pass. It contains some . . . well,'
he leaned forward, as one man of the world to another, 'some
material that might cause a stir. But you know how that goes
– once it has been performed *somewhere*, the people cause a
stink, they want to see it too, pressure is brought to bear. I
needn't draw you a picture, I'm sure.'

'What material?' The coronet was feeling a little less secure.

'Oh, you know the kind of thing. Devils, a few devils . . .'

'Devils? We've done devils before. Tom—'

'I was going to ask you about Tom. How is he?'

'You know Tom,' Henslowe clicked his tongue. 'Can't keep
a young dog down, eh? He'll mend.'

'There you are, then,' Marlowe beamed, keeping to himself
the thoughts that Meg might have more to do with the time of
Tom's return than Tom. 'Nothing to worry about. So, my plan
was to get it put on in a private house. You know how these
titled lot go on, always having revels and such; Ralegh, he's
always ripe for a revel. House on the Strand. Nice and central.'

'I don't know him, though.'

'You know Strange.'

'Everyone knows Ferdinando Stanley.'

'Well, there you are, then. Speak to him. Tell him you have a new play . . . oh, and another thing. Can you tell him Shaxsper wrote it?'

Now Henslowe's eyebrows all but disappeared. 'Now, Kit, that is too much! No one could take your work for Shaxsper's.' He dropped his voice again. 'Have you *seen* any of *Henry the whatever*?'

'Sixth, I think.'

'Is it? He keeps changing it.'

'Some of it is all right.' Marlowe tried to keep the doubt out of his voice.

'But *Shaxsper?* Why?'

'I want to hide my light under his bushel. To see if my line is mighty enough for recognition if the playgoers don't know it's me.' Marlowe dropped his eyes in mock modesty.

Henslowe was silent for a long moment, looking at his cash cow from under heavy brows. Then he sat forward, suddenly, bringing both palms down on the table with a crack. 'Let's do it!' he cried. 'Do you have the pages with you?'

Marlowe smiled, the smile of a spider who has only to wrap up the fly before sucking it dry. 'Not with me. But you shall have them tomorrow. After the performance. I want them in rehearsal as soon as possible after that. This play . . . it is topical, it won't keep.'

Henslowe wagged his head. 'Hmm . . . I think that could work. How many in the cast?'

'Not many. You'll need Alleyn, of course. Burbage. Some walking gentlemen. Jenkins . . . Shaxsper, I suppose . . . and I thought I might take a small part myself, nothing major, just for fun.'

Henslowe was already taken up with the thrill of it all and forgot for a moment Marlowe's nominal acting skills. It would undoubtedly be all right on the night.

Marlowe stood. 'So, Master Henslowe . . . can I leave it with you?' He hoped the answer was yes. He desperately needed to get home to Hog Lane and have a lie down. He wasn't even sure whether he would be able to make the stairs.

'Yes, yes,' Henslowe's head was still full of coronets. 'Oh, Kit, before you go. I found this on my chair this morning.' He paused for a moment as a thought struck him. The parcel he was now holding out to the playwright had not been there when he had locked up the night before. And yet, there it had been when he unlocked that morning. He shook his head, deciding that sometimes the least said, the soonest mended. 'It's addressed to you. By hand.'

Marlowe took it with a sigh. 'It's probably some would-be playwright, showing me his work. Although . . .' he weighed it in his hand, 'it is a heavy piece of work, if that is so. May I open it here, Master Henslowe? Then I can leave it here for kindling, if I am right.'

'Of course.' Henslowe cleared a space.

Marlowe undid the knots and folded out the waxed cloth that wrapped the contents, secure against the elements. A pile of parchment and papers were inside, not looking like any play Marlowe had ever seen. On top was a folded note, sealed with a blank spatter of wax. He opened it and read silently, glancing up at Henslowe as he did so, but the theatre owner was already jotting down some figures on the corner of an old playbill and had lost interest already in Marlowe and his parcel.

'Kit,' the note said, in scrawled, uneven letters, 'I write in haste. Cecil's men are on the way to search my rooms. They have already been to everywhere I lodge and these papers are not safe with me any more. Take them. Read them. Hide them somewhere secure. They will come for you, next. Believe me. Faunt.' He turned the paper over and saw another line, in faint graphite, on the back. 'I am on his trail. I will have him soon.' Cryptic, so cryptic, it was unclear whether it was meant for him or was just a note on the other side of an old piece of paper.

Marlowe folded the parcel up and tucked it under his arm. He had a feeling that Faunt's warning had come too late for Tom Sledd. Suddenly, the assault on the Mermaid made some sense. Henslowe looked up. 'Is it any good?' he asked, pointing at the bundle.

Marlowe shrugged. 'Too soon to tell. I'll look at it at home.' He hitched the parcel tighter under his arm. 'Well, goodbye,

Master Henslowe. I will deliver those pages tomorrow.' And with that, he was gone, clattering down the stairs.

'Alleyn?' Richard Burbage could roar for England when the need arose and it *always* arose at the mention of his rival's name.

'Of course, Alleyn.' Philip Henslowe stood his ground while flapping his hands for quiet at the same time. 'He always plays the leads in Kit's plays; you know that.'

'Why?'

Henslowe looked at the boy. What was he? Twenty-two? Twenty-three? Towering ambition in one so young was downright embarrassing, but Henslowe had been here before – with Ned Alleyn only three years ago. The theatre was a young man's world, but God give him strength, he could kill for a little maturity. And he didn't have all day to explain the secrets of the theatrical universe to a boy who hadn't finished shitting yellow. 'You've got Mephistophilis, Richard,' Henslowe wheedled. 'It's a plum part. Head Devil.'

'I thought Lucifer was head Devil.' Burbage had petulance written all over him this morning.

'Technically, yes, but not the way Kit's written it. I'll tell you how unimportant Lucifer is – I've cast Jenkins.'

Burbage's expression changed. 'Oh, I see. Well, put like that . . .'

'Burbage?' Alleyn thundered a little later and in another part of the theatre. 'You've given Burbage a role?'

Henslowe's hands were flapping again. 'I had to, Ned; you know how it is.'

'No, Henslowe,' Alleyn looked at him from under his best leading man scowl. 'Suppose you tell me.'

Henslowe looked at the actor. Ned Alleyn, it was true, was *everybody*'s leading man – tall, handsome, assured. Winchester geese flocked to him (no payment required); titled ladies sent their manservants with offers of trysts in romantic places, often accompanied by a diamond clip or two. Alleyn wasn't choosy – no sensible offer was refused. But Henslowe didn't have all day and had no idea of how to even *start* to give Alleyn a sense of his own perspective.

'Faustus, Ned,' he murmured in his ear, like the good angel that Marlowe had conjured up. 'A magus with power to raise the Devil himself. Kit based the character on you.'

'On me?' Even Alleyn was surprised by that.

'Only someone of your gravitas,' Henslowe grinned, hoping that some of Marlowe's Muses would rub off on him, 'your raw sensual power, could carry a part like that. It'll be something they'll talk about for years, trust me – "I saw the great Ned Alleyn play Faustus". Can't you hear it?'

'Edward,' Alleyn said. He thought of posterity often. 'The great *Edward* Alleyn. Has more of a ring.'

'Absolutely.' Henslowe knew he had got him.

'So, it's a comedy, then?'

Henslowe frowned. Perhaps he hadn't got him after all. 'Er . . . no, Ned. It's a tragedy – *The Tragical History of Doctor Faustus.*' The impresario closed to his leading man. 'It's a true story.'

For a moment, Henslowe believed he saw the colour drain from Alleyn's cheek, but it may have been a trick of the light. The actor fumbled in his purse and hauled out a large crucifix on a chain, which he hung around his neck. He caught Henslowe's glance.

'Can't be too careful,' he said. 'Don't worry, I'll remember to take it off when I play *The Jew* tomorrow.'

'Lots of thunder, Tom,' Henslowe beamed at his stage manager; but, if truth were told, he didn't like the look of him. He was still carrying all the signs of his stay with Master Topcliffe, but it was almost time to stop making allowances, in Henslowe's opinion. Allowances cost money. 'Lightning, a dragon, apparently. Is that going to be all right?'

Sledd tried to shrug, but gave it up as too damned painful. This was a Kit Marlowe production; miracles took longer. 'I suppose I should be grateful it isn't the whole thing,' he said. 'Have you seen the stage directions he has in mind for the full play?'

Henslowe shook his head.

'If you take my advice, don't. Dragons and thunder are only the beginning. But . . .' a sudden thought had struck him. 'We aren't doing it here, are we?' It would be an absolute nightmare if they were. It was already bad enough, with the cast corpsing in their lines on stage in *The Jew* because they had got confused with their lines from *Faustus*. If he had to have two lots of scenery stored backstage as well, he might as well throw a lighted taper in first as last and hope that Henslowe would embrace an early retirement.

'No, no, don't you worry.' Henslowe patted his shoulder, forgetting that it had been dislocated by various and cunning means not so long before. 'Sorry. No, it's a private performance. At Durham House. That's Sir Walter Ralegh's place, you know, along the Strand. There'll be a few fat purses there or I'm a friar's codpiece.' He swept away and clapped his hands, ignoring the scowls that Alleyn and Burbage gave each other. 'Places, everyone. Where's the bloody Chorus?'

'Our Puritan friends wouldn't approve,' Walter Ralegh murmured in Ferdinando Stanley's ear. 'If this gets out, they'll want Durham House closed down.'

Strange laughed. 'I'm looking forward to this. Good of you to lend your place, Walter, and good of Henslowe to find me a new playwright after . . . well, you know, the whole Marlowe business.'

'Yes.' Ralegh's face was dark for a moment. 'Who is it?'

'Well, that's just it. I may have met the man. I can't remember. Shakespeare. William Shakespeare.'

'What a ludicrous name!' Ralegh laughed.

'Warwickshire, apparently. County's thick with them.'

'Do you know this story, Walter?' Thomas Hariot leaned across from his makeshift box.

'No. It's all about raising the Devil, apparently. And a scholar who signs a pact with him.'

'The Great Lucifer?' Henry Percy leaned across from his box, next to Strange. 'Are you not taking a part, Walter?'

'No, no,' Ralegh chuckled, flashing his fondest smile to where Bess Throckmorton sat with a bevy of her ladies and Jane Dee, all in their finest velvet. 'You know how I detest being the centre of attention.' He pretended not to see Percy's and Strange's eyes roll upward.

For a whole day, Tom Sledd and his people had been sawing, hammering, gluing, creating the Rose's O in Ralegh's Great Hall overlooking the river. The stage manager was annoyed with himself. Ever the perfectionist, Sledd knew he could never do justice to Marlowe's new work in somebody's house. On the road, with the strolling players of Lord Strange's Men, it was difficult and everybody allowed a little latitude. True, this was not the finished *Faustus*, Marlowe had told him. It was a work in progress, but the stage manager was to give it his all – the more terrifying the better – and Marlowe had insisted the performance be at night rather than the usual afternoon.

Now, all was ready. A thousand candles, it seemed – reflected in Ralegh's window that looked out over the darkling river – shone in the eyes of Bess Throckmorton and her friends, who fluttered their fans and made those eyes at the gentlemen sitting in their boxes across the stage from them. Bess, of course, only had eyes for Ralegh, now that they had kissed and made up, as he had told Marlowe they would. The others sighed at the elfin locks of Henry Percy, the strange, lovelorn young man who, even now, had his nose in a book. There was the dashing Lord Strange, the friend of actors and mountebanks and to some extent rather a dark horse. The ladies of Court had certainly heard of Derbyshire where he spent much of his time, but had no intention of actually going there. There was the downright peculiar mathematician, Hariot, who had numbers for brains, and the odd little foreigner Salazar, who was watching the stage so intently. In the centre of them all, one of them yet apart, the Queen's magus, Dr Dee, with his snow-white beard and glittering eyes. Could any company on the stage match the one that sat in the audience?

In Sledd's temporary green room, more usually Ralegh's armoury, the players prowled the space. Will Shaxsper, as surprised as the next man to find his name on the bills as author, was gowned as a scholar playing Cornelius, Faustus's friend. His high forehead was covered in a shapeless Piccadill and his ruff was giving him gyp. Richard Burbage stood on tiptoe, his face and hands a vivid scarlet and horns protruding from his hair, Mephistophilis to the life. Tom Sledd had seen it all in his time with Lord Strange's Men and at the Rose. Even some of the rough plays he had put on – when the only audience were some passing shepherds and their sheep, their only scenery a sheet with some bushes scrawled across it in charcoal – had had some scary moments, for anyone willing to let mummery carry them away, but he felt his hair crawl when he looked at Faustus's Devil. He had to glance at the Good Angel, old Ben Kent, complete with wings and a halo, to keep his feet firmly on the ground. Ned Alleyn was increasingly edgy. The more he read Marlowe's words, the less he liked this part. He was as blasphemous as the next man, in his cups and in the Mermaid, but this was on stage, within feet of the great and good. There were two earls in the audience, the Queen's favourite and the Queen's magus. And he was playing a man rejecting God and supping with the Devil. *It's only a story*, he kept telling himself, *only a story*. Such things can't happen. Even so, he fingered the crucifix, bright at his throat.

Not even Sledd could recognize Belzebub, his face and hands black, a flash of lightning running like a livid scar from his forehead to his jawline. Kit Marlowe had never played in his own works before. He had rarely played in anybody's works before. Tom Sledd was not the only person who had noticed the metaphorical broom up his backside as soon as he walked onstage and his opportunities had been few even when he was trying to make a name for himself. But tonight was different. Everybody sensed it. This was no ordinary performance. This was no ordinary play.

'Kit.' Shaxsper was still struggling with his ruff, whispering to Marlowe backstage. 'Don't think me ungrateful for the billing, but why . . .?'

Marlowe stopped him with a raised hand. 'Patience,' he said. 'All will be revealed.'

'It's just that this play, this Faustus story . . . well, it's a bit . . . near the knuckle, isn't it? One thing's for sure; it'll never get past the Master of the Revels.'

Marlowe was peering through Sledd's flats of Faustus's study at Wittenberg, watching the audience as they waited. 'The Master of the Revels is the least of our worries tonight,' he said.

Shaxsper caught sight of Helen of Troy, a beautiful girl with grey eyes and golden hair. It was her presence that bothered him most of all. Not only was it illegal to have women on stage, it was bad luck. They were all risking God's wrath with Faustus as it was; no need to frost the cake. But Marlowe had insisted. There were a number of young lads who could have taken the role – after all, Helen had no lines. But Marlowe had insisted, ignoring the protestations of almost everybody. Not only was Helen to be played by a girl; she was to be played by *this* girl, whom Marlowe himself had found.

'And what's all this about Helen?' Shaxsper had to ask again.

'When she comes on,' Marlowe whispered, 'watch if you can, the face of the magus. You'll understand.'

Shaxsper sighed heavily. He'd like that. He'd like to understand *something* that was going on tonight.

The Heavens crashed and roared. There would be no music for *Faustus*, no orchestra cluttering the stage. Just Tom Sledd and his thunder-box. One or two of the ladies shrieked and the men were secretly glad of that – it hid their own fears. The windows rattled and the candles guttered, half of them going out with the blast. Henslowe had dispensed with the Chorus to open the play. The man wasn't very good and, anyway, he had had to leave town very suddenly when the father of a young lady he knew arrived at the Rose with two enormous sons and several large clubs. So the scene settled on Alleyn, sitting alone in his study, surrounded by charts, circles, numbers, hieroglyphs and a brass object that looked very like Hariot's perspective trunk, pointing through Ralegh's windows to the Heavens.

Marlowe watched him. Hariot would not show that he was impressed. How the Devil . . .?

'Settle thy studies, Faustus,' Alleyn began, talking to himself as all the School of Night did in their laboratories. He had his instructions from Marlowe. With various lines, he was to pause and look at certain members of the audience. He just hoped he'd get that right. Aeneas, Tamburlaine, Barabbas; all his great roles had had their challenges, but *this* was something else.

'Yet,' he said with the voice that had held thousands in the sound, 'art thou still but Faustus and a man?' He half turned in his chair to face Salazar. 'Couldst thou make men to live eternally, or, being dead, raise them to life again . . .' He paused, long enough for Salazar to hear his own heart thump. What knavery was this? His innermost secrets spilled on to the world's stage. What was going on?

'*Stipendium peccati mors est*,' Alleyn murmured, staring into the eyes of Walter Ralegh. 'The reward of sin is death.' Ralegh's eyes flickered, first to Bess, then back to Faustus, who had the attention of them all.

'These necromantic books are heavenly.' Alleyn threw a few of them about, unaware of Henslowe cringing backstage. They had cost him an arm and a leg. The actor fixed his stare on to Hariot. 'Lines, circles, scenes, letters and characters; ay, these are those that Faustus most desires.'

The mood of the audience lightened measurably when Ben Kent came on as the Good Angel. They had all seen Mystery Plays in their childhoods. It was like coming home. 'Oh, Faustus,' Kent intoned, doing his best vicar impression, 'lay that damned book aside and gaze not on it lest it tempt thy soul . . . Read, read the Scriptures; that is blasphemy.' But the audience dipped again when it was clear that dear old Ben was wasting his time; Faustus was having none of it. Alleyn stood up and walked slowly to the stage's apron. Now he could touch any of the School of Night, at least with a sword. He was happy to see that none of them carried one.

'Philosophy is odious and obscure,' he said, looking each man in the face. 'Both law and physic are for petty wits; Divinity is the basest of the three.'

Salazar decided to brazen it out. Whoever this Shakespeare fellow was, he was playing games with them, having a laugh at their expense. Well, he for one could cope with that. He clapped his hands several times, slowly. But Ned Alleyn had trod the boards of London's theatres for years and nothing could throw him. He leaned forward to Salazar. ''Tis magic, magic that hath ravished me.'

'Going well,' Skeres muttered to Frizer as they scampered across the stage behind Lucifer, all cloven hoofs and thrashing tails. Even so, he wasn't ready for another of Sledd's thunderclaps when it came and he bit his tongue. Thank God he had no lines in this bit.

It grated on Burbage that *his* first line should play second fiddle to Alleyn, but there it was. 'Now, Faustus,' he boomed, 'what wouldst thou have me do?' The greatest actors of the day circled each other on the stage. The audience had long ago got over the usual fidgeting and casual conversation. They were silent, rapt, intent to catch every word. It was what both Alleyn and Burbage expected – complete, unadulterated adulation.

'Where art thou damned?' Alleyn asked Burbage.

'In Hell,' came the reply.

'How comes it, then,' Alleyn closed to the Devil in front of him, 'that thou art out of Hell?'

It was Burbage's turn to face the School of Night. 'Why, this is Hell, nor am I out of it.' They all shifted in their seats, Ralegh stony-faced, John Dee regretting that he had let Marlowe and Henslowe talk him into this. It was at this point that things turned ugly. Alleyn had not been happy about it. He was all for realism, but a *real* knife? A *real* cut? Marlowe had told him not to worry; there would be a doctor on hand to staunch the blood. And anyway, it was nothing that Alleyn had not experienced a dozen times when things got out of hand at the Mermaid.

'Lo, Mephistophilis,' Alleyn held the dagger high, 'for love of thee, I cut mine arm,' he sliced the blade through his velvet sleeve and the skin beneath and held the hand downwards. '. . . View here this blood that trickles . . . and let it be propitious for my wish.' He scowled across at Salazar.

There was an inrush of breath from the audience.

'How do they *do* that?' Percy asked Strange, as though the man with his own acting troupe would have the answer. Viscosity he understood; tricks of the theatrical trade, not so much so.

'He's done it,' Strange murmured, lost in the action. 'He's made his pact with the Devil.' He crossed himself. 'God help him now.'

A drum rattled from the wings, slowing to a solemn beat, like a heart in its last moments and walking gentlemen moved to a slow galliard in their Devils' robes, bowing in turn before Faustus and leaving gifts at their feet. It was Ralegh's turn to clap ironically. Around Alleyn, tobacco pipes were placed and tobacco leaves scattered. Expensive wines, in their dusty bottles and straw, joined them and lastly, as Frizer turned to bow to Hariot, a sack of potatoes.

'Walter . . .' The mathematician leaned across, fear and fury etched on his face.

'Shut up, Thomas!' Ralegh commanded, every bit as imperious as Mephistophilis himself.

When Alleyn's Faustus demanded books from Mephistophilis, each one of the School of Night was ready to leave, but none of them could, riveted as they were by the play unfolding in front of them.

'Spells and incantations,' Alleyn spoke directly to Salazar. 'All characters and planets of the heavens,' he spoke to Dee. 'All plants, herbs and trees that grow upon the earth,' he spoke to Strange. The night grew dark. No one heard Sledd's thunder any more, or saw the smoke crawl along the ground. Marlowe, black as Belzebub, stood on stage now and introduced to Faustus the seven deadly sins, the number of the chairs that night at Dr Dee's house. Pride, envy, wrath, covetousness, gluttony, sloth and lechery, all of them in dazzling costumes bowed before Faustus and told him their stories.

'Bell, book and candle,' Alleyn intoned, 'Candle, book and bell. Forward and backward, to curse Faustus in Hell.'

A mighty line and one that, for most of the audience, regular playgoers as they were, seemed to sound the end of the Act. But they sat back down again as the action swept on, numbed by Sledd's thunder, Alleyn's acting and, unknown to them all, Marlowe's words. Friars wandered the stage, holding their crosses high, pulling back their cowls as they chanted *'Maledicat dominus'* over and over. May God curse him. And the School of Night looked at each other. Were they not all cursed by God?

The assassins circled each other on the stage, peering out into the audience looking for their target. Three of them carried knives, the fourth an axe. 'Then, gentle Frederick,' Benvolio said, 'hie thee to the grove and place our servants and our followers close in an orchard there behind the trees . . .'

Elias Carter found himself nodding. He still remembered the near miss as the crossbow bolt had all but parted Marlowe's hair. In the wings, Will Shaxsper, still struggling mentally with his *Henry VI*, scribbled the name down. Benvolio. That was good. He could do something with that.

'Here will we stay to bide the first assault,' Benvolio went on, cradling his axe. 'O, were that damned Hell-hound but in place, thou soon should see me quit my foul disgrace!'

Hell-hound, Shaxsper scribbled. Better and better. Alleyn, all innocence, wandered across the stage and the killers fell on him. They scuffled together, Alleyn's boots scraping on Sledd's timbers.

'Groan you, Master Doctor?' Frederick asked, but he was looking at Dee.

'Break may his heart with groans!' Benvolio came back. 'Dear Frederick, see, thus will I end his griefs immediately.'

Twice, thrice the axe fell, thudding into the woodwork. An arc of blood sprayed sideways and Faustus's head bounced across the boards to disappear behind a curtain. Perfect. While there were screams from the ladies and cries of disgust from the gentlemen, Tom Sledd congratulated himself on a job well done.

'Excellent, my boy,' a delighted Henslowe whispered in Sledd's ear. 'The groundlings will love that bit.'

As for Ned Alleyn, he stayed crouched behind his murderers, grateful for the fact that Marlowe hadn't insisted on real blood for this scene in the play. Actor extraordinary he well may be, but beheading would be something hard to come back from. The assassins sat facing the audience. Benvolio's axe blade glistened with blood. 'Come,' said Frederick, 'let's devise how we may add more shame to the black scandal of his hated name.'

'We'll pull out his eyes,' a delighted Benvolio suggested, 'and they shall serve for buttons to his lips, to keep his tongue from catching cold.'

'An excellent policy!' Martino laughed. 'And now, sirs, having divided him, what shall the body do?'

Alleyn's feet twitched once, twice. Then his knees flexed and he sat upright. It hurt like Hell, straining the muscles of his back, but it impressed the audience. Bess Throckmorton, pale and ill looking, screamed again. Jane Dee looked at her husband for reassurance.

'Zounds,' Benvolio really didn't need to tell anyone. 'The Devil's alive again.'

Nearly as rattled as the audience when he turned round, Frederick yelled, 'Give him his head, for God's sake!'

'Nay, keep it,' Alleyn bellowed from inside his ruff. He thrust upwards and his head reappeared. 'Faustus will have heads and hands . . .'

Strange squinted, leaning forward. He'd seen some trickery in his time, but this was beyond him. Percy breathed out a sigh of relief. Of course it was all a play, smoke and mirrors. Of course; it had to be. And yet. And yet . . .

No one was ready for the beautiful and silent girl who was led forward by the scholars later. Strange rubbed his eyes. Ralegh did a double take. It actually *was* a girl, wasn't it? The Master of the Revels would never stand for that; he'd close Henslowe down and the Rose too, in all probability.

'Was this fair Helen,' the second scholar asked, 'whose admired worth made Greece with ten years' war afflict poor Troy?' He took her by the hand and brought her forward to within feet of John Dee. The old magus was on his feet, his mouth open, a solitary tear trickling down his cheek.

'Was this the face,' Alleyn asked, watching them both, 'that launched a thousand ships and burnt the topless towers of Ilium? Sweet Helen,' he closed to her, nodding briefly to Dee, 'make him immortal with a kiss.' The girl leaned forward, taking the magus's face in both her hands and their lips met. In the silence that followed, the girl's eyes were closed but Dee's were wide open. Only he understood it fully. Only Jane understood it partially. She had seen the portraits of John's first wife, Nell, whom he called Helene. Only Dee and Jane knew that Kit Marlowe had once promised to make her live again, in a play. Dee spun silently on his heel and left Ralegh's hall, Jane in hot and frightened pursuit. What had just happened?

Everyone was on the edge of their seats as the Devils gathered. The echoing drum gave them their marching rhythm, but the march was an inversion of what men did. They dragged their long, clashing tails and snarled their words.

'What,' Burbage had great delight in taunting Alleyn, kneeling, a broken man centre stage, 'weep'st thou? 'Tis too late; despair! Farewell: Fools that will laugh on earth must weep in Hell.'

'Stay,' Alleyn roared, reaching out with both hands. 'Stay, thou monstrous crawling thing.'

Burbage looked down at him. This wasn't in the script, not the one he'd seen, anyway.

'Grant, in mighty Lucifer's name, one last request of mine,' Alleyn begged.

Burbage had never been asked to make up lines before and he stood there, open-mouthed. When he got off stage he was going to cut Ned Alleyn a new arse. Meanwhile, that idiot Jenkins had taken his name for a cue and was capering and posturing across the stage. There was a strange smell of burning as well; he would be having a word with Sledd too; extra stage props should not be left to every Tom, Dick and Jenkins.

'I would exchange it all,' Alleyn dragged himself upright, using Burbage as a crutch, 'for one boon.'

'Name it,' Henslowe mouthed from the wings, directly in Burbage's eyeline.

'Name it,' Mephistophilis repeated, with as much gravitas as he could in the circumstances.

Marlowe crept nearer, his black face glistening with the sweat of the greasepaint and the gleam from the candles. He wasn't watching Burbage. He wasn't watching Alleyn. He was watching the School of Night. All of them. They were all rigid, unmoving. Only Dee had gone and Marlowe would make his peace with him later.

'At this eleventh hour, one man must die,' Alleyn said and found himself being answered not by Mephistophilis but by Belzebub.

'Name him,' Marlowe said.

'One close to the Queen and closer to himself.'

'You wish him dead, this servant royal?' He had crossed to Alleyn now and the two men faced each other. To Burbage, this was intolerable. He was just standing there like a walking gentleman, his tail dangling.

'I do,' Alleyn nodded, 'and all his Puritan kind.'

'How will you have it done? With ball or blade?'

'With poison,' Alleyn grunted, 'from the shores far West of here.'

Marlowe turned to face the audience. From where he stood,

he could see clearly the faces of both the men who had been to the far West. Ralegh, who had brought the Nicotiana plant. Hariot who had found the tuber. And he could see someone else too, someone standing half in the shadows behind the others, shifting imperceptibly, listening to the mighty lines from the Muse.

'I'll bring you poisons that will stop the blood,' Marlowe said. 'The weeds that kill the great and good. 'Tis best you mix them simply in the dark . . .' He paused, watching the shadow slide sideways on the far wall, 'With all the skills you learned in godless Prague.' He was shouting now, his eyes wide, his finger pointing at them all, yet only pointing at one.

No one was ready for the crash that shattered the window behind Marlowe's head. Henslowe spun round, wondering how the Hell Tom Sledd could have done that. But Sledd was as nonplussed as his master. He gaped beyond the curtain, shattering the illusion of the moment as Marlowe dashed through the audience, kicking over chairs and scattering the School of Night as he went. Everyone was on their feet now, shouting at each other, screaming, wondering at the spectacle they had just witnessed.

Only two pairs of feet thudded along Ralegh's passageway beyond the Great Hall. Only one pair of hands slammed into the unforgiving oak doors. The echoes that usually rang with the chattering of ladies taking their exercise in inclement weather now returned curses that would make a sailor blench.

'Not that way, Carter.' Marlowe had stopped running and waited for the man to calm and turn. There was a wheel-lock in the servant's hand, but he had already fired the shot that had shattered the window and he could never reload before Marlowe's knife found him. His shoulders sagged.

'How did you know?' he asked. 'About Prague, I mean?'

'I am Machiavel,' Marlowe said, as others, the men of the Rose and the School of Night, came at the double. 'More than that, I am Belzebub. How could I not know?'

SIXTEEN

'Gentlemen,' Marlowe did not turn to face them, intent as he was on watching Carter. 'I give you the murderer of Sir Francis Walsingham.'

There was a silence.

'I thought you had *us* in the snare for that,' Percy said.

There were murmurs all round. They were all still reeling from the revelations on stage.

'Cecil will have to be informed,' Ralegh said. 'In the meantime, if it's not too late to knock up Master Topcliffe . . .'

Strange gave a bark of laughter. 'I have never known him sleep,' he said. 'I wager we will find him awake and blowing on his fires to keep his pincers hot.'

'Tie him,' Hariot said. 'He has beaten the best minds in England for long enough to make me fear he can elude us yet. Let me make the knots; I have studied the art of it.'

'Typical,' Salazar muttered. 'It is one thing to have looked in books on knot-making, another to be able to do it. Give me a moment and I can bind him fast by magic.'

Carter, at bay against the door, smiled. He should have known that he could have relied upon these arrogant fools to fight amongst themselves. His fingers crept, inch by inch, to the latch and, when Marlowe's attention was taken for a moment by Strange threatening to knock Hariot and Salazar's heads together, he snatched at it, wrenched the door open and was gone, into the night-held Strand.

Across the roadway from the gates of Durham House, a tree spread its boughs over the wall of the Convent Garden. Under it, two lovers stood, wrapped up in each other, though not touching. Their heads were bowed, their voices low. Love enveloped them in their own world and, although the man, John Dee, would never see his youth again, his wife could only see the man she loved above all things, wrapped in a pain he had thought had gone.

'I love you, Jane,' he murmured. 'You and the children, more than life itself. But . . . Helene . . . I had never thought to see her again although, the Heavens know, I tried and tried. For months after her death, I did nothing but try to bring her back. It's wrong, but . . .'

She reached out a hand and stroked his cheek, feeling the old skin parchment under her fingers. 'I don't care, John,' she whispered. 'I know you love me. And I love you because of your love for her, not despite it. Come here,' she held out her arms. Then, her head turned as a rout came running out of the gates of the erstwhile Bishop's Palace. 'What the . . .?'

Dee stepped in front of her to protect her. 'It's Marlowe!' he said over his shoulder, 'with the entire School of Night at his heels. Whatever did he have those mummers say next that they are all after him?' He shook his head. He had warned the man, after all.

'No.' Jane's younger, sharper eyes had seen the other man, perhaps six paces ahead of Marlowe, but making ground fast as he jumped over the ruts of the road. He was heavier than the playwright, older certainly, and yet he ran with a fixity of purpose which gave his feet wings. 'No, look. Look, there. It's . . . John, it's Carter! Why are they chasing Carter?'

Dee felt a white-hot anger rise in his chest until he thought it would choke him. Two men he trusted were running towards him, one in pursuit of the other. There was no question of what to do next. With a power and speed which surprised even him, he launched himself out of the shelter of the tree and tackled Carter around the knees, bringing him down so that his head smacked on to a stone in the roadway and he lay still, stunned.

'John!' Jane screamed and ran forward.

By the time the School of Night caught up, many of them puffing and blowing, though Ralegh managed to still look cool and collected, Marlowe was hauling Carter to his feet and Jane was supporting Dee on her shoulder.

'Doctor!' Marlowe could not hide his surprise. 'I never knew you had it in you.'

Dee smiled. 'Nor did I,' he said. 'Although . . .' he flexed his leg and winced, 'this knee might need some tender loving care.'

'I have a poultice which will do the trick,' Jane said, in such a tone that Marlowe looked away, embarrassed by the naked love on her face.

Carter was bloodied, but had only been stunned for a moment, so stood, straight and tall, with Marlowe holding his arm up behind his back. He had not meant to run at all. Ever since his plan had come into his mind, he had always told himself that, should exposure come, *when* exposure came, because he had not presumed to escape scot free, he would take his punishment like a man. And so now, there would be no more struggle, no more flight. Whatever happened to him, would happen. He closed his mouth in a mirthless smile and let his enemies do with him what they would.

There was an unseemly scramble to take the miscreant back into the house, but this was Ralegh's house and it was Ralegh's ropes they lashed around Carter's wrists, steward Scranton giving orders to his minions left, right and centre. Each of the School of Night decided to take their own carriages to the Tower, Ralegh having care of Carter, leaving Philip Henslowe and his players to de-rig the makeshift set, the play unfinished, Faustus still this side of Hell.

Bess Throckmorton and her ladies had had time to overcome their panic and they soon found themselves the centre of the attention of not one great actor, but two. Faustus and Mephistophilis were all too grateful to drop their demonic possession and become arrogant peacocks again, the roles they played the best.

'But that's enough about me,' Alleyn purred to one of the Queen's maids of the bedchamber. 'What did *you* think about my performance tonight?'

Outside, back in the shelter of the nuns' tree, Marlowe and the Dees stood, the magus still leaning heavily on his wife. They stood in silence for a while, all wrapped in their own thoughts.

'I'm sorry about Carter,' Marlowe said, eventually, for want of anything else that would fit the bill.

'No,' Dee said. '*I* am sorry about Carter. I gave him to you to watch you and keep you safe. And, all the time . . .'

'You weren't to know,' Marlowe said. 'You did what you thought was for the best. As did I.'

Dee's voice cracked a little. 'You said you would bring Helene back,' he said. 'I didn't think you meant to taunt me with it.'

Marlowe stepped forward and put an arm around the old man, holding him tight for just a heartbeat. 'She walked tonight to taunt you, yes, and I am sorry. But I promise you, she will walk again, and when she does, the whole world will marvel.' He stepped back again. 'I promise you. *Pactum factum.*'

Dee nodded. 'A promise fulfilled, indeed.'

Jane leaned forward and pulled him to her, kissing him on the cheek. 'We believe you,' she said. 'But now,' and her voice changed, from the soft lover to the efficient housewife, 'now I need to get my husband home to tend to his wounds. And you,' she pointed over Marlowe's shoulder, 'you need to hail one of these carriages, or they will carry your man off to the Tower and take the credit. There! Go! Hurry!'

Marlowe looked as the carriages turned out of the gates, their horses' eyes rolling, hoofs clashing on the stones, drivers flicking their whips. Strange's carriage slithered to a halt and Marlowe jumped in. As it gathered speed, heading east, he looked behind him and saw the Dees still under the tree, her hand raised in benediction. Jack shall have Jane, naught shall go ill . . . it needed work, but the playwright was never far beneath the skin and a good line was, after all, a good line. He fell back against the leather of the carriage seat and he and Strange spent the short journey in silence, alone with their thoughts.

Striking a set was always an emotional time for Tom Sledd, but he had no real connection with this one. It had, after all, been in existence less than half a day. Even if it had been a run of months, the last few minutes would have rather taken the gloss off in any case; so he set to with pliers and wrench, saws and hammers, dismantling the stage and Faustus's study with a will. Henslowe himself snatched up the expensive leather-bound volumes and the polished brass tube that doubled for Hariot's perspective trunk, whatever that was. Around him, actors and walking gentlemen milled around, some still in costume and make-up, some looking like a mad chimera of man and actor. Sledd was quite sad; Kit had been right. Even without the flight of a murderer from among the audience, there was no possibility that this play would ever be put on again. Anywhere. It was a shame.

The ladies of Bess Throckmorton's entourage had slowly drifted away, driven by the assault on their ears from the hammering and scream of nails being withdrawn from damp timber. In their absence, Alleyn and Burbage had taken their argument to new levels, as everyone knew they would, and a small crowd was gathering to see who would punch whom first.

'What *was* that supposed to be in Act Two, Alleyn?'

'That was *acting*, dear boy,' the great tragedian bridled. 'You really should try it sometime.'

Sides were drawn up, with money changing hands, but everyone with money on Burbage as the aggressor was feeling confident. They noticed that he had managed to obtain not one, but two ladies' favours a few moments ago and was clearly at the top of his form. The two dramatic lions circled each other, their mannerisms becoming more and more arcane, their declamations more stentorian. After a while it became a moot point whether one would strike the other, or that they might explode in a flash of fire that not even Tom Sledd could produce.

Into the chaos limped a small, dejected figure, leaning on two crutches. It had a large bandage around its head and two whalebone struts were taped fore and aft, to protect and straighten its back. Of the face, one eye and the mouth were the only parts visible.

'Excuse me,' it croaked, to no avail. 'Excuse me.' But no one heard. By dint of hopping round carefully – it clearly could not turn its head – the poor beleaguered thing found a friendly face. Tom Sledd had stopped his de-carpentering and had eased himself to his feet. He came nearer.

'Can I help you?' He was doubtful; it looked as though aid had long ceased to be an option.

'Tom?' The creature's cracked lips could hardly form the word. 'Tom? I went to the theatre but the caretaker said you were here. Sorry I'm so late. It's a long way when you can only hop.' The man – for it seemed almost certain that this had once been a man – lifted a heavily bandaged foot and would have fallen over, had Sledd not steadied him.

It seemed unkind to add to his woes, but Sledd had to ask. 'I'm sorry,' he said, leaning close to the bandaged ear. 'Do I know you?'

The single eye turned to him, filled more with sorrow than with anger. 'Tom?' he whispered. 'Do you really not know me? I'm Jenkins. I just got out of the Tower, just this afternoon. I came . . .'

But Tom Sledd was not listening. 'Jenkins?' he asked. 'Jenkins the *actor*? *My* Jenkins?'

It may have been a nod, it may not; it was so hard to tell. But the eye looked brighter and the dry lips tried to smile.

'But . . .' Tom looked at the back of the stage, where costumes had begun to pile up. On its own, draped across the back of a chair, was a red costume, clearly a tight fit for even the slimmest, its tail trailing disconsolately across the floor. 'But . . . who played Lucifer?'

No one took any notice. They were still all watching Alleyn and Burbage.

Sledd clapped his hands. 'No, people, stop.' He put his fingers in his mouth and whistled; everyone spun round. 'Stop a minute. You can punch him later, Dick. Here's . . . Jenkins.' He extended an arm to where the man hung between his crutches.

The actors immediately gathered round.

'What happened to *you*?' Burbage asked, almost accusingly.

This was followed by a silence as the same thought dawned in a dozen heads.

'But more pertinently,' intoned Alleyn, '*when* did it happen to you?'

Jenkins cleared his throat, sounding like two coffins grinding together in a charnel house. The damp in Master Topcliffe's second level had played merry Hell with his chest. 'I don't remember. What day is this? I've been in the Tower since . . .' and he was racked with a cough which made everyone wince, 'since the first performance of *The Jew*. How long is that?' His eye looked out pleadingly.

Burbage leaned in, condescendingly. 'Quite a long time,' he said slowly. 'Will someone get this man a seat? A drink?' Then, having captured the moral high ground of being the most caring actor in the place, he beckoned everyone together and he whispered, 'So . . . who played Lucifer? Come on. No one will be cross.' He looked Skeres in the eye, as the one most likely to be messing about. 'It was you, wasn't it?'

'No, it was not!' Skeres automatically denied everything, but this at least had the virtue of being the truth.

Sledd made his way into the centre of the circle. 'We'll settle this the old way,' he said. 'Everyone close their eyes. Go on, do it.' He waited until everyone's lids were squeezed tight. 'Now, the one who did it, the one who played Lucifer, open your eyes and look at me. I won't tell. Dick is quite right. No one will be cross.' But no one looked him in the eye. No one was admitting to playing Lucifer.

'Can we open our eyes now?' Alleyn asked, petulantly. He was a great actor, for God's sake, not a child.

Sledd made a decision. 'Yes. Yes, open your eyes. And,' he wagged a general finger, 'don't do anything so stupid again.'

'Who was it? Skeres asked.

'I promised not to tell and I won't. Everyone back to whatever you were doing, unless it was fighting, in which case, stop. Here, you,' he clicked his fingers at Frizer. 'Pass me that costume, will you? That red one, there, on the chair.'

Frizer looked at him penetratingly. No one can con a conner, but he did it all the same.

Sledd went out into the gallery and stood in a window embrasure, finding the last of the dying light, and examined Lucifer's costume. It was made, as all the Rose costumes were, of cheap stuff dyed to suit, with stitches inches long and wishful thinking as to sizing. The inside seams hung ragged with frayed threads. The tail of this one was stuffed with straw. The horns . . . were not there. Instead, there were two jagged holes, burned around the edges. The whole thing smelled of sulphur. Sledd screwed it up and tucked it under his arm.

'Just popping out for a moment,' he called to a heedless room. He ran out of the back door of Durham House and down the garden to the river's edge, the costume clutched to his chest. Looking frantically around, he found a large stone and, spreading the costume on the ground, placed the rock in the middle. Using methods he had seen Meg use in diapering little Zenocrate, as he tended to think of her still, he wrapped the stone up and tied it with the tail. And threw it into the water. And watched it sink. The bubbles exploded upwards for a moment, then, with one, large, noxious pop, the surface was still again, old Father Thames going about his business. Sledd heaved a sigh and walked quickly back up across the sheep-cropped grass, trying, not always successfully, not to look back.

It wasn't often that the Queen's rack-master had *two* noble earls in his outer sanctum. Men like Percy, Strange and Ralegh often came to the Tower, but they came with the Privy Council on matters of state, not in their finery of a night out and *never* as late as this. Dogs barked and torches erupted into flame, the shafts of lanterns darting that way and this. Topcliffe's men, with their master at their head, bowed in recognition of their honoured guests and took Carter into custody, barrelling him along passageways that glistened with the slime of the centuries.

'Henry, Ferdinando.' Ralegh, for all his inferiority of rank, took command. 'Send your fellows to Whitehall. Be sure they're there when Cecil wakes. The imp will no doubt be delighted. As for you, Marlowe . . .'

In a body they turned to face the playwright, still painted black as he was from the stage. The lightning flash had blurred a little, but he was still an arresting sight. Belzebub held up his hand. 'Lords,' he said, 'gentlemen. I crave your pardons, all of you. I believed, wrongly now as I see, that any one of the School of Night could have carried out a crime like the murder of Walsingham. The craftiest man in England could only have been despatched by those whose crafts are . . . dare I say, diabolical?'

'That's outrageous!' Ralegh said, looking hard into the dark eyes of the man who had nearly killed him just days ago.

'It may be,' Marlowe said, 'but ask yourselves, gentlemen; are you not out of joint with the times? There may come a day when every man has his own laboratory or your arcane science is taught to little boys in our schools. God help us, Master Hariot, but that, one day, *girls* will love numbers as you do. Perhaps, Lord Strange, we will all take physic from the hedgerow and there will be no such thing as witchcraft, black, white or what colour you will.'

He had stunned them all to silence.

'But, until that day, we have an order of things, don't we? The planets float around the earth. God created the world in six days and on the seventh, he rested. He made man in his own image and we have spent the last four thousand years trying to live up to that. And if some of us can't accept that . . . if we doubt Scripture . . . if we believe,' he looked at Ralegh, 'that Moses was but a conjuror, they will continue to hound us, to give us to Master Topcliffe, to burn us in a town square.'

The School of Night shifted uncomfortably. 'Isn't that why you hide your perspective trunk, Master Hariot? Why you fear your shadow, Lord Strange? Why you trust your arcane library only to good, honest men like Michael Johns, my lord of Northumberland? Why you harm your animals and yourself, Master Salazar? Why I . . .' he dropped his eyes, 'hide behind the greasepaint and the written word, letting other men speak my lines for me? We are all members of the School of Night,' he said, 'and we are all afraid of the dark.'

One by one, they wandered away, making for Topcliffe's gate that led to the Green.

'There was no other way,' Marlowe stopped them as the first one got there. 'Remember the left hand, Sir Walter, in our little contretemps?'

Ralegh nodded. 'I had to do something desperate,' he admitted.

'So did I,' Marlowe said. 'Tonight at Durham House. I had tried everything else I knew, shaming you to your faces, driving you to fury. Nothing worked. So,' he wet his thumb and wiped a smear of greasepaint off his cheek, 'I called up Belzebub and Mephistophilis, Lucifer and all the guardians of Hell. And the frightening thing is, gentlemen, it worked.'

Ralegh was the first to nod. He walked across to Marlowe and shook his hand. 'It did, Marlowe,' he said, 'and we'll all of us sleep easier in our beds for it. Until the next time, play-maker. You and I must talk poetry again. And Moses . . . let's not forget him.'

Henry Percy was next. 'I underestimated you, Muses' darling,' he said, 'and I'm sorry for that.'

'And I'm sorry for the fact that I still have two books of yours, Your Grace.'

Percy blanched as only a bibliophile can. 'You have?'

'*The Historie of the Damnable Life and Deserved Death of Doctor John Faustus* for one. The other, a small volume of hedge magic.' Marlowe smiled. 'The first I took because I could not resist it. The second, I kept as a clue, which I would have turned against you, had things fallen out differently.'

'Keep them,' Percy said. 'For the first, I have the German original. For the second; I find I am not so fond of poisons as I was.'

Marlowe frowned. 'I thought you didn't read German, Your Grace.'

'Really?' Percy cocked an eyebrow. 'Whoever told you that?' And he was gone.

'I knew it all along, of course.' Ferdinando Strange shook Marlowe's hand.

'My lord?'

'*Faustus*, that it was you, not this Shakestick fellow, or whatever he calls himself. The mighty line is unmistakable. I'd take it as an honour if you'd write again for Lord Strange's Men.'

'The honour would be mine, my lord.'

Strange smiled then, as he passed, he turned. 'Perhaps not *Faustus*, though, eh? I couldn't help noticing that the ladies were a little . . . alarmed.'

'Potatoes,' Hariot took Marlowe's hand. 'Ferdinando has been telling me all about them; I had no idea. Do you think, Marlowe, that a man can stretch himself too thin? Do you think I should stick to numbers, the music of the spheres?'

'I think that would be impossible for a man like you, Master Hariot. *Wlibamkanni.*'

Hariot laughed his short laugh. 'Ha, Master Marlowe. Will you never cease to amaze me? *Adio, wli nanawalmezi*, I think is more correct, but, yes, in certain tribes, *wlibamkanni* is certainly acceptable.' And, chuckling, he slid through the gate, anxious to be back to his numbers.

'I'll not shake your hand, Marlowe,' Salazar slunk towards the gate, 'but I'll give you a lift, if you like. You have no carriage.'

'And no manservant. And probably, with Walsingham gone and *Faustus* performed for its one and only time, no future either. Thank you, but my way isn't far. I'll walk.'

'I did it, though, didn't I?' Salazar had a strange look in his eye. 'Conjuring the spirits? You saw it, didn't you? You and Dee? You saw Walsingham's face?'

Marlowe nodded, his skin crawling. He would see Walsingham's face in Salazar's blood for the rest of his life.

When they had all gone, Marlowe turned. He trudged into Topcliffe's lair, past the tools of the man's trade and found the rack-master sitting alone by candlelight.

'Angels and ministers defend us,' Topcliffe muttered when he looked at the black face, the shining horns still jutting from Marlowe's hair.

'That's a curiously Papist oath from a psalm-singing Puritan,' Marlowe said. 'I have a favour to ask. Give me five minutes with Elias Carter before you rack him.'

'Rack him, Master Marlowe? No, no, nothing so crude. I . . .' he tapped the side of his nose, 'No, no; no trade secrets tonight, especially to a blasphemer who told me he had never crossed a theatre's portals.' He stood up suddenly, a bunch of keys at his waist. 'Five minutes,' he said. 'No more.'

He patted Marlowe's costume roughly, checking for weapons, phials of glass, Papist literature, *anything* his suspicious nose had been sniffing out for years. He took the candle and led the playwright along the blackness of a passageway, past grim doors without number. At one, he paused, clicked the key in the lock and swung it open. It caught on the uneven stones and he kicked it until it stood ajar.

'The Devil's come for you a little early, Carter,' he chuckled and closed the door, leaving Marlowe alone with a killer.

'You've brought the candle, Master Marlowe,' Carter said. 'No bell or book? I'm disappointed.'

'Just tell me why,' Marlowe said, facing the man already shackled to the wall. 'Why Walsingham?'

'And Jorge,' Carter said. 'Don't forget Jorge.'

'Him too?'

'Oh, an accident, I assure you. The *pastel de nata*? I hoped you would accept Master Salazar's offer of some to take home for later. When you didn't, Jorge ate them. Like too many good men, he was expendable.'

'Tom Sledd is a genius,' Marlowe said. 'But not even he could have pulled off the crossbow stunt, so I must assume that that too was you. How did you work that?'

Carter managed a laugh, echoing through Topcliffe's caverns. 'No magic, believe me. Just the magic of gold. Money wasted, as it turned out. The Percy retainers are a loyal lot. I told one of them you meant His Grace ill and paid him handsomely, but I either didn't pay the bastard enough or he was a useless shot. Either way, he missed.'

'And Ralegh?'

'Ah, yes. That turned out quite well, didn't it? I knew that the Great Lucifer "entertained" Mistress Throckmorton most mornings and I knew how badly he would take it if he were interrupted. I half expected your corpse to be rolled out into the Strand, or to join the nameless things floating in the river. Alas, that was not to be either.'

'All right,' Marlowe nodded. 'So I was getting too close to you for comfort. But why Walsingham? You're no Papist.'

'You know why,' Carter said. 'You knew it even before that little charade at Ralegh's house.' He chuckled. 'You rattled them, the School of Night – I'll give you that.'

'I didn't know,' Marlowe admitted, 'not entirely. And I had to know that you had acted alone. As Dee's factotum, you could slip in and out of the corridors of power with impunity. Seething Lane, Whitehall, Barn Elms, wherever Walsingham was. Dee is the Queen's magus; Walsingham was her Spymaster. No one doubted you, did they? No one doubted the man who took his brother's death so stoically. And you nearly got away with it. So keen was he to sweep like a new broom that Robert Cecil swept away any crucial evidence in your case. Fortunately, he swept it into the hands of Nicholas Faunt, who swept it into mine.' Marlowe looked with something like compassion at the man fettered to the streaming wall. 'He was an assiduous note-keeper was Francis Walsingham. I'm working from memory now, you understand, from the notes Nicholas Faunt managed to keep hold of and left to my safe-keeping, so forgive me if I'm a little hazy. I only had an hour or so to look through them before hiding them elsewhere. Your brother was Zebulon Carter, who worked for the Merchant Venturers in godless Prague. Except, he didn't, did he? That was just his cover story. In reality, he was an intelligencer, one of Walsingham's golden lads. One of us.'

'Yes,' Carter grated. 'Yes, he was. And Walsingham got him killed. He *could* have pulled him out; it was getting too dangerous. He *should* have pulled him out; he had a wife and children. Instead, nothing. Not so much as a kiss my arse.'

'It's not Walsingham's way.' Marlowe knew what he was talking about. 'What are any of our lives against that of the Queen? Our futures measured against England's?'

'Well, it's not my way,' Carter growled, turning his head away. It was easier to tell when he wasn't looking into Marlowe's face, with its expression of more sorrow than anger. 'The doctor was in Prague, in Golden Lane with the other deviants and their black arts. Oh, don't misunderstand me. I'd have walked through fire for that man, but you know my views on priests of the sun.'

'I do,' Marlowe nodded.

'I signed on as his man, knowing he would return to England one day. And patience always was a virtue of mine.'

There was a scream of iron as the hinges worked and the door opened, Richard Topcliffe filling the space. 'Time's up, Master Marlowe,' he said.

'The science,' Marlowe ignored him, 'some of it, at least, must have rubbed off from Dee.'

'Needs must,' Carter said, 'when the Devil drives. Didn't I hear that on the stage tonight, Master Marlowe?'

'You might have done,' the playwright said. 'You might have done.'

'Come on.' Topcliffe had taken Marlowe by the arm and was leading him out of the cell.

'One last question,' Marlowe said and Topcliffe paused. 'Did you really work alone?'

Nothing.

'Was any of the School of Night involved, in any way?'

Carter smiled and the door slammed shut.

'See you in Hell, Marlowe,' were the last words Marlowe heard him say.

SEVENTEEN

The tenter-grounds stretched white under the moon as Kit Marlowe trudged along Hog Lane. No watchmen patrolled this far north and only the stray cats of Norton Folgate haunted the alleys. But there was a black shape ahead, almost filling the width of the lane. It looked like a carriage and the snort of waiting horses confirmed it. A cloaked figure sat hunched on the perch and another rested against the side, blowing smoke from an elegant curved pipe.

'I didn't expect to be having our chat about Moses so soon,' Marlowe said. 'I was hoping to get to bed.'

Walter Ralegh straightened. 'We have more pressing problems than the Old Testament, Marlowe,' he said. 'Cecil's missing.'

'Missing?'

'When I left the Tower, I went to Whitehall. Percy's people and Ferdinando's wouldn't have had the nerve to knock the little pygmy up, so I decided to do it myself. He wasn't at home.'

'Hatfield, then. The Cecils own half of England, one way or another.'

'I thought that too. Until I saw the state of his chamber. The place had been turned upside down, cupboards thrown open, papers strewn about.'

'What did Cecil's people know?' Marlowe asked. Both men were talking in whispers. Disappearing members of the Queen's Privy Council were not often a topic of conversation in the streets of Norton Folgate.

'Piss all!' Ralegh snapped. 'You'd think, after Walsingham, they'd look to their locks a little more.'

'Percy's people?' Marlowe thought it worth asking. 'Ferdinando's?'

'As I suspected, standing like good little children until His Tininess got up. Except he'd already got up. And gone.'

Marlowe felt the hairs on the back of his neck crawling. 'Faunt,' he said softly.

'Who?'

'May I beg a lift, Sir Walter?' Marlowe hauled himself up into the carriage, making it rock. 'I'll explain as we go.'

'Good,' Ralegh said. 'That's why I came here. You don't keep a tame projectioner and ignore his skills. Where are we going? I only ask so I can tell my man.' He pointed to the roof of the carriage.

'Of course,' Marlowe said. 'It's either Barn Elms or Seething Lane.' He squinted out of the window, looking up above the tall houses to the night sky. 'It'll be dawn before we get upriver.'

'Seething Lane it is, then,' Ralegh said. He rapped on the carriage roof and shouted to the driver. They were rewarded by a mighty lurch of the carriage and the echo of a cracking whip.

Marlowe caught sight of his face in the polished ebony behind Ralegh's head, opposite him on the seat and he scrubbed at the greasepaint with a cloth he found on the cushions next to him. It was soft and velvety, just perfect for the job in hand, but he froze in horror as he realized it was Ralegh's cloak. To replace it would cost him the same as a year's rent. He smoothed it out as best he could. 'Sorry,' he muttered.

'Don't worry about that old thing,' Ralegh said. 'It's been in more puddles than you've had hot dinners.' He picked it up and passed it back. 'Carry on.' He peered in the gloom. 'I think you've missed a bit. Just there; along the hair . . .' Marlowe plied the cloth, gingerly, as though the damage was not already done. 'That's better. Now, why Seething Lane?'

'Or Barn Elms,' Marlowe pointed out. 'There's not much of the poet in Nicholas Faunt, but he does like neat endings. Except, this time, he's got the wrong man.'

They rattled through the night, Ralegh agog with the story Marlowe told him now, as he had been agog with the story of Faustus earlier in the evening. The tenements of Houndsditch rolled by and dogs ran by the wheels, barking and snapping at the horses' hoofs. Down Gracechurch they raced, the wind blowing the driver's cloak and whipping off his hat. The carriage tilted disturbingly by St Dunstan's in the east, then righted itself and came to a screeching, rattling halt in Seething Lane.

Marlowe was out before Ralegh, hammering on the door he had entered so often. There were lights burning in the upper storey. No one was asleep in Walsingham's house tonight. The door opened and Francis Mylles stood there, blinking and confused.

'Master Marlowe,' he said, surprised, and recognized Ralegh at once. 'Sir Walter.' He half bowed.

'No time for niceties, Mylles.' Marlowe barged past Walsingham's man. 'Where are they?'

'Where are who?' Mylles played the innocent.

Marlowe spun to the old man, pushing him against the wall and holding him there. 'I know where your sympathies lie, Mylles,' he said. 'You want Sir Francis's murderer brought to book as much as the rest of us. But Faunt's got the wrong man.'

For an instant, Francis Mylles' life flashed before him. For years he had served the Spymaster faithfully and well and for years, strange and dangerous men had been knocking at this very door. None more so than the four who had come knocking tonight. 'Upstairs,' he blurted out. 'Sir Francis's Inner Sanctum.'

Marlowe and Ralegh raced each other along the passageway, Ralegh's pattens clattering and echoing as they ran. If they had hoped for the element of surprise, that was gone now. Marlowe knew the way, if Ralegh didn't, and he put his shoulder to the second door on the left. It crashed back and in the guttering candlelight, Nicholas Faunt was holding a wicked-looking blade at the throat of Robert Cecil.

'Nicholas!' Marlowe screamed. 'No! It's not him!'

Faunt's eyelids flickered but nothing else moved, least of all the dagger tip that tickled the man's windpipe. 'Of course it is,' Faunt said. 'It has to be. Stay out of this, Marlowe.'

'It's Dee's man, Carter,' Marlowe said, edging nearer. 'He's confessed.'

'Dee's man,' Faunt frowned. 'But I thought—'

'That Sir Robert had Walsingham dispatched so that he could take his place,' Marlowe finished the sentence for him. 'Yes, I know.'

'I told him what rubbish that was,' Cecil squeaked, trying to speak without moving his throat. He cut a ridiculous figure in his nightshirt, his cap askew, pinned over Walsingham's desk as he was. Faunt looked down at him and applied a threat more pressure to the dagger; Cecil shut up and closed his eyes.

The Spymaster's right-hand man assessed his options. He may or may not be able to handle Marlowe. He was pretty sure he could handle Ralegh, but *both* of them? What were the odds against that? Other things began to dawn on him. Marlowe was wearing some sort of costume, but was he armed? Ralegh would be – the dagger at his back – and Ralegh would have people, a coachman at the very least. Old Mylles, who accepted fully what Faunt was about to do, would have no chance.

'Do you know this man?' Ralegh spoke for the first time, looking at Faunt.

'Marlowe?' Faunt frowned. 'Of course I do.'

'Do you trust him?'

Faunt chuckled. 'Your end of the court is far away from mine, Sir Walter,' he said. 'Best you don't involve yourself.'

'Listen to him, Faunt,' Cecil rasped, feeling a trickle of blood run warm and sticky down from his throat and soak into the ruffled collar of his nightshirt.

'You are projectioners both,' Ralegh went on, 'you and Marlowe. I don't pretend to know what all that means. I know that the service you give is secret and that, under Walsingham, you kept the Queen safe. You *do* trust each other because you have to. Your lives and that of the Queen depend on it. If Marlowe says you're wrong, Faunt, then you're wrong.'

Faunt looked at Marlowe, ignoring the terrified Cecil altogether. There were the dark eyes he had looked into before, the mind as sharp as his own but with that flash of genius. Under the strange costume beat a heart that sounded, in its way, to England's drum, as did his own. He heard Ralegh's words echo and re-echo in his head. 'If Marlowe says you're wrong . . . you're wrong.'

He took a deep breath, then he jerked back the dagger, tossed it in his hand and slid it into the sheath up his sleeve in one lightning movement. Everyone breathed a sigh of relief, not least Robert Cecil, who clutched his throat and scuttled across the room.

'Kill him, Marlowe,' he screamed, pointing at Faunt. 'He's a traitor!'

'He's no such thing, Sir Robert,' Marlowe said. 'He just thought you were.'

'Ralegh!' Cecil shouted. 'You're the Queen's favourite. You can't just stand there. You saw. Faunt tried to kill me.'

The Great Lucifer shrugged. 'I've just come from the theatre,' he said. 'As far as I'm concerned, this is just the Chorus, winding things up neatly.'

Cecil subsided. He'd get nowhere with these two, that much was certain. 'The cyphers,' he snapped at Faunt, holding out his right hand. 'I'll have them now.'

For a long moment, Nicholas Faunt hesitated. Then he dug into his purse and pulled out the royal seal and that of Walsingham. He slapped them both into the new Spymaster's hand.

'Nicholas Faunt,' Cecil said, his voice back in its usual register now, 'your services are dispensed with. Your house, your estate and the movables thereof are forfeit to the Crown. If you come within the verge again, I'll have you hanged for a traitor. You will die like a common thief. Do I make myself clear?'

'As crystal, Sir Robert,' Faunt sneered and spun on his heel.

'Now, Marlowe, tell me what the Hell is going on. First, I'm dragged from my bed by this lunatic at knife-point and brought to this jakes of a place . . .'

'It was the Spymaster's home, Sir Robert,' Marlowe told him flatly. 'Sir Walter, would you do the honours? I want a word with Faunt.'

The projectioners met at the bottom of Walsingham's stairs. Francis Mylles stood there, a wheel-lock pistol in his hand. Faunt saw it, took it gently from the old man's hand and smiled, patting him on the shoulder. 'You won't be needing that, Francis,' he said. 'All's well that ends well.'

There were tears in the old man's eyes. 'Thank you, Master Faunt,' he said. 'If you're sure.'

'I'm sure,' Faunt said and Walsingham's faithful retainer shuffled off into the darkness of the house.

Faunt looked out of the open front door. 'Dawn,' he murmured. 'A new day.'

Marlowe nodded. 'And what will it bring for you, Nicholas?' he asked.

Faunt laughed but there was no mirth in it. 'From today, Kit,' he said, 'I am a masterless man, one of the many-headed monster. This day has been long in coming. Mistress Faunt has had bags packed for years, waiting for the axe to fall, hopefully metaphorically, on my neck.'

Marlowe always forgot there was a Mistress Faunt. Her husband knew how to keep a secret; who better? 'I can't believe Cecil *really* means to let you go, though,' he said. 'All your skill. Your experience . . .'

This time, the laugh was genuine. 'Can't you?' Faunt said, flipping his hat on to his head. 'You were there just now, damn it. I had my blade at his throat. If it weren't for you, he'd be dead by now. And you heard him – if I come within the verge . . . if I'm within twelve miles of the Queen, he'll have my head. *And* he'll enjoy doing it, nearly as much as our friend Topcliffe. There's nothing for me here now,' and he stepped out on to the cobbles of Seething Lane.

'But, a man of your skills . . .' Marlowe followed him. It all seemed such a waste.

Faunt half turned. 'I'll go North,' he said, 'to the King of Scots. I'm told the Highlands are very beautiful at this time of year. Mad Jamie can always use a spy or two. In the meantime,' he turned back to Marlowe and shook his hand, 'the Cecils rule England now and that's not good news. You watch your back, Kit Marlowe.'

'I always do, Nicholas Faunt,' he said.

Upstairs, when Marlowe joined them, Cecil and Ralegh were deep in grim conversation.

'It seems, Marlowe,' Cecil said when he saw him, 'I owe you not one vote of thanks, but two. You saved my life a moment ago and, rest assured, a Cecil never forgets.'

'It's nothing, Sir Robert,' Marlowe assured him, but he was starting to regret it now.

'And as for the other thing,' the new Spymaster went on, 'all England thanks you, for bringing Walsingham's murderer to book.'

'When do you expect the trial?' Marlowe asked.

'Trial?' Cecil frowned. 'Don't be ridiculous, Marlowe; there'll be no trial.'

'What?' Marlowe could scarcely believe what he was hearing.

'I don't intend to give the Papists a whiff of air over this. Carter's motives may have been personal, but Rome will twist that. He'll be an avenging angel striking a blow against the Protestant Church and the Jezebel of England – I can hear their damned presses churning now. No, they'll make no capital out of us. Francis Walsingham, God rest his soul, died of apoplexy. Natural causes. It was his time; God called him; what you will – but not murder.'

He looked at the men in the room with him; two of the most dangerous men in England, in their different ways. 'I want your word,' Cecil said, 'both of you, that not a whisper of this business will get out. I don't suppose, Marlowe, there's any point in asking you to swear on a Bible?'

'No point at all, Sir Robert,' the playwright said.

'Ralegh?' Cecil looked at him.

'You have the word of the Great Lucifer,' Ralegh said. 'Let that be enough.'

'Marlowe?'

There was a silence, then the playwright said, 'You have the word of Machiavel,' he said. 'Of Tamburlaine and . . . of Faustus. Of the Muses' darling. And that will have to suffice.'

Cecil looked at them both, dark and enigmatic. One knew all the secrets the Queen had to offer. The other; who knew what secrets he had locked inside his head? They would take watching, of that the new Spymaster was certain. With as much dignity as he could muster, he straightened his nightcap, adjusted the hang of his nightshirt and made for the door. On the landing, he turned.

'Sir Walter,' he said. 'I wonder if I might trouble you for a ride back to Whitehall?'

Ralegh looked rueful. 'I am *so* sorry, Sir Robert,' he said and almost sounded as though he meant it. 'I'm not going that way.'

And with that, shouldering the Queen's imp aside, the privateer and the playwright clattered down the stairs.

Marlowe sang as he made his way through the abandoned vegetables in the groundlings' pit at the Rose. They would be gathered up later and divided half to Master Sackerson and half to the families of the cleaning crew; it seemed an equitable arrangement that even Henslowe didn't quibble with often. He had slept the clock round and was feeling human again and although his projectioner's mind knew that thinking all was well with the world could only be a childish fancy, it was as well as he could expect of it and that would have to be enough. The first person he bumped into was Henslowe.

For once, the theatre owner was stuck for an opening. 'Er . . . a very . . . good evening at Sir Walter's, I thought, didn't you?'

It was difficult to see quite how it could be good, but Marlowe was listening.

Henslowe laughed, a little nervously. 'I was asked by two gentlemen there if I could provide a private showing for them. Quite . . . lucrative, in fact.'

Ah, *that* kind of very good. Marlowe smiled and waited. There seemed to be a 'but' on the horizon.

'But . . . of course, they think it was Shaxsper who wrote the play. So . . . well, to cut a long story short, Kit, one of them approached him directly, so . . . I don't really know how to put this, but . . .'

'He said yes. Don't worry, Master Henslowe,' Marlowe was still glowing from his twenty-four hour sleep, 'let Shaxsper have his moment in the sun. My back is broad. I don't need to write private plays for gentlemen.' He patted the man's arm. 'Just make sure you get the proper fee. I wouldn't like you to be out of pocket.' He laughed involuntarily; that was such a stupid remark and he didn't usually make stupid remarks.

Henslowe looked at him for a moment and then also burst out laughing. He could be heard laughing, all the way to the Lombards, with his concealed purse of money.

Shaxsper was next, creeping out from behind some stored flats, inky and anxious.

'Kit?' he hissed. 'Do you have a moment?'

Marlowe smiled. He had been expecting this. 'Of course, Will. How may I help you?'

Shaxsper flushed. 'I was approached at Sir Walter's . . .'

'Oh, I am sorry,' Marlowe said, playing the innocent. 'Those ladies of the bedchamber!' He clicked his tongue. 'Some of them have no shame!'

'No, no; not that.' His pride got the better of him; wife notwith-standing he was, at bottom, a ladies' man. 'Not that I didn't *get* approached by several, of course. No, this was a guest at the performance. He wants me to write a play, to be performed at his house.'

'Wonderful, Will, well done. But,' it seemed cruel, but his bubble must be burst, 'was that not on the strength of *Faustus*?'

'Um . . . yes.'

'The play *I* wrote?'

'Yes.' Shaxsper was becoming less excited.

'With *your* name on it.'

Shaxsper looked rueful. 'I understand, Kit,' he said. 'How shall we manage this? Shall I write it and pay you? Shall you write it and I pay you?' It was clear that, with all the options, Shaxsper paying Marlowe would be the upshot.

Marlowe looked at him severely and then laughed. 'No, Will. Shall we say you write it and keep the money? That sounds the fairest way to me. After all, I did steal your name to hide behind. If things had gone differently, you could be in the Tower by now.'

Shaxsper bridled. He hadn't thought of that.

'Is that it?' Marlowe pointed to the sheaf of paper under Shaxsper's arm.

'Yes. It's my *Henry*.'

'Ah, yes . . . I believe you have shown me this before. May I . . .?' He held out his hand and Shaxsper passed it reluctantly over. 'Yes . . . oh, I see you have made a few of the changes I suggested. Hmm . . .' he riffled through the sheets. 'I believe the quick answer here, Will, is that you take one of the more . . . shall we say *charismatic* characters and concentrate on him. Because, you must see it, Will, Henry VI is a *little* on the boring side. Stark raving mad, of course, but without being even remotely interesting. Look, let me choose one at random.' He fanned the pages and stopped them with a forefinger. 'Here we are, this one would do. Richard of Gloucester. Why don't you write a play about him? It would be a riot.'

'Richard of Gloucester?' Shaxsper's interest was piqued. 'I'll look him up. I should think Holinshed would have something about him, wouldn't you?'

'For certain, Will. If you go to the Earl of Northumberland's house at Blackfriars and ask for the librarian there, he will help you. Say I sent you.'

Shaxsper scuttled off, a man on a mission.

Marlowe didn't get much further before he heard his name being called from the stage to his right. He looked up, shielding his eyes against the piercing summer light pouring in through the skylight.

'Tom?' he said. 'Is that you?'

'Yes,' an unexpected voice said. Tom Watson jumped down into the pit. 'Fancy you recognizing me and here of all places. They're right what they say about you, Kit; you *are* a genius.'

It was pointless to tell the man that it was Tom Sledd he had expected, so Marlowe smiled politely. 'Tom. Back from . . .'

'Scadbury, yes. It was a nice rest, some time in the country, fresh air, birds, that kind of thing. But, well, you know me, Kit; I crave the city. The bustle. The hustle.'

'The women.' Marlowe could not forget Watson's greatest pleasure.

A slow smile crept over the poet's face. 'Oh, Kit! Don't forget the country is full of milkmaids. Farmers' daughters.' He grew reminiscent. 'There was one in particular, she had the . . .'

Marlowe held up a hand in protest. 'Tom, please! Do you remember why I asked you . . . no, ordered you, as I recall . . . to leave my house?'

Watson was puzzled. 'Not really, no.'

'It was the women, Tom. The constant stream of women. So, now we have met by chance like this, can we see if this short conversation – because it will be short, Tom – can be without a recitation of a woman's charms.'

'But, Kit. You should have seen her! She had . . .'

Marlowe turned to go.

'Sorry, sorry Kit.' Watson grabbed his sleeve. 'I won't mention women, I promise. I came to give you this.' He held out the papers.

Marlowe didn't take it. 'What is it?' he asked, dubiously.

'It's a play. I wrote it down in Scadbury.'

'About?' Marlowe could not take much of Tom Watson, although in a pinch, he would fight a battle and die for him if necessary. That's what friends were for – it wasn't necessary to actually like them.

'Well . . .' Watson paused. 'You know who owns Scadbury, of course? My patron.' He lingered over the beloved word. 'My patron, Thomas Walsingham?'

'Yes. I do know that.'

'Well, his cousin died, you know.' Watson peered into Marlowe's face. 'Ah, I can see you *did* know that. An apoplexy, poor old chap. Well, I got to thinking, what if he were *murdered*? So . . .' he pointed to the papers. 'I wrote a play about it. I want you to read it.' He proffered it again and this time Marlowe took it.

'Do you know, Tom,' he said, 'I do believe I will.' He tucked it securely in the crook of his arm and stepped round his erst-while lodger. 'Meanwhile, you might want to make yourself scarce. That dresser . . . what's her name, now? Emily, isn't it? She seems to be heading this way. She really *has* packed on the weight. Still, fashion is a funny thing – one minute the girls all want to be thin, the next . . . Tom?'

But Watson was away, heading for the wicket gate and freedom.

Chuckling to himself, Marlowe made his way backstage, into a chorus of greeting and congratulations. Even Alleyn slapped him on the back and said how much he liked the part he had played. Burbage was less effusive; he wouldn't remember the first performance of *Faustus* as his finest hour, but he had had a very memorable evening with one of Bess Throckmorton's ladies, so he was minded to be generous.

Finally, Tom Sledd and Marlowe were as alone as it was possible to be, in the pre-performance hubbub that was the Rose.

'That was exciting,' Sledd said. 'At Durham House, I mean. Do you mind if I ask you something?'

Tom and Marlowe went way back. 'Of course not. Ask away.' No jokes today about just one question.

'Do you know who played Lucifer?' It was still eating at Tom Sledd.

'Um . . . Jenkins, wasn't it?'

Sledd nodded, very slowly. He gave a nervous little laugh. 'Of course it was. Silly me.'

'I'm thinking of completing *Faustus*, you know. A few more characters. A servant, for instance. I was thinking of calling him Wagner.'

'German? I suppose that's where it's set. But you know my boys; not very good on accents.'

'A few more bangs and whistles.'

Sledd smiled. He was always ready for more bangs and whistles.

'It will never get past the censor,' Marlowe mused.

'No,' Sledd laughed. 'But won't we have fun trying?'

EIGHTEEN

Another sell-out performance of *The Jew of Malta* was drawing to a close and Kit Marlowe sat on the wall of Master Sackerson's pit, having a word with the bear. The more he saw of humans, the more he was drawn to the animal kingdom. Except dogs. He didn't think he would ever come to love dogs. He threw apples down to the moth-eaten creature and listened with a smile to his grateful grumblings, the soft, winter-stored fruit not giving even the bear's toothless old jaws any trouble. The juice dripped on to his paws and he licked them greedily.

'That's all,' he told the animal as he threw the last one and the bear mumbled in reply.

'Looking for some intelligent conversation, Kit?' a voice asked, right in his ear.

He spun round. 'I wish you wouldn't do that when I'm leaning over!' he protested. 'I could have fallen in.'

Nicholas Faunt looked over the wall. 'It isn't far to fall,' he said. 'And I don't think a toothless bear would do you much damage.'

Marlowe smiled. 'And we are good friends,' he said. 'But, what are you doing here, Nicholas? The Queen is at Placentia. You are well within the verge, here.'

'Come now, Kit,' Faunt said. 'You know how slowly the wheels of government grind. I doubt that Cecil has even written the order yet, let alone let anyone know to look out for me. In fact,' he looked at him, his head on one side, 'as far as I know, only you and Ralegh know about my banishment.'

'And I won't tell,' Marlowe said, managing to make it sound almost like a question.

'No, Kit. You won't tell. Are you going to work for Cecil?' Faunt asked, suddenly serious.

'I don't know. I'm thinking of giving up the spying game. Get myself a little cottage in the country somewhere. Roses around the door.'

'A little wife, baking bread? A tribe of children?' Faunt cocked an eyebrow.

'Perhaps not that,' Marlowe conceded. 'But, why are you here, Nicholas? Have you just come to say goodbye?'

'I wondered if you had time for a chat,' Faunt said, a little wistfully. 'Where I'm going, there will be nobody to remember the old days.'

'Nicholas, I would love to,' Marlowe said. 'But I have promised a couple of the walking gentlemen I will dine with them. I could put them off, but . . . I feel rather guilty. I feel sure I know them from somewhere, but I can't quite put my finger on it.'

'We meet a lot of people, in our line of work,' Faunt remarked.

'That's true, but . . . Nicholas, let me put them off. Some other time will suit them just as well, whereas you . . .'

'I have places to go, Kit, people to see. Don't let me keep you.'

Marlowe was stricken. It was true that every moment Faunt stayed in the verge he was in danger, but . . . and Marlowe would have to check on this, but he thought he may be his oldest friend. 'Why don't you join us?' It would keep him longer in the verge, longer in danger of his life but, in for a penny, in for a pound.

'No. It's tempting, but I really can't stay. The papers I left for you. The ones I . . . unfortunately . . . misread. The ones that put you on to Carter.'

'What of them?'

'You know how it is, dear boy.' Faunt became confidential, even catching Master Sackerson's eye for a moment. 'Nothing incriminating. No hard evidence . . . but paper can hang a man.' And he heard Marlowe delivering that last line in perfect choral speech alongside him.

'They're in the Rose somewhere, Nicholas,' Marlowe told him, 'along with the plays the hopefuls keep longing for me to read. Will you trust me to find them and burn them? I can guarantee that the pile is high and they are buried deep; no one ever reads so much as a page, I promise.'

Faunt hesitated, then made his decision. 'Of course, Kit. I'd trust you with my life.'

'Gratifying,' Marlowe smiled.

Faunt shook his hand and turned to go. Suddenly, he turned back. 'Tell me something, Kit,' he said. 'Do you miss Sir Francis? I do. He was . . . if you will forgive the cliché for a moment, he was like a father to me.'

'Well . . .' Marlowe cast his mind back. He had never had a father to whom he could really look up to. As he recalled it, he was about four when he realized that the angry, volatile presence in the house would never love his mercurial son, or indeed any of his children. 'I didn't know him as well as you did, of course, but . . . yes, I do miss him. I wish I'd had time to say goodbye.'

Faunt looked down and, if it had been any other man, Marlowe would have suspected that there was a tear in his eye. After a moment, the ex-spy looked up and smiled. 'He looked peaceful,' he said, 'when I got there. Although it may surprise you, I don't think he had any regrets at the end.'

Marlowe thought of Carter and his hatred, nurtured over the years against the man who was only doing his best. 'I'm glad,' he said, patting Faunt's shoulder. 'But now, Nicholas, I worry . . .' He looked up and down Maiden Lane, always expecting the unexpected.

Faunt raised a hand. 'You're right,' he said. 'I must go. Go and dine with your walking gentlemen. There will be another day for us, I know, Kit. Going somewhere nice?'